I would like to thank my editor Mike at Bloomsbury and my agent Rachel for all their tremendous help, support, enthusiasm and lunches.

The spinning-wheel that Sleeping Beauty pricked her finger on arrived in Aberystwyth around the middle of the seventeenth century. Technically it's known as the Saxon wheel, though no one ever calls it that. There are four main parts: the wheel, the spindle, the distaff and the foot pedal or "treadle". This is a story about the treadle. Or, more precisely, about that sorry army of girls who pedalled it during the years after the flood. The girls came mainly from the farms up beyond Talybont — chancers who didn't know a loom from a broom but flocked to the lights of Aberystwyth to make it big modelling on the tops of the fudge boxes they sold to the tourists. They called them treadle trollops but normally they never got to peddle anything except their sweet young bodies down at the druid speakeasies on Harbour Row. You won't find much enchantment in this story. And since it all took place in the shadow of Aberystwyth Castle and not the one described by Hans Christian Andersen there aren't any knights in shining armour. Just me, Louie Knight, Aberystwyth's only private detective and more frog than prince. Not many of the people in it lived happily ever after either. But at least half of them lived, which was a good average for the town in those days . . .

1

CHAPTER
ONE

I needed to find a druid, which in Aberystwyth is like trying to find a wasp at a picnic. I wasn't fussy about which one, no more than you care which one lands on your jam sandwich, but Valentine from the Boutique would have been good. In his smart Crimplene safari suit, Terylene tie and three-tone shoes, the druid style-guru should have been the easiest to spot. But tonight he seemed to have gone to ground, along with the rest of his crew; and during my lonely sweep of the Prom I met no one except a couple of pilgrims who asked directions to the spot where Bianca died.

I pulled up my collar against the wind and turned back, and wandered disconsolately down past the old college and on towards Constitution Hill. In the bed-and-breakfast ghetto the shutters squeaked and banged and a chill low-season wind blew old newspapers down the road. There were vacancy signs glowing in all the windows tonight and here at the season's end, as September turned into October, they would be likely to remain that way for another year. Even the optimists knew better than to try their luck now. In this town the promise of an Indian summer often meant the genuine article: a monsoon.

Misplacing Valentine was no great hardship, but the word on the street said he had tickets to Jubal's party and without a ticket there was only one way in: I would have to use the scrap of paper that lay crumpled up in my coat pocket. I'd bought it half an hour earlier from a streetwalker down by Trefechan Bridge and paid a pound for it. She assured me it would open Jubal's front door faster than a fireman's jemmy; but I somehow doubted it. I'd used tricks like this before and either they didn't work at all and you wasted a pound; or they worked so well you ended up getting a sore head. Which would it be tonight?

Jubal Griffiths was the mayor at the time and also head of casting for the "What the Butler Saw" movie industry. This was about as close as you could get to being a mogul in Aberystwyth and his house was easy to find: one of those stately Georgian piles on North Road, overlooking the bowling-green with a distant prospect of the pier. They were the sort of houses that had high ceilings and real cornices and a bell next to the fireplace to call the servants. In most of them, too, there was an invalid rotting away upstairs who could still remember a time when you rang and someone answered.

I banged on the door and a Judas window slid open. The sound of music drifted out, along with muffled screams and the aroma of smoky bacon crisps. Two eyes peered at me through the slit and before I had time to wonder what sort of mayor needs a fixture like that in his front door a voice said, "Sorry, mister, members only." I laughed. It didn't even convince me, but on a night like this it was the best I could do.

"Someone tickling you, pal?"

I chuckled some more and said brightly, "No I was just thinking, normally to get a drink in this town you just need to be a member of the human race."

"Yeah, well we've had a lot of trouble with that particular organisation." The little door slid shut.

I walked down the side of the house to the back door, opened the letterbox and shouted, "Coo-ey!" Carpet slippers slithered down the hall. The door opened slightly, held by a chain. Two old, grey, watery eyes peered at me.

"Yes?"

"I've come for the speakeasy."

"The what?"

"The speakeasy. I hear it's a good party."

The old lady knitted her brows together and said with the sort of acting you get at a school play, "Oh I'm afraid you must have made a mistake, there's nothing like that here."

She began to close the door and I wedged my foot in and leaned my shoulder against the wood. It opened a few more inches. She would have been about five foot two in her socks and was wearing a dust-coloured shawl over an indigo wool skirt. She had opaque,

5

flesh-coloured stockings the colour of Elastoplast and on her feet were those felt relaxation boots — trimmed with fake fur at the ankle and a zip up the front. The same outfit worn by a thousand other old spinsters in this town. It fooled no one.

"You're the one who's made the mistake, lady, there's a party going on and I'm invited."

She switched to Welsh. "*Beth ydych chi eisiau? Dydw I ddim yn siarad Saesneg . . .*"

I could speak in tongues, too. "*Edrychwch Hombré, agorwch y drws! por favor.*"

She tried pushing the door on my foot, switching back to English. "I can assure you there's nothing like that going on in my house."

"You must be in the wrong house, then. Just tell Jubal I'm here. Tell him I've got a message . . ." I peered at the slip of paper in the palm of my hand, "from Judy Juice."

At the mention of the name the old lady's demeanour changed. She stopped pushing the door and considered me through narrowed eyes.

"Miss Judy?"

I nodded.

"Who shall I say is calling?"

I handed her a card. It said, *Louie Knight, Gumshoe.* She took it and I removed my foot. As she closed the door I bent down and shouted through the letterbox, "And drop the confused old biddy act, it stinks!"

I waited on the step for a while and thought about the piece of paper. Two words that meant nothing to me but the whole world, apparently, to Jubal. She was, they said, the one girl in town he wanted but couldn't have. And such is the eternal perversity of man's heart that because he couldn't have her he wanted her more than all the others in the world put together. The door opened and two men in rugby shirts with chests the size of wardrobes leered at me. They were the sort of men with no necks, just extra face. They motioned with their heads and we walked down the hall, the sound of the party getting louder. One of the side-doors burst open and an old man in satyr trousers rushed out pursued by an elderly, giggling woman. I peered into the room: a crush of people standing up, talking and drinking; a buffet on the sideboard with vol-au-vents, crisps and those pineapple cheese things impaled on miniature plastic swords. Girls in stovepipe hats and not much else wandered through with trays of punch. Before I could see any more the two tough guys grabbed me and pulled me along.

At the end of the corridor was a study. Inside were three other muscle men in the same rugby-club shirts; a bored-looking blonde in Welsh national dress and fake leopard-skin coat; and a man sitting behind a desk. The girl stared mesmerised at a light-fitting on the ceiling and chewed cuds of spearmint with regular wet, clickety-clack sounds. The man behind the desk was Jubal. Short and tubby, with a hunchback and a small round head stuck on to the hunch like a pea on a lump of dough. A man with a finger in more pies than Jack Horner. He was holding my card gingerly between his two index fingers, and contemplating it as if it had just scurried out from under his fridge. Then he tore it into two bits, dropped them at his feet, and looked at me myopically through a pair of tortoise-shell spectacles. He blinked. "I appreciate your candour, Mr Knight. Most of the peepers who come sniffing round my business usually have a card that says they've come to read the meter."

I smiled at him.

"Unfortunately that's the only thing about you I appreciate. Would you care to give me the message you claim to have."

"No." It was just one tiny syllable but it produced a synchronised gasp from everyone in the room. Jubal stared at me inquisitorially.

"I hope you've got something good up your sleeve, snooper . . . for your sake."

"I'm not willing to give you the message, but I might exchange it . . . For information."

"What sort?"

"I'm looking for a man called Morgan."

"And?"

"Dean Morgan. This is the bit where you say you haven't heard of him." Just to spite me he said nothing, so I filled in the silence. "He went missing as people often do in Aberystwyth. And, as people often do, someone asked me to find him."

"I'm struggling to see the connection to me. It's going to be very painful for you if you don't have one."

"He was last seen at one of your parties."

Jubal removed his spectacles and polished them on the girl's leopard-skin coat. "Is that it?" he spluttered, his gorge rising. "He came to one of my parties? You bust your way into a private gathering, drop some old tart's name at the door as a calling card and that's all you've got?"

"Who says she's a tart?"

"They're the only sort of girls I associate with." He slapped the knee of the blonde. "Ain't that right, Toots?"

The girl dragged her gaze away from the ceiling and treated him to a smile that came and went faster than a flash from the lighthouse. "Sure, honey." Then she pressed her head against his chest and cooed. Jubal spoke across the top of her head.

"She wants to be in one of my pictures; they all do."

"It's probably more fun than watching them."

He flinched slightly and said, "Tell me what you really want, peeper, is it money? And please dispense with the witty dialogue, it's tiresome."

I didn't know what I was doing there, really; just looking to see if the Dean's name induced any reaction. So far it hadn't produced even a flicker. So I said, "I've come to ask why your boys threw Dean Morgan in the sea."

He addressed the rugby-shirt crew. "Have any of you boys thrown a man called Dean Morgan into the sea recently?"

They exchanged questioning looks among themselves and then said in unison, "Not us, Boss."

"Looks like there's been a mistake," said Jubal.

"Your boys are probably confused. His name's not actually Dean, that's his title. He teaches at the college in Lampeter. He was found last night floating face-down in the harbour."

"How tragic, I hear the tides can be very strong."

"They must have been, they broke his neck."

There was a slight heightening of tension, and an air of mild surprise at the news of his death, which was understandable because I had just made it up. The people in the room turned their attention to Jubal. All except the girl, who was rubbing her cheek against his chest and making a long drawn-out "Mmmmm" sound. Jubal laughed. Not the hammed-up stage-laugh of someone trying to conceal something. But the carefree laugh of someone who knows you've thrown in your wild card and you couldn't have been further from the truth if you tried.

"Well, shamus, he seems to have made an excellent recovery from his broken neck. He telephoned me five minutes ago."

I thought for a second about an appropriate expression. He could have been lying and probably was. But then again so was I and he knew it; just as I knew that he was, and he knew that I knew that he was, and I knew that he knew that I was. I put on the bright wide grin of an idiot.

Jubal said, "Tell me, peeper, do you really have a message from Judy?"

"Of course."

"Why would she give it to you?"

"She's a friend of mine."

"Is that right! A close friend?"

"Oh so-so."

"This is really interesting. What does she look like?"

I hesitated, caught in the headlights of an oncoming train.

Jubal laughed. "Go on describe her."

"Er . . . well, you know . . ."

"Come, come, shamus! It shouldn't be too difficult, I'll give you a clue: tonight she's wearing a leopard-skin coat . . ."

The girl turned and gave me a sickly-sweet smile. And then everyone in the room except me laughed. As the tears slid down his reddening face, Jubal waved a hand at me and said to one of the tough guys. "Throw this trash into the sea."

That was the signal for them to take out their blackjacks, put a hood over my face, and play a tune on my head.

When I regained consciousness I was lying at the base of Constitution Hill, a cold tongue of sea-water licking my face like a faithful dog. Dawn was breaking through thick woolly cloud and my head was throbbing. They had dumped me just above the high-water mark which meant that, all things considered, they must have liked me.

CHAPTER
TWO

The battered, green Crossville bus pulled up with a sigh of brakes and disgorged an old man in a cheap suit. He put two suitcases down on the floor and then squinted at the morning sun glittering on the sea. From the bus shelter, a mother and a little girl eyed him suspiciously. The man took a breath and said, "Smell that, Señor Rodrigo?"

A voice answered from the suitcase, "Back in Aberystwyth. Same old smell."

The man looked down at the case. "Yes, the same old smell."

"We said we'd never come back."

"We always say we'll never come back."

"But here we are again."

The woman grabbed her little girl by the arm and dragged her briskly up the Prom, casting doubtful looks behind as they went. The old man watched them go for a while, his face lined with the wistful sadness that is the lot of the lifelong outcast. Then he bent down, the whole world on his shoulders, and picked up the cases. They were covered in faded stickers and the most faded of all said, "The Amazing Mr Marmalade".

"Need any help?" I offered.

He shook his head. "Been carrying them for forty years."

"I could take the small one."

He jerked slightly. "Yeah, I know, and throw Señor Rodrigo in the sea." He strode off, crossed the road, and entered the Seaman's Mission.

I remained standing there for a while and then walked up the rest of the Prom to the wooden jetty by the harbour. The autumn wind was warm and blustery and held in it the promise of a season about to change. At the end of the jetty, I turned, and contemplated the vista of the town steaming in the morning sun as if still damp from its soaking three years ago.

Looking back, it was surprising how well the old place had stood up to the great flood. The waters had passed over Aberystwyth like a giant car-wash and picked it cleaner than an alley-cat does the bones of a kipper. But not much had actually been knocked down. We all held our breath that fateful night, closed our eyes, and when we opened them again most of the town was still there. True, most things that could be moved had gone. All the tables, chairs, spinning-wheels and grandfather clocks; all the Coronation mugs with their hoarded sixpences; all the tea cosies, the dioramas and stereoscopic views of Llandudno; all the ointment from the backs of drawers, and the lengths of orthopaedic hosiery; the china figurines, brass elephants and hairbrushes with four generations of matted hair. And, from the their picture frames atop the steam radios, a sepia generation of young men from the Great War were lost again, only this time at sea. It was all sucked out into the insatiable drain of the ocean. Even the seaside rock disappeared in a lurid pink slick before slowly sinking to rot the teeth of the bottom-dwelling fish.

But the buildings remained, by and large. Here and there — like missing teeth — there were gaps in the rows of shops on Terrace Road and Great Darkgate Street. Little squares of rubble, filled with oily puddles, flapping polythene and broken dressers housing families of rats. And bounded on each side by the image familiar from the photos of the Blitz — sides of houses torn away to reveal the contents, floor by floor, like dolls' houses open to view.

The city fathers from Dresden who came to advise on the rebuilding found little to advise upon. You call this a moonscape? they said. This is a walk in the park! Just do what we did in 1945. Gather together all the Old Master oil paintings with views of the town; all the watercolours and prints of the main civic buildings; all the etchings and lithographs and work from that; rebuild. Roll your sleeves up. Don't dwell on it, move on. And so we did. In the absence of canvases by Canaletto and engravings by Dürer we resorted instead to something more modest: a nationwide appeal for old holiday snaps and postcards of Aberystwyth. Predict-ably it produced its fair share of pictures of the Sphinx and the leaning tower of Pisa because, as anyone who's ever been stopped by a traffic cop knows, everyone's a comedian these days. But the steady stream of ash-trays, salt and pepper shakers, and souvenir barometers with views of the town were enough to get us started.

We were also helped enormously by the Bucket & Spade Aid concert put on by the end-of-the-pier performers. From all round the coasts of Britain they came — birdsong impressionists, organ-grinders, ventriloquists, stand-up comedians, skiffle practitioners — all joining in to raise funds under the slogan, "I say, I say, I say, my dog's got no nose!"

By the time I returned to the bus stop my partner Calamity Jane was there waiting for me. She was wearing a shiny black leather coat and a black beret and looked ready to assassinate someone. Not even seventeen and so well versed in the ways of the street, a girl who in many ways knew more about it than me, who always got to hear the word, whatever it was, long before I did and always paid a lot less for it. An hour late and holding a new camera with a strangely furtive air.

"Calamity!"

"Hiya! Where've you been?"

"Where have *you* been, more like, we've missed the bus."

"I've been testing my new camera. Do you like it?"

She pushed it towards me.

"Will it squirt water in my eye?"

"Nope."

"Then I like it a lot better than the old one."

She grinned. No matter how hard she tried to act the wised-up bingo-hall hustler, the imp in her always bubbled through. I couldn't resist smiling when I saw it. The sly cunning that mingled strangely with that charming innocence, the look of bright wonder and belief that the tarnished streets couldn't cloud. That look in her eye that Eeyore said made putting on a silver star still worthwhile.

We'd been partners now for three years, and I'd done my best to look out for her, to stand in for the father she didn't have and keep her on the right track. It wasn't always easy, as the newly acquired camera proved. The black market that sprang up in the aftermath of the flood had proved an irresistible lure to a girl like Calamity.

I looked sceptically at the camera. "That looks like quite an expensive bit of machinery."

She gave it an appraising look. "From one of my debtors."

"What do you need it for?"

Calamity moved half a step closer and took a quick look up and down the Prom.

"I'm taking Aunt Minnies."

"That's good."

She nodded in agreement. "I think so too." She pointed the camera upwards. "It's got an East German lens. They're the best for this sort of thing."

"Aunt Marjories, eh?"

16

"Minnies."

"Aunt Minnies?"

"Yep."

"I was just thinking we should probably get some more of those."

"I'm going to put them on file."

"You're just dying for me to ask, aren't you?"

"What?"

"You know what."

The next bus was over an hour away so we went to the Cabin coffee bar in Pier Street and sat in one of the booths looking out on to the street. After extracting as much mileage as she could from my ignorance on the subject, Calamity explained what an Aunt Minnie was.

"It's a word the spies use; it means pictures that tourists take that then become of interest to the intelligence community because they accidentally include something top secret in the background. Like a Russian missile or a defector."

"And who's Aunt Minnie?"

"They call them that because there's always someone's aunt in the foreground."

"It's a bit of a long shot, isn't it?"

"You never know. Some of this stuff will prove useful one day, take my word for it."

I handed her a photo of Dean Morgan that had arrived in the post. "We'll just have to hope no one defects this afternoon, we've got a real job. If we're lucky, we might even get paid."

Calamity scrutinised the photo. "Preacher man, huh? How boring."

"This is the sort of preacher man who would be right up your street. He's from the Faculty of Undertaking."

"They teach that?"

"You have to learn somehow."

"So what did he do?"

"He's been teaching the Undertaking course out at Lampeter for thirty years. Then one day he decides to visit Aberystwyth. He hasn't been heard of since. The worry is, he might have become part of the curriculum. The client is a girl called Gretel. She's one of his students."

"You'd think she'd be pleased her teacher had done a bunk."

"They're not like that out at Lampeter."

Gretel had called three days ago. I told her to come to town, my office was on Canticle Street, but she giggled at the very idea and said, "Oh but I couldn't!" as if Canticle Street was in Gomorrah. So I agreed to go to Lampeter and asked her for a description. She said she would be wearing a brown Mother Hubbard, a black headscarf and big wooden beads. And she was quite fat. I thought that shouldn't be too difficult but when our bus turned into a main street lined with dreamy old sandstone colleges, I saw six other girls just like it.

The pub on the high street was easy to find. The Jolly Ferryman, two doors down from the souvenir shop selling bonsai yew trees. A pub with olde worlde bow windows and panes of glass like the bottom of a milk bottle — the sort that make your vision go bleary even before you've taken a drink. When I walked in a fat girl in a Mother Hubbard waved from the window alcove.

Gretel introduced herself and her friend Morgana and asked us what we wanted to drink. Morgana said amiably, "You and your daughter must be tired after your long journey from the city."

"I'm not his daughter," said Calamity. "I'm his partner, I'm a detective."

"What city?" I said.

The girls broke into a peal of giggles like silvery bells, and covered their mouths with their hands.

"Why, Aberystwyth of course!"

A number of people in the pub looked round sternly at the mention of the name. I ordered a rum and Calamity ordered a whisky sour which I changed to a ginger beer. When the drinks arrived we chinked glasses and I said, "So why undertaking?" The girls paused politely as if allowing the other to go first. Gretel said, "Strictly speaking, I'm not doing 'undertaking' as such. I'm doing media studies."

"Are you hoping to write for the parish magazine?"

"Oh no! Not that sort of media. I mean I'm studying to be a medium."

I said, "Ah." And then after I'd thought some more, added, "I didn't know you could do that."

Gretel smiled and looked down at her clogs. "You don't believe, I can tell."

"I didn't say that, I've got an open mind."

Morgana nudged her friend. "Make some ectoplasm, that'll shut him up."

There was another peal of giggles and this time they both laughed so much the wooden beads clacked.

"Oh I couldn't!" squealed Gretel. "Not after what happened the last time."

The barman threw a suspicious look in our direction as if he'd read our thoughts and didn't need any reminding about the last time. Gretel added, "Besides, it takes me half an hour just to get an eggcupful!"

"I expect a little goes a long way," I said helpfully. "Tell me about the Dean."

Gretel picked up her beads, fingered them for inspiration and, prompted by subtle but insistent nudges from Morgana, gave me the background. He'd been at the college for many years and in all that time hadn't said boo to a goose. There wasn't any record of him ever having said anything to a goose, in fact, but if he had you could be sure it would have been more polite than boo. Then one day, out of the blue, he astonished everyone by announcing his intention to go away for a few days.

This revelation led to looks of disbelief being exchanged between the two girls. I was about to say it didn't seem like such a big deal when we were interrupted by raised voices at the next table.

A young man put down his glass sharply. "Oh really, Jeremy, next you'll be telling me, like, Osiris never happened or something!"

"I'm just saying —"

"Perfumed unguents, wax, spices . . . you know all that goo they make balm out of. Alexander the Great preserved in honey . . ."

"Oh sure, spare me the O level stuff please! All I'm saying is wrapping in cloth and burying in dry sand was accidental and wasn't a chief mortuary concern . . ."

"And I suppose the settlements at Abu Qir don't exist either?"

"Sssh, you two, keep it down!" said some of the other students at the table. "You'll disturb the other drinkers."

There was a murmur of approval round the table. "Yeah, it's getting late anyway, we'd better go back and study." They began to finish off their drinks.

We turned back to our own conversation.

"Maybe the Dean just felt like a holiday," said Calamity.

Gretel blinked in disbelief. "But Dean Morgan would never do anything as frivolous as that! And besides, he didn't say he was going to Aberystwyth, that's the funny part. It was Gwladys Parry the cleaner who saw him just by coincidence on the Prom, coming out of the Excelsior Hotel. Well, we couldn't believe it. The Dean in Aberystwyth! I rang the Excelsior Hotel straightaway and they said he had already checked out. Then a few days after that he rang me from that number I gave you —"

"The speakeasy?"

"Yes. But when I called him back it was really strange, I could hear the sounds of . . . well . . . a party

21

or something in the background and the man who answered said . . ." She half-closed her eyes as she tried to remember the exact formulation, " 'It is the club policy to neither confirm nor deny the presence of any patrons on the premises.' But I knew it must have been a wrong number because the Dean would never go to a party."

"It's unheard of," said Morgana.

"What did he call you about?"

"Oh, he said to cancel his milk and I was to take his cat and the litter of kittens she'd just had and drown them."

I took out the photo. It was just a stiffly posed shot of a priest in a dog-collar, taken for some yearbook or catalogue and obviously cut out of one.

"That's the best I could find."

"Maybe he just wanted to go and play bingo or something," suggested Calamity.

"But why would he want to do that?"

"For some light relief. Must be pretty spooky looking at stiffs every day."

Gretel gave an understanding sigh. "Yes, I know what you think — we must be really boring because we do what we do, not like those students in Aberystwyth. Everyone thinks the same."

"Or they think we're really ghoulish," said Morgana. "Just because we do experiments with worms and flesh."

Gretel nudged her friend. "They're disappointed because we're not like the Bad Girl."

They giggled again.

"Who's the Bad Girl?"

"Oh," said Gretel throwing her nose up. "We don't talk about her."

"And you're wrong anyway," added Morgana. "Undertaking's a lot more exciting than you think. Do you know . . ." she exchanged a conspiratorial glance with Gretel, "we each get a cadaver at the beginning of term to practise on, just like being a real doctor. Fancy that!"

"Yeah," said Gretel. "And some of the ones from Aberystwyth have died violently. I found a bullet hole in mine."

"And mine had a crushed larynx!"

"And we get to go on some great field trips — the catacombs or crypts . . . at Easter we're going to Golgotha."

"All the same, none of this is any reason to think he's in trouble."

Morgana nudged Gretel. "Tell him about the other thing."

Gretel took a breath and leaned closer in. "A week after he went, a man came looking for him. A really strange man."

"You mean strange for Lampeter," asked Calamity, "or strange for a normal town?"

I kicked her under the table.

"He was dressed funny and was unfriendly," said Gretel.

"Rude," added Morgana.

"What did he look like?"

"We couldn't see his face," said Gretel, "because he wore a muffler and had a wide-brimmed hat pulled down low —"

"With a black feather stuck in it."

"And he wore a long black coat like the ones the medieval Jews wore — you know, like the ones they sell in Peacocks for nineteen ninety-nine."

"The gaberdine ones."

"Then a few days later the Dean called again, and I told him that a man in a Peacocks' coat was looking for him and he sort of cried out and said, 'Oh my God, I'm doomed!'"

"What I don't get," said Calamity, "is why he contacts you and not a secretary or something?"

"Because", said Gretel, "we're his friends, we do voluntary work for him and things."

"What sort?"

She shrugged. "Oh nothing special, alms-giving mostly. Just like students anywhere, really."

I let that one pass.

They paused and then said together, "And of course we do his laying out."

I fought the reflex to choke. "You do that for the Dean?"

"Well, you can't expect him to do it himself, can you?" said Morgana huffily.

"And he pays us for it," said Gretel. "We're lucky to get it. I mean, how else are you supposed to survive on a grant these days?"

★ ★ ★

As the bus drove up the main street to turn at the top we saw through the back window a fracas on the neatly trimmed lawns of the college. The two students who had been arguing earlier in the pub were trading blows, surrounded by the rest of their group who were excitedly egging them on. From the cloisters on either side of the lawn, scholars and tutors poured forth in a flapping black gale of academic gowns, like starlings or startled bats, running like the wind and shouting dizzily with excitement, "Scrap! Scrap! Scrap!"

CHAPTER
THREE

The Excelsior was one of those crumbling, fading hotels that stood in a gently curving row on Aberystwyth Prom facing the sea. It was a hotel that spent the summer dreaming of better days, and wore its four stars on either side of the main door like combat medals. Like the motoring organisation that awarded the stars, it was a refugee from the world of A and B roads and button B telephones. A world in which a lift was considered an American contrivance and shared bathrooms at the end of the corridor were the norm. People still wore jackets and ties here and took luncheon and, perhaps most damning of all, it was the world that gave us Brown Windsor soup. Inside the hotel the floors creaked as you walked, like the innards of a wooden ship. It was an old, rickety dowager of a hotel and if it were possible for a building to get arthritis and walk with a stick this one would. I knew all this because once, for a season many years ago, I had worked there as the house John. An underpaid sleuth with a cubby-hole and a nightstick and a remit to keep one eye on the shifty characters who walked in off the street and an even beadier eye on the dodgy ones who worked there.

In the old days, as with all hotels with pretensions to grandeur, the door had been opened by a man dressed as a cavalry officer from the Napoleonic wars. But he had long since gone and today I had to push the heavy brass and glass door open myself. Inside the lounge, little had changed. The swirly carpet, the antimacassars; the horse brasses . . . And the same cast of characters: the greasy manager's son at the bar in a tatty white shirt and bow tie, eternally polishing a pint glass; in the bay windows sat members of that travelling band of spinsters and widows who spent their lives wandering from hotel to hotel in a predetermined route round the coast of Britain. Shrivelled old women who appeared at the same time each year with the predictability of migrating salmon and who insisted on the same room and ordered the same food. And every day at dawn they crept downstairs to place their knitting on the vacant armchairs signifying possession for the day like the flag on Iwo Jima.

The only other residents were the travelling shawl salesmen and the doily traders. There were two sitting at a table near the bar, talking doily shop in the impenetrable slang of their trade. Strange words and familiar ones used in strange ways. The weave, the whorl, the matrix, the paradigm; a disc, a galaxy, a web, a Black Widow and White Widow; a Queen Anne and a Squire's Strumpet . . . I listened to them talk for a while. These were the strange, forlorn men you sometimes passed when you went for a drive — parked

27

in a lay-by and crouched over a map. Next to it, a local newspaper opened to the death announcements with one of them circled in ballpoint. A grubby life lived according to the simple credo that with doilies, like snowflakes, there were never two alike.

I walked over and spoke to an old lady in the bay window. She was sitting in the chair with the exaggerated erectness of posture that no one knows how to do any more, just as no one can do algebra or decline a Latin verb. Her nose had a slight but permanent snooty tilt and she was peering through a lorgnette at the people walking past, trying to get as much disapproval in before her nap.

"I bet you get a good view from here," I said.

She turned her gaze to me with painfully deliberate slowness. Her mouth was gathered together and clamped so tightly shut it distorted the rest of her face.

"I mean, you can see everyone who comes in and everyone who goes out."

I waited and waited, the smile slowly withering on my face, until after an eternity she finally opened her mouth and said, "Maybe." Then she returned her gaze to the street.

The detective's cubby-hole was on the second floor in the same place it had been fifteen years ago. There was no one there but the soft sigh of steam from the recently boiled kettle told me he couldn't be far away. I stepped in from the corridor. The room had been designed originally as a utility room and was mostly filled by a wooden desk. Pictures of nude women torn out of the tabloids were pinned to the wall, and on the desk, next to the kettle and chipped china mug, was a set of keys. I walked round the desk and opened the drawer. There were a few knitting patterns in there, no doubt left behind by guests, a sock, a cheese sandwich and an ice pick. The floor outside creaked and I looked round and found him staring at me with an air that suggested he'd been doing it for quite some time.

He was dressed in a dirty vest covered in dried egg, had four days' growth on his glistening mauve jowls and his trouser flies were half-undone. His face was gummed up with sleep and he was so fat his hips almost touched both walls of the corridor. The cosh in his hand swung gently with an exaggerated casualness that suggested this was the sort of hotel where you could get coshed just for complaining about the soup.

"You looking for something?"

I smiled bashfully. "I was just checking the fire escape."

He sniffed the air. "Is there a fire? I can't smell anything."

"Not at the moment but there could be — it happens in the best establishments."

"We should be pretty safe here then."

"You've got four stars outside the front door, that means you're good enough to burn down."

He lifted the blackjack and scratched his cheek with it. "Fire escape, huh? Mmmmm." He gave the matter some deep thought and then brightened, saying, "The mistake you made was to look for it in the drawer of my desk. We don't keep it there." He squeezed into the room and threw some cleaning rags off the only other stool and motioned me to sit. I obeyed and he went to sit in his chair, giving the desk drawer a slam as he did. "I've been in this business twenty years now, and in my experience the place to look for the fire escape is outside the window."

"That was the first place I tried but I couldn't see it."

"That's because it isn't there yet. Special arrangement with the fire brigade — if there's a fire they'll come and put a ladder against the wall."

"That's reassuring to know."

"All part of the service." He pointed the blackjack at me. "Now we've sorted the fire escape out, perhaps you'll tell me if there's anything else I can help you with."

I took out a hip-flask. "Do I look like I need your help?"

"You look like a peeper to me."

I nodded. "Well I guess you would know. Drink?"

He pushed his teacup across and I filled it and poured a shot into the cap for myself. He took a gulp and then nodded appreciatively. I took the photo of the Dean out and slid it across the desk. The John made no effort to look, just took another gulp of the rum, and another until it was empty and pushed the cup back towards me. I filled it. He took another drink and then picked up the photo, took one look, put it down and said, "Yeah, I've seen him."

30

I put a pound coin on the tabletop and he picked it up and examined it as if it were a foreign coin he hadn't seen before. "Funny, you're not the first person to ask about him."

I waited for him to carry on but he didn't. Instead he smiled. I put another coin down.

"After he checked out a man came round dressed in a long black coat like they sell in Peacocks. Had a black feather in his cap. Wasn't as polite as you."

I nodded. "Did the Dean leave any forwarding address?"

"Not strictly speaking."

I put another coin down which met a similar fate to the other two. "What about speaking unstrictly?"

He scratched his chin again with the blackjack. "He didn't say where he was going but the funny thing was he was dressed differently when he left. Completely different, almost as if he was trying to leave in a new identity — we often get idiots like that. Now once you know what he was dressed like, you can guess where he was going." He stopped and looked at me blankly.

I put my last coin down. He shook his head. "This one I have to charge by the syllable."

"How many words is it?"

"Just the one."

I sighed. "OK, surprise me."

"Ventriloquist."

I walked up Great Darkgate Street and through the castle grounds towards the bed-and-breakfast ghetto down by the harbour. This was where the ventriloquists tended to stay, along with the out-of-work clowns, the washed-up impresarios and the men who ran away from the bank to join the circus. At the castle, I wandered through the piles of shattered stone and climbed up on to the hill by the war memorial. The sky was filled with bulbous shiny clouds hinting of a storm to come and churning the sea into soapy dishwater. Down below I could see Sospan's new kiosk — repositioned and re-established after the short-lived fool's errand of selling designer coffee to a town that hungered only for vanilla. And south towards the harbour, but moving north towards Sospan's stall, with the slow but inexorable tread of a glacier, was my father, Eeyore, and the donkeys. Every day he would be there, even in the depths of winter when there were no tourists, plodding up and down the Prom, from Constitution Hill to the harbour and back. A pendulum of fur, wound by a key of straw.

I walked down and Sospan hailed me.

"*Bore da!* Louie. Usual, is it?"

"No, give me something I haven't tried before."

He wagged his index finger at me. "Got just the thing for you." He turned to the dispenser and I turned too, placing my back against the counter, and stared out to sea. Down below, etched into the slimed rocks, were the remains of an Edwardian sea-water bathing-pool. Less than a hundred years old and already there was almost nothing left: just an outline in the rocks like the bones of a fossil; proof that the poison that did for Nineveh and Troy had no intention of sparing

Aberystwyth. Sospan handed me a pale green ice cream. "You'll like this!"

I licked. It was like nothing I'd ever tasted before. "What is it, frog?"

"Absinthe."

"You're kidding!"

"Lick it slowly now!"

He made one for himself and leaned forward to join me.

I said, "I thought we'd lost you for a while — given up on the ice-cream trade."

He pulled a wan face. "You never really can, though, can you? It was like running off with a dizzy blonde. You know, fun for a while but she can't cook and after a time you find all you really want is a nice bowl of *caawl* and someone to wash your socks."

"I don't think I've ever had a woman wash my socks for me since my mother died when I was a baby."

"You've missed out on a fine feeling there, Louie; washing a man's socks, it's what love's all about in the end."

"I'll slurp to that."

"You've just missed Father Seamus. He was asking after you."

"That's nice of him."

"He loves the new absinthe — of course I don't tell him what's in it. I say it's green tea."

I looked at the faint, impenetrable smile that Sospan wore to meet all occasions. The same smile worn by the undertaker and the brothel-keeper and others with a professional understanding of the hearts of men and a

33

policy not to interfere. It was good to have him back in business, we'd felt his absence keenly, just as we still miss the song of Myfanwy that no longer echoes down the streets at night.

"I thought Father Seamus liked to take his ice down the other end of the Prom," I said.

"Oh very sad, that is," said Sospan, hissing softly in sympathy. "It's on account of this rejection of the teachings of the Church you find nowadays. A lot of the other kiosks refuse to serve men of the cloth."

"That seems a bit drastic, doesn't it? It wasn't the Christians who started this flood, it was the druids."

"I know, but they're upset, aren't they? Because there was no rainbow this time as a mark of His covenant. A lot of people are angry about that. 'What's wrong with us,' they say. 'Why don't we get one?'"

"He probably just doesn't want to waste a good rainbow."

"That's what I tell them."

"Still, it's nice of you not to go along with the rest of them."

"You know me, Louie, I never take sides."

"Your kiosk is a moral Switzerland."

"Everyone's welcome, you know that. It's an understanding I have with Evans the magistrate: I won't judge you and he won't serve ice cream in court."

I looked at him. It was the first time I'd heard him attempt a joke and for once his smile almost became warm.

Eeyore arrived and ordered a 99. We nodded to each other and I patted the flank of Sugarpie and tied her halter to the lamppost. Eeyore had worked for the police for years before retiring to the gentler company of the donkeys. The only animals in the world, he once told me, with absolutely no agenda. In his time his fingers had been worn smooth from fingering the collars of the local hoodlums and he still had an encyclopaedic knowledge of their ways. I asked him if he knew anything about men in ankle-length Peacocks' coats, with black feathers in the cap. He nodded and a troubled look stole over his old, lined face.

"Yeah," he said with a heaviness in his voice. "I've seen something like that, once, a long time ago. He was a druid assassin called the Raven. The feather was his badge of office. Ravens were special agents, skilled philanderers, trained to seduce female agents and then kill them."

"Do you think this could be the same guy?"

Eeyore shook his head wearily, the memory was obviously painful. "No the Raven I arrested got five terms of life and died seventeen years ago in a knife fight in the maximum-security wing of Cwmtydu Pen. But these are a class of agent, a type. There are always more. For most of the time they live among us as sleepers. Lying dormant, in a sort of hibernation — going about their everyday business like you and me. Sospan here could be one and we wouldn't know." He indicated the ice-cream man with his half-eaten cornet. I looked at Sospan who was polishing the Mr Whippy dispenser and pretending not to be listening. He smiled. Somehow I couldn't see him as a sleeper, except in the ordinary sense of the word.

"Then someone activates one and you can rely on some pretty unpleasant things happening. These men don't get activated for commonplace jobs."

"They sound grim," I said.

Eeyore nodded. "They are. The worst thing is, once you set one loose, they can't be recalled. The mission can't be aborted. Even the person who activates them can't do it."

The Seaman's Mission had been built by the church in the last century with a non-specific Episcopal architecture of bare stone arches and dark stained wood. The word "seaman" had widened in scope since those days and now referred to any of the human flotsam shipwrecked by life and washed up on the shore of Aberystwyth. Vagrants and veterans of the Patagonian War; sea captains and stokers lost in a world where there is nothing left to stoke; monks on the run from their order at Caldy Island; lighthouse men whose lights had been doused or automated; and always there was a smattering of unemployable ventriloquists.

Downstairs there was an empty room with a notice-board and some hard seats set against a wall. Behind, towards the kitchen from which there came the strong odour of boiling cabbage, was a refectory-style dining-room. Five pence for a meal and don't forget to help with the washing-up. Upstairs there were dormitories and private rooms for those with modest

36

means; and in the corridor outside was a lady in a housecoat and headscarf mopping the tiled floor. I asked after Father Seamus who ran the place but she said he was out. She also said the Amazing Mr Marmalade was in Room 3 at the top of the stairs.

The door at the top was slightly ajar and the sound of soft sobbing came from within. I hesitated. I could also just hear the squeaky voice that I'd heard coming from the case.

"There, there, Mister Marmalade. Everything will be all right, just you watch."

"It's finished Señor Rodrigo, I tell you. All gone."

"Say not the struggle nought availeth, Mister Marmalade!"

"Where did the years go, my dear friend?"

"For a while we held them in our fist, Mister Marmalade, we held them close to our hearts, we did!"

There was a half-chuckle of remembrance. "Yes, we certainly did! But we couldn't stop them, we couldn't hold them for long."

"They fled like the pages of a torn-up programme blowing down the street."

"Yes, that's exactly it, blowing down the street . . . staining the cold north wind with . . . with . . ."

"With the shadow of our passing."

"Oh the shadow, yes!" He chuckled again.

"Happy days, Mister Marmalade."

They chinked glasses.

"We've been through a lot, Señor Rodrigo."

"We've seen them all, we have, we've seen them come and seen them take their bow."

A floorboard creaked beneath my feet. Mr Marmalade and Señor Rodrigo suddenly stopped talking.

"Who's there? Who's that?"

"It's a peeping Tom!"

I pushed the door open. "I heard a cry, so . . ."

Mr Marmalade squinted at me and then put on his glasses. "Oh, it's you."

I walked in. They were seated on either side of a cheap coffee table with spindly legs sharing a tea. Next to the table was an electric bar-fire, but only the flame-effect bulbs were switched on and the bars were cold and grey like rods of ash. Mr Marmalade was in his undershirt and trousers, braces hanging loose by his sides. Opposite him sat his dummy, Señor Rodrigo. He was wearing a pair of toreador trousers and a little matching jacket was folded neatly over the arm of his chair. He was also in his undershirt, thin wooden arms sticking out. They were sharing a tin of Spam, although Señor Rodrigo had not touched his.

Mr Marmalade spoke, "Heard a cry, did you say? No one crying in here. Did you hear anything, Señor Rodrigo?"

"Must have been when you got that speck of dirt in your eye."

"Oh yes! That would be it. I got a speck of dirt in my eye." And then he added uncertainly, "Honest I did."

38

I took out the photo of Dean Morgan and held it out. "I don't want to interrupt your party, I'm looking for this man."

Mr Marmalade lifted up his specs to rest them on his forehead and brought the photo up to within five inches of his eyes.

"I don't think I know him. Is he your friend?"

"I'm investigating his disappearance. I'm a private detective."

"I told you it was a peeping Tom," said Señor Rodrigo.

"Now, now," admonished Mr Marmalade, "there's no need for that." And then, lowering the photo, "I don't know him — is he in trouble?"

"He might be. He's just a harmless old man who might be mixed up in some trouble, the sort he probably doesn't know how to handle. I think he might be disguised as a ventriloquist."

Mr Marmalade pulled a face. "An impostor! We don't like them do we, Señor Rodrigo?"

"They always mean us harm."

I took out my card and picked up the photo. "If you should see him, or if you know anyone who might know something, you can reach me at this address."

On my way out the cleaner brushed past me and pressed a piece of crumpled paper into my hand. I waited until I had turned the corner at the end of the street and then read it. It said: "Meet me tonight at the Game if you want to find out about your friend."

And then the inevitable Aberystwyth afterthought: "Bring plenty of money."

When I got back to the office, there was an empty police car parked outside. The two occupants were already waiting for me in my office. One was Police Chief Llunos, and the other I didn't recognise. Llunos reached out and shook my hand as usual, although maybe there was a strained air about him. The other cop just watched with a look on his face that suggested there was a bad smell in the room. I gave him a curt nod and without a word fetched three glasses from the kitchenette and poured out three rums on the desk. Neither of them made a move.

"Thirsty?" I asked.

The new cop said, "It won't help you."

I took a sip from mine and then said to Llunos, "Who's the tough guy?"

He winced. "This is DI Harri Harries from Llanelli. He's up here on attachment to . . . er . . ."

"To wipe your nose?"

"They said I'd have trouble with you," Harri Harries said sourly.

"It looks like they were right."

"No." He walked up to me and positioned his face six inches away from mine and looked up. He was about seven or eight inches shorter than me and wearing the standard-issue CID crumpled suit and shabby raincoat. And he had been eating salami. "No, pal, they were wrong. I told them no shamus ever gives me problems. Not twice anyway."

Llunos sat on the client's chair. "Detective Harri Harries will be helping me out for a while. I'd appreciate it if you'd give him all the co-operation you can."

I ducked out of the way of the salami breath. "He won't get anything out of me until he improves his manners."

"Go on, cross my path, snooper, you'll be doing me a favour. I'm already bored of this dump, I could do with some entertainment."

I looked at Llunos. "Do they learn this dialogue in Llanelli?"

He shrugged. Harri Harries took a half-step to me until his coat was brushing lightly against my wrist. I could feel the heat from his body and detect the faint sour reek of Boots aftershave and unwashed ears.

"Llanelli, Carmarthen, Pontypridd . . . fine towns. You want to know why? Because there are no peepers in any of them. There used to be, but I cleaned them all out."

I turned to Llunos. "What do you need him to help you for? You seem to be doing a fine job all on your own."

Llunos didn't answer but the discomfort was evident on his face. Something had happened to make them send this monkey to sit on his back.

"Getting the whole town washed away in a flood is doing all right in your book, is it?" sneered Harri Harries.

"That's history."

"Oh, you don't like history? How about something hot off the press? Like some cheap shamus busting into a private party and trying to put the frighteners on the Mayor?"

"Or what about the Mayor ordering his men to beat up the shamus and chuck him unconscious into the sea?"

Harri Harries paused for a second. It seemed Jubal had omitted to mention this aspect of the night's entertainment. I could see Harri Harries didn't like that. Didn't like the fact that the Mayor was handing out unauthorised beatings, or that he had pulled the wool over his eyes. He didn't like it, but he didn't like it less than he didn't like me being at the party.

"Shouldn't have been there in the first place, should you?" he snarled.

"Nor should the Mayor. They sent you all the way up here just for that?"

"No, there's this other thing."

"What other thing?"

He stopped and looked at Llunos who stared solidly at his shoe.

"None of your business. Although I don't suppose you know what that phrase means, do you?"

"I could learn."

"Oh you'll learn all right!"

He walked to the window. At the desk he picked up the photo of Marty.

"Who's this, your wife?"

I said nothing and Llunos jumped slightly. "Hey, that's . . . er . . ."

The new cop held the picture close to his face and then turned it round and read the back. "Hey, I know who this is, it's the schoolkid isn't? The one that died on the cross-country run —"

I looked at Llunos who said simply, "He didn't get that from me."

Harri Harries sneered. "No I read it in your file, peeper. I bet you didn't know you had one, did you? So I know all about your little pansy friend freezing to death during games." He dropped the photo into the bin. "Tragic. No reason to push your games teacher out of an aeroplane, though."

"I didn't push him, he fell."

"What's the difference?"

"Not a lot to you, perhaps. But a lot to me. What happened to him was an accident; but what he did to Marty wasn't." This was a lie, of course. He fell out when I hit him with a cricket bat. I glanced quickly at the bat which was standing in the corner of my office and then at Llunos who had been in the plane; he didn't seem inclined to contradict me.

Harri Harries sneered, "Stop breaking my heart, snooper. Kid has a weak heart, dies on a cross-country run, so what? It happens. Doesn't give you the right to charge round town on a white horse all your life and throw mud at the Mayor."

"And what the hell gives you the right to tell me what to do? You haven't been in town five minutes yet!"

"I'm the law round here, that's all you need to know."

I walked to the door and opened it. "Thanks for coming, tough guy."

He walked through. "Keep your nose clean, peeper, or I'll clean it for you."

Llunos stood up and followed him. At the door he stopped and looked at me with the helpless expression of a friend who wants to explain but is struggling for the words. For years there had existed a sharp animosity between the two of us. Like most cops he didn't like private operatives, but since that time we fought side-by-side in the plane a warm bond of friendship had arisen. Strengthened, I liked to think, by his growing awareness that despite the different approaches we were still on the same side. I waved him to go. I knew how much he hated this, he didn't need to say.

As their footsteps receded down the wooden stairs I took the photo of Marty out of the bin and replaced it on the desk. For some time now the colours had been gradually lightening — a slow cinematic fade to white that echoed the moment in the fourth year when he disappeared into the blizzard. Only in my mind is the image still vivid. That day when the games teacher, Herod Jenkins, rejected his medical note and sent him on the cross-country run. Marty the consumptive schoolboy who never stood a chance. I picked up the cricket bat and took a swing, re-enacting the scene from three years ago when I finally avenged his death: when I faced up to Mr Jenkins in the fuselage of the plane and delivered the stroke that knocked him for six and sent that horizontal crease in his face they called a smile spinning out of this world. Since then I had lost count of the number of former pupils who had sidled into my office on account of it. Men who stood there in shabby suits, ill at ease and unsure how to say what they'd come for. They always smiled with relief when I said I understood and, without a word, handed them the bat. Howzat! they would shout as I bowled a piece of crumpled-up paper. Often the only other words they uttered before shaking me solemnly by the hand and leaving down the echoing, bare wooden stairs, were, "I was there from '70 to '75."

I poured the untouched drinks back into the bottle, sat down and cradled my own glass and swirled the drink round. And wondered what this other thing was, the one that Harri Harries had mentioned and then didn't want to talk about. The one that was none of my business. I was beginning to get that faint prickly sensation on the back of my neck. The one that said trouble ahead. There weren't many certainties in the job I did. But there was one prediction I could make that was copper-bottomed. When some tough guy told me something was none of my business it always ended up being plenty of my business.

CHAPTER
FOUR

Considering the number of garden sheds and herbaceous borders that were swept away, how much of the season's jam-making was ruined, there was surprisingly little rancour against the people who bombed the dam. Most people agreed justice had largely been done. Dai the Custard Pie, whose own joke shop had disappeared completely, was now imprisoned in a specially adapted dungeon, deep beneath Aberystwyth Castle. A clown of evil, doomed like a troglodyte never to see the face of the sun again. Mrs Llantrisant, the woman who swabbed my step for so many years, now exiled like Napoleon on Saint Madoc's Rock fifteen miles out to sea. Lovespoon the druid and Welsh teacher, missing presumed drowned. Herod Jenkins, last seen falling from the plane. Only Dai Brainbocs had escaped. The evil schoolboy genius and chief architect of our soaking. Somewhere at large now in South America, the traditional holiday destination of fugitives and renegades: Butch Cassidy and Sundance, the officers of the Third Reich, the Great Train Robbers, and now Brainbocs. And with him also, that most unlikely moll — the girl who should have been mine — Myfanwy.

* ★ ★

The cleaner from the Seaman's Mission had hardly been specific. Meet me at the Game. But it was enough. There might be many games in town but only one began with a capital G: "Mrs Beynon Says", also known as Fishwife's Chess. The contest that depended on knowing more about your neighbour's secret vices and indiscretions than anyone else in the street. It had once been a harmless parlour game played for matches at Christmas, but nowadays an entire week's pension or a dead husband's war medals could be staked on it. I wandered off in search of tonight's game, somewhere in the ghetto. Down some back alley, under a line of washing and through a hole in a fence where the touch of creosote was just a memory, like the scent of an old love letter. But which washing-line and which fence?

I could hear the ghetto long before I reached it. That far-off sound of carousing sailors found in all the world's great ports. And mingling with it, incongruously, the sweeter strains of the Sweet Jesus League out on their own shore patrol, singing hymns and warning the men of the dangers of unbridled fornication. A mixture of sounds that perfectly encapsulated the contradictions of the hour — captured the spiritual divide that the receding waters had left behind. To the puritans, the disaster had been a well-deserved punishment for our ill-defined iniquity. You saw them every night, singing hymns and carrying torches through the streets like columns of monks in a Gothic painting. Sometimes you caught the eye of one, who

47

tried to avoid your gaze, and you'd think to yourself, isn't that our postman? For other people, it was all just a reminder that our tenure here is short and that we should make the most of it. So the people of Aberystwyth gulped their pleasure giddily for a while, like Paris in La Belle Epoque or Berlin in the Roaring Twenties, dancing like the marionettes on a music box playing at the wrong speed. Sospan capitalised on the mood with that innate understanding of the *Zeitgeist* by creating new recipes based on a suggestion that life is precious and fleeting: Dance of the Mayfly, Gossamer Happiness, and the ever popular Lost Eden. Or the saucy one that caused all the trouble with the Sweet Jesus League, Hornucopia. This was also the time when the Chief of Police had to confiscate a lot of large-print pornography.

As I walked up Bridge Street, the battered old Bentley belonging to the Philanthropist swept past. A cat darted across the road. There was a squeal of tyres quickly followed by a soft furry thud and the sad but comic sight of an inert cat cartwheeling through the air. The car stopped and the chauffeur got out. He picked up the cat by its tail and, with a loud clattering noise, slung it into a rubbish bin. Then he slapped his hands together and drove off. I strolled on and thought of some lonely old lady sitting at her kitchen table tonight, looking round sharply every time the wind blew open the catflap, a saucer of unlapped milk standing on the tiled floor. Or was it a little girl walking down the street with her mum, pinning notices to the trees saying:

"Have you seen Bathsheba?" Aberystwyth could get to you sometimes.

In the old days, of course, if we wanted to gulp our pleasure giddily we just went to the Moulin — Wales's most notorious nightclub. A place that had stood for so much that was good and bad about the town. But they hadn't reopened it, had moved it instead to the end of the pier. I'd never been and I said I never would. The Moulin without Myfanwy was Troy without Helen. The gods obviously thought so too because the swooping new Perspex entrance to the pier funded by the Bucket & Spade Aid concert blew away in a storm. And since then the front had been permanently obscured by builders' plywood.

But tonight I needed only information. The sort that was supposed to be impossible to obtain, but could be bought in any of the pubs in the ghetto. I walked into the Angel.

It was crowded, hot and dark. And reeked of beer. Fishermen and sailors rubbed shoulders with town councillors and ladies of the night. Added to that was the usual haul of holiday-camp impresarios, bingo callers, whalebone dealers, shawl salesmen, out-of-work actresses from the "What the Butler Saw" movie industry, and here and there, looking even more furtive than most, a few monks from Caldy Island. A typical early-evening crowd in the Angel. I pushed my way to the bar and ordered a rum and went to sit in the corner by the fireplace.

A figure detached itself from the shadows leaning against the wall and sauntered over to me.

"Are you enjoying your holiday, love?"

The voice was soft with a husky rawness, the sort of rawness a voice gets when you see more before you are nineteen than most people see in a lifetime. The girl was wrapped up in a fur coat. The silky brush against my wrist suggested it was real, though probably full of moth-holes.

"Like that, huh?" she said when I didn't answer, and sat down next to me. A syrupy thud filled the room as someone, somewhere, clumsily dropped a needle on to a record, and after a few seconds Jim Reeves struggled to raise his voice above the bacon-frying hiss and sing, "Welcome to My Home".

"It's not a lot of fun, really, I know," said the girl. "The summer's much better and that's not a lot of fun either."

I smiled. There seemed something familiar about her, although there was almost nothing physical to see in the darkness. Reflections of flames dancing in her eyes, an edge of gold outlining her cheek, giving her the air of a wench in a Rembrandt painting. It wasn't her voice that was familiar and since I couldn't see her face I couldn't put it down to that, but still there was something. And when you work as a private eye in Aberystwyth you learn not to worry too much about where your hunches come from.

"I could show you round if you like . . . show you things."

"So you're a tour guide, are you?"

"Well not exactly . . . no . . . well yeah, in a way."

"Is there much to see?"

"There's the castle. I could show you that."

"And I bet you know all about it, don't you?"

"Yeah, of course."

"Who built it, then?"

"The Romans."

"The Romans!"

"Yeah, I s'pose. Or Robin Hood or someone. I don't know — who cares?"

She took out a cigarette and a lighter and the flame gave her young features a tender wash of light. When the cigarette was alight she flicked the lighter again and held it up to my face. Through the harsh hot glare I could see the glints of her eyes as she scrutinised me. The flame went out.

"You're Louie, aren't you?"

"Yes, how did you know?"

"I've seen you about. I'm Ionawr." She grabbed my hand in the darkness and shook it gently. "Nice to meet you." The hand was cold and smooth like a pebble on a beach.

"Do I know you?"

"We haven't met, but I know you through my sister."

"Is she here?"

"She's dead."

I peered at her intently through the blackness.

"My sister was Bianca."

★ ★ ★

We found the game in a cellar on Prospect Street. Ionawr, who had sold me the information for the price of a drink, insisted on coming with me, saying I wouldn't get in otherwise, which was hard to believe. But she refused to come in herself, knowing better than me what sort of reception a girl like her would get in this crossroads for the world's gossips, shrews, scolds and harpies. Inside, the air was fetid and moist, filled with the gamy fug of wet hair drying, infused with cellar smells of old stored potatoes, and Mintos, and camphor, cheap scent from grandsons at Christmas, ointment . . . and everywhere the air tingled with an intense, feverish mood of anticipation. It was partly the buzz you get at any big fight but also there was the build-up of static brought on by the rustling of pacamacs, and which had on occasion, so they said, given rise to the appearance of ball-lightning at these events.

The two contestants sat at a small kitchen table either side of a pot of tea. The audience was gathered round in rows of seats. We sat down as the umpire clumsily shuffled a pack of very big cards and called on a woman in the front row to draw. These were the Pleasantry cards and carried bonus points. The woman took three and the umpire read them out. "Well, that's what I heard, anyway" (murmur of disapproval from the crowd and shouts of "easy"). "Well you can't be too careful now, can you?" (more grumbling). And, finally, one that drew a ripple of applause: "'E'd have bloody flattened her if he'd found out, wouldn't he!"

52

The bell dinged and the lady in the red scarf started.

"Well, anyway, Mrs Beynon was just saying that it's not her first one that Mrs Jenkins was talking about. It's the elder one — she's got two, hasn't she? — the youngest one is still in Penweddig, isn't it? And the eldest is out at Talybont married to the chap whose father ran the garage that was knocked down, anyway it wasn't him it was his brother whose two boys were in the same class as the daughter of the one from the woman who lives above the bakers in Llanfarian —"

There were cries of "Logic! Logic!" from the blue corner and after a quick conference among the judges the charge was upheld and points were deducted for logic. The woman in the red scarf picked herself up off the canvas and came out fighting: "Anyway, it was her niece what made the jam for the 'bring and buy' after her husband came back from the mines with emphysema —"

There was a roar of delight from one section of the crowd and the other section looked on stony-faced. Two ladies in front of me turned to each other and swapped disapproving nods. Another lady in front of them turned round and said, "It wasn't emphysema at all — it was nothing to do with the aureoles as such —"

"I heard it was viral," said another spectator, "but they weren't quite sure what."

"You'd think she'd test her weak spot with mumps and measles or something first, wouldn't you!"

"Or maybe sciatica, that's always a good one, that is."

"You watch!" the first one scoffed. "Mrs Jenkins will trump her now with the pneumoconiosis."

People in the other rows turned round and told them to hush and I saw the cleaner from the Seaman's Mission waving to me from the adjoining room.

I walked in and bought two paper cups of beer served warm from a party-sized can and handed one to the woman. She took a drink and let out a satisfied "Ha!" as she patted her chest.

"Needed that, I did." She nodded towards the next room. "Just the warm-ups, the real stuff isn't until after eleven. Hang around a bit and . . ." Her words trailed off as her attention was caught by the entrance of another woman. A very old, shrunken woman who carried herself with the regal air of an abdicated queen. Her face was bony and almost skull-like, with fine white strands of hair stretched with painful tightness across the dome of her head. The woman serving at the bar instantly poured out a gin and put it on the counter for her, saying "Evening, Champ!"

The cleaner nudged me. "It's Smokey G. Jones. Won the treble in '62. Fifty-eight bouts and never lost."

I tried to look impressed and then asked her about the Dean. Tearing her admiring gaze away from the Champ, she licked her lips. "Well," she said, switching instantly into disapproval mode, "I knew straightaway there was something funny about him, like. He wasn't like the usual ones you get at all. Always giving himself airs he was and saying the bathroom was dirty and moaning about the breakfast and he never wanted to watch the same TV programmes as everybody else. Well, I could see he wasn't going to last long. 'I didn't know we had a member of the royal family staying with us,' I said to Mrs Jenkins so he could hear. But he didn't take the hint of course. Them type never do. I mean if he was so high and mighty, why wasn't he staying at one of the posh hotels down by Consti?"

I yawned. "You expect me to pay for stuff like this?"

She jerked her head back indignantly. "Well I'm not doing for me health now, am I?"

"This isn't gossip, it's ancient history."

"I should hope so too, I'm not one to gossip." She leaned closer and whispered, "I haven't got to the best bit yet."

I forced another yawn. "Don't tell me, let me guess: some man in a long back coat turned up asking questions about him."

"Yes," she hissed. "But the point is, what did he want to know?"

I shrugged.

"The valise! He wanted to know what had happened to the valise."

"What's a valise?"

"A case, you idiot!"

"Why didn't you say that?"

"I thought you were a private dick, that's how they speak."

"Where?"

"In LA."

"This is Aberystwyth."

She snorted. "Fat lot of good you are."

"So tell me about the valise."

"It belonged to the monk."

"What monk?"

She leaned back slightly and beamed at me. Her eyes were making dramatic downward movements and, following her gaze, I spotted her left hand tucked in tightly to her side, palm up, and making fluttering motions with the fingers as if she was trying to tickle a trout. I put a pound coin on her palm and the hand disappeared into the pocket of her pinny.

"I knew straightaway he was a monk," she continued seamlessly. "Even though he was pretending not to be. We've had his type before. Up from the monastery on Caldy Island for a good time. They were room-mates, you see."

"So what was in the valise?"

"How should I know, I don't go looking in other people's cases."

"Not much you don't!"

She flushed. "Well of all the . . . any more of that and I won't tell you the rest."

I nodded her to go on.

She held out her hand and tickled another trout.

I shook my head and turned to go. "Sorry, I can't afford it."

"But don't you want to know what happened to the valise, it's the best bit."

"What was inside it was the best bit, but you say you don't know. I don't believe you, by the way. I don't believe there's a single bag, case, coat or drawer in that crummy hovel you haven't stuck your nosey beak into.

But if it makes you feel better to deny it, that's up to you."

"Oooh you dirty rotten chiseller!" She sniffed forcibly. "I should have known what to expect from the son of a donkey-man. Well suit yourself. Now you'll never know what happened to the valise."

"I already know. There's only one thing that could have happened to it." I walked out and threw over my shoulder as I left, "The Dean must have taken it, otherwise you wouldn't have mentioned it."

As I left the house I bumped into someone arriving in a hurry. It was the old lady from the bay window at the Excelsior. She was heavily wrapped-up to disguise herself and pretended not to know me, but it was her all right. I could feel the hot smothering shame that, underneath all the finery, the lorgnette and the etiquette, she was the same as the rest of them. Borne in on a floodtide of longing that she could no more defy than the beaver can stop himself from building a dam. That eternal drive to gather round the village well and pour scorn on her neighbours for failing to live up to a code that no one else had ever managed to live up to either.

I walked out into the street as the room behind me thundered with the explosive percussion of five hundred orthopaedic boots stamping on the boards, accompanied by shrill Red Indian whoops. Above the tumult, a voice rose exultantly, crying, "E'd have bloody flattened her if he'd found out, wouldn't he!"

Out in the street Ionawr came up to me from the shadows and put her hand in mine. I could see now in the yellow streetlight she was dressed much like any other kid of her age. Faded jeans flared at the bottom over absurd platform shoes, too much make-up and too little on underneath the fur coat: a skimpy halter-neck top that didn't reach down as far as her navel. You saw girls like this all the time walking down the street hand in hand with men old enough to be their fathers or even grandfathers. And they really could be were it not for that furtive air that marks them out and gives the game away: that strange awkwardness that comes from having to concentrate on the simple task of walking; and from the insane overwhelming belief that everyone in the street that night can read your thoughts. The walk of shame that only dissolves when the bedroom door slams gratefully shut.

The cold had deepened and stung our cheeks like the kiss of a jellyfish. We cut through the castle and headed for Pier Street. There weren't many dining options at this time of night — if you discounted the 24-hour whelk stalls on the Prom.

"We could go to the Indian," Ionawr said hesitantly, reading my face to gauge my reaction.

"That's not the sort of place to take a lady, even one . . ."

"One what?"

"Oh nothing."

58

"I know what you were going to say. Even one like me."

"No I wasn't."

"Yes you were. Don't deny it, it doesn't matter. I know what I want to eat: something traditional Welsh like my grandmother used to make when I was a kid."

"That's a bit of a tall order."

"They do *caawl* at the Chinese." She took my hand and pulled me. "Come on."

I hesitated.

"What's wrong?"

"Did you hear that?"

"What?"

I thought for a moment and then said, "Oh nothing." We carried on. And then I stopped again.

"We're being followed."

"Are you sure? I can't see anyone."

"I've felt it since we left the game."

I sent Ionawr on ahead and slunk into a doorway and waited. The footsteps got louder and louder. When the guy passed I grabbed him and threw him into the doorway.

"Oh my Lord!" said a voice. It was Smokey G. Jones, her tiny head projecting from the collar in her coat like a light bulb. "Don't kill me, please!"

"Mrs Jones! What are you doing? I thought you were following me."

"I was. Only I didn't mean any harm. I just wanted to ask you. No harm at all."

"Ask me what?"

"If you'd have a word with her, please, Mr Knight, just a word. This arthritis is something terrible. It's all them cups of tea in me fighting days."

"Have a word with who?"

"Miss Calamity. She's cut me supply down. I need me placebo, Mr Knight, I can't get through a day without it. But she's gone and cut me supply."

Just then Ionawr reappeared and Mrs Jones stopped and looked at her. "Hmm." She sniffed. "What baggage." She walked off.

It was often mayhem in the small take-away but tonight it was quiet. A few students, a few locals sitting on the hard-backed chairs, stupefied by drink into a morose silence, killing time softly like holidaymakers at a strike-bound airport. At the counter a Chinese girl in her mid-teens was doing her homework, a curtain of silky black hair falling forward to protect her from the gaze of the customers, falling in a delicate curl like the clef on a musical score.

I coughed and she looked up.

"Can I help you, sir?"

"I hear you sell *caawl* now."

"Yes," she said. "Would you like some?"

"Is it good?"

"People who know about these things say it is. Personally I've never tried it."

"Quite an unusual dish to find in a Chinese restaurant."

60

"We Chinese have to adapt." She wrote down the order and handed it through the serving-hatch. "And it brings in the crowds."

"Isn't it a bit dishonest?"

She shrugged. "I don't know, is it? In my grandmother's province they have a tree that gets pollinated by bats, so the tree gives off a perfume of dead mice. No one complains about that."

"Except maybe the cats."

She smiled and took our money. "Anyway, lamb stew with lumps of cheese — it's not so very hard to make."

"Ah! but the cheese has to be added with love," I said.

Someone by the door farted and his mates burst into crude guffaws of laughter. I fought the urge to look round and waited for the prickle of shame to subside.

The girl said, "We add all our ingredients with love, our customers deserve nothing less." She took the cartons of *caawl* and placed them carefully in the paper bag. "I've seen you before somewhere, but you're not a regular."

"With my father, maybe, on the Prom. He's the donkey-man."

"Ah of course!" She handed me the food. "You round-eye are so sentimental about your animals. *Bon appetit!*"

On the Prom the wind roared past our ears like a tube train rushing out of a tunnel. The tide had risen and each time the water thundered into the base of the sea-wall, spray flared up like a series of jack-in-the-box ghosts. I had one arm over Ionawr's shoulders, clutching her against me for warmth, and I held the brown paper bag with its cargo of hot *caawl* at arm's length like a lantern — two wayfarers lost in the night.

"Do you know what she was talking about?" I said. "Asking Calamity for some placebo?"

"No idea, but if she's getting it from Calamity, who knows what it is."

Electro-illuminated dwarves danced drunkenly on the swinging cable overhead, and down by the bandstand we heard the sound of youths jeering. We walked on and as we got closer the jeering of the youths became punctuated by faint Spanish cries, "No, please leave us alone, *Señores*!"

The lads were dancing round in a circle, and in the centre there lay a man. Next to the man, on the floor, was a ripped-open suitcase.

"Hey!" I shouted. Slightly wrong-footed by the intrusion, they stopped and turned to face us. There was silence for a while, except for the sea exploding like distant artillery, and then I heard the Spaniard again, squeaking above the muffled roar. "Please, sir, we are just humble peasants!" It was the dummy, Señor Rodrigo, and lying on the floor, battered and kicked and covered in cement grime, was Mr Marmalade. Ionawr gasped. One of the youths was holding Señor Rodrigo by his ankles, upside down over the railings. His eyes had rolled upward in their sockets and in the garish mix of bright lights and shadows thrown by the streetlamps and the overhead illuminations, his wooden face had acquired a cast of terror.

The youth gave him a shake and the other lads cheered. Mr Marmalade was making desperate attempts to get up, but every time he half-raised himself one of the lads would shove him back down with the sole of his boot.

"Gottle of fucking geer!" they shouted. Mr Marmalade was clutching his chest above the heart and gasping.

"*Somos solamente campesinos pobres, mi amigo!*" wailed the dummy.

"You leave him alone, you bullies!" shouted Ionawr. The leader of the youths shouted, "What the fuck do you want?"

"*Somos solamente campesinos pobres, mi amigo!*"

"And shut that fuckin' dummy up!"

The kid smashed the dummy's head twice against the metal of the railings. One of the eyes came out. Ionawr screamed. Mr Marmalade was now making obscene sucking sounds and holding his chest, his eyes bulging as if something was pushing them out of his head from the inside.

"*Somos solamente campesinos pobres, mi amigo!*"

I stepped forward and punched the lead yob. Despite the swagger and posturing, he was probably not much more than eighteen or nineteen and slightly built. He fell sprawling on to the pavement. I kicked him viciously in the stomach and he grunted in pain. Across the road a casement window screeched open and a woman in a nightie leaned out and cried, "I've called the police, you bastards, they're on the way!" And as if in confirmation we heard the distant wail of a siren starting up. None of the lads had the guts to make a move on me. The leader got to his feet and, seeing the distant blue flash of the approaching prowl car, took to his heels, followed by his gang.

We kneeled down by Mr Marmalade. Over by the railings, like the dummy that continues talking as his master drinks a glass of milk, the shattered mannikin continued to plead for their lives.

"*Somos solamente campesinos pobres, mi amigo!*"

Maybe it was the wind plucking strange notes from the musical stave of the seaside railings. Or maybe the terror of the night, working on our own dark fears and imaginings, had somehow transformed the voices of the approaching cops. Or maybe we just dreamed it. Because as we kneeled in the grime and Ionawr cradled Mr Marmalade's head it was clear that the old ventriloquist's heart had already given out and instead of milk he had drained the cup of life.

"*Somos solamente campesinos pobres, mi amigo!*"

CHAPTER
FIVE

It would be naïve to say Aberystwyth ever had much innocence left to lose, but the death of the Amazing Mr Marmalade struck many people as a watershed. Old man kicked to death on the Prom, they said, never thought I'd live to see that. Perhaps it was all those fresh graves on the side of Pen Dinas dug in the wake of the flood that contributed to the mood, or maybe just the casual brutality of the attack. Or perhaps it was the recognition that the optimism that many people felt after the flood had deceived us. As a town we had stared death in the face and prided ourselves on the fact that death had blinked first. But the murder of Mr Marmalade confirmed what we secretly suspected all along: it was all at best a reprieve, a stay of execution. The optimism was snake oil.

Walking home after the attack, I kept thinking about what a senseless act it was, and how easily it could have been avoided. What was an old man like Marmalade doing there at that time of night? Where did he think he was going? It didn't make sense. When I got home I found the answer. It turned out he had been going to see me. There was a note from him saying he had called

65

and that he had information. And I had to wonder, was this a coincidence, a motiveless attack of the sort that could happen to anyone? Or did it have something to do with me? As far as I knew, the police didn't know about his visit but they soon would, and once that happened they'd haul me in for questioning. The smart thing to do was tell them before they found out, that way they would know I wasn't holding out on them. Trouble was, holding out on them was what I did for a living. It was part of the unwritten code: protecting the client's privacy. But I could only go so far and murder was definitely beyond the line in the sand. Not that the new broom at the police station would be much for fine distinctions anyway. His type were always itching to revoke your licence. And they generally had a preferred technique for doing it: making it fall out from your pocket as you tumbled down the police station steps.

I let Ionawr take my bed and I took the sofa. And then I put Myfanwy's LP on the turntable, unscrewed the cap on my friend Captain Morgan, and tried to beat back the louche imaginings that all men feel in the presence of a girl who sells herself for a living. The look of reproach in her eyes didn't help. That sweet, sharp pang and slight surprise that you maybe don't find her attractive . . . ah if only she knew! As if any man would not ache and burn inside for such a lovely girl. But you cannot say it, because the act of protecting her has no meaning if you say the words. I'd love to but . . . it's not that I don't want to but . . . But what? Your sister died in my arms once? To speak the words is to ask to be absolved. To disavow your cake on moral grounds and then eat it anyway. Bianca's sister, probably not much more than eighteen. The same age as Bianca when she walked into my life and almost immediately out of her own. A waif from the Moulin who, they said, never did anything from a pure motive, but who tried to help me on a case without any motive at all other than kindness. A quality so rare in those days most people didn't recognise it when they saw it. I couldn't save her — had to watch helplessly instead as they ran her over down at the harbour. And of all the cars in town they could have chosen to kill her with, they chose mine. So sleep alone, Ionawr, and don't ask why; in case the answer you get is the simplest one: that three years ago I shared the same pillow with your sister. Captain Morgan stared at me. I didn't know who he was but I could guess what he would be doing right now in my shoes. He winked and I turned the bottle round and forced my thoughts elsewhere, far away from Aberystwyth Prom, to Myfanwy, stuck with the creep Brainbocs in some cockroach-infested cantina in Patagonia. Singing those bitter-sweet ballads of love and loss to the half-Welsh half-Indian mestizos. On the front of the record cover, for no apparent reason, the characters were spaced out: M.Y.F.A.N.W.Y. Seven scarlet letters running through the seaside rock of my heart.

Next morning I put a call through to Gretel's hall of residence. It was a bit early to expect students to be up but they were made of different mettle in Lampeter and the porter told me she was out giving alms. I left a message for her to call me before evensong at the latest. Then I made some coffee and called Meirion, the crime reporter at the *Gazette*. He'd heard about the attack on Marmalade but no one knew what the story was. The police were just treating it as routine. He promised to let me know if he heard anything. I asked him about the man in the Peacocks' coat. Did it ring any bells? He chuckled. We both knew that on matters like this he had a whole cathedral belfry at his disposal.

"I seem to remember some sort of incident out at Ysbyty Ystwyth a while back," he said. "Something to do with the military, called the Ysbyty Ystwyth Experiment or something. Apparently some civilians saw something they shouldn't have and afterwards they got a visit from someone dressed the way you describe. I didn't cover the story so I don't know much but I'll dig up what I can."

I thanked him and went downstairs to fetch the post. There was a card from Mrs Llantrisant. If ever there was a demonstration of the fact that we never really know anyone, she was it. Ten years swabbing my step and general cleaning and all along she had been planning to blow up the dam at Nant-y-moch. She'd been on Saint Madoc's Rock for eighteen months now, standing, they said, all day long on the cliff-top like a statue from Easter Island, staring out towards Aberystwyth. On fine days you could charter a boat from the harbour and look at her through binoculars. She must have earned some privileges through good behaviour to be allowed to send mail. This was the second in four months.

> A pair of puffins have taken up residence in the eaves of the old wool shed. I have called them Gertie and Bertie. They dote on each other madly. Their cooing and billing fills me with joy in the gleam of the morning sun. But when evening falls and a gentle melancholy descends upon their preening a fear creeps into my heart and I have to close the shutters and banish them. Ah yes! love, that beautiful demon that devours us all in the end. I think of you and all that has passed between us and I forgive you freely with my heart because only love — for that harlot whose name I will not utter — could have made you betray me the way you did. Banished from the hearths of those I love and confronted daily with the rubble of my life, this is the truth I publish abroad: love will corrupt us more assuredly than sin.
>   Yours Gertrude Ophelia Llantrisant

I dropped the card on to the table and said to the empty room, "Wow!" Despite all that had happened I found no hatred in my heart for her. Only pity. Was her middle name really Ophelia? I put on my hat and coat, left Ionawr sleeping, and walked out.

It was a grey, damp morning and the light on the end of the harbour jetty winked sleepily. I walked to the very end of the Prom and then doubled back, my steps taking me unwittingly, or perhaps because they knew better than me where they wanted to go, to the place on Harbour Row where Bianca had died: the stigmatic stain in the tarmac that commemorated the short blasted life of an Aberystwyth harlot. The mark had faded now but the faith that her outline would return was strong among the pilgrims. The nearby guest-houses were already booked out for the week of the anniversary next summer and it didn't matter how much Domestos the ladies from the Sweet Jesus League poured on the tarmac. There was a man standing at the spot, staring down and deep in thought. It was Father Seamus. He bent down and picked up a wreath, one of the donation from the Abergavenny Rotary Club, and put it in the bin. He looked slightly embarrassed to find himself observed.

"Best place for it," he said lamely.

"You think so?"

"We could do without this sort of nonsense."

I nodded. "You're a sceptic, then?"

"Don't tell me you're not, Louie?"

I shrugged. "I am, of course, but it really did look like her, you know. And this is the exact spot where it happened."

"It's just a stain. You could probably find one on your toilet floor that reminded you of someone if you screwed up your eyes and stared long enough. And had enough to drink."

"True, but no one has been murdered on my toilet floor."

70

Father Seamus took my arm and led me away. "This sort of thing doesn't help, Louie. I really don't think so. These people have very pressing needs, real problems of squalor and sickness and hunger and overcrowding. Dickensian problems even . . ." We walked along towards the Seaman's Mission, Father Seamus still holding my arm, although I didn't feel comfortable with him doing it.

"These people need concrete solutions. Looking to ghosts for their deliverance won't help them."

"I'm sure you're right, Father."

"I know it's hard, but sometimes we have to face facts, no matter how unpalatable."

"But what are the facts, Father?"

He raised his hand and put it on my shoulder and leaned in, faking a look of deep, pained seriousness. "Sometimes when a prostitute dies in brutal tragic circumstances, it doesn't make her a Mary Magdalene, it just makes her a dead whore."

I winced and in that moment I hated Father Seamus. No one who knew Bianca could have used words like that about her. But I said nothing because forcing a smile on to a face that sees little reason to smile and getting on with it is all part of the job.

After Father Seamus disappeared from view I walked down the alley between the two buildings to the Rock Wholesaler fronting the harbour. The door was ajar and I entered, my nostrils filling instantly with an intense suffocating sweetness. It was an Aladdin's Cave of confectionery: millions of pink crystalline rods, neatly stacked and rising to the ceiling like alabaster columns in a mosque. The light had a soft pink translucency, almost hypnotic, like you get from staring at the bright sun through an eyelid, spidery red veins showing through like the scarlet letters a.b.e.r.y.s.t.w.y.t.h.

After the flood the stockpile had been replenished with the same urgency that they rebuild stocks of coal at a power station following a strike. And now, all around, men scurried like ants with sugar, toiling to keep it topped up. I passed through another door into an antechamber where I came upon the same scene except for a minor difference. A door was open at the back and men were lifting crates on to a lorry. Off to one side, with a Biro stuck behind her ear, Calamity was sitting on an upturned crate, punching numbers into an adding machine.

"What do I do with the *Blackpool*, Miss Calamity?" said a warehouseman.

"Stack it behind the rainbow-coloured ones," she said without looking up.

I took a step forward, my shadow falling across her gaze.

"Oh hi, Louie! How's it going?"

"What's this, contraband seaside rock?"

"Just skimming off some surplus production."

"Didn't I tell you to stop all this wheeling and dealing?"

She sighed. "I know, you did, Louie, but it's just not that simple."

"Where's the hard part?"

"You can't roll an empire up overnight. I've got people relying on me."

"One of these days you'll get into trouble."

"Everyone's paid off, don't worry. They're all looking the other way."

"And what's all this about Smokey G. Jones and some placebo?"

"I'm trying to cut her down — she's getting through three bottles a week."

"That's not what I meant."

She shrugged. "You know how it is. She took part in a trial at the hospital for some new drug and they gave her the placebo. She said it worked a treat. Placebos are the —"

"I know what they are."

"Faith can move mountains, Louie."

"But you can't go round prescribing drugs."

"It's only vitamin C. And anyway, she's hooked now, I can't stop it."

The sound of a man unconvincingly barking like a dog cut through the air. The noise set off a frenzy of activity. The men stopped unloading and scurried hither and thither, slamming doors and flinging tarpaulins over crates. Shouts of "police" and "stop" came from the other room. Calamity grabbed her stuff and fled to the far side of the hall. In less than two seconds I was alone. Calamity rushed back, grabbed my arm and dragged me to the cupboards where they stored the protective clothing and pulled me inside.

★   ★   ★

We stood in the dark cupboard and held our breath, listening intently to the sounds from outside. Footsteps approached. Stopped. The door was pushed slightly, teasingly. And then opened. It was Llunos. He made a soft gulping sound as he recognised us, his eyes jumping in their orbits. We smiled. He closed the door. Five minutes later, a piece of paper was slipped through. It said, "Not you as well!"

CHAPTER
SIX

The death of one of the ventriloquists had shaken the others quite badly and some had agreed to talk. I was shown into a room upstairs at the Seaman's Mission in which sat two very old men, with fine wisps of white hair on their shiny pates, and old suits that had stayed the same size for years as they both gradually shrank. They were drinking tea and still chewing their breakfast with grizzled unshaven jowls and false teeth that suggested that necessary lip control to be a working vent was no more than a distant memory for them. They were twins, Bill and Ben.

"Few years ago he probably performed at their birthday parties," said Ben. "Their little faces glowing with excitement."

"All pink and freshly scrubbed, their hair neatly combed and everyone smelling of vanilla," said Bill. Then he turned to me again as if just remembering something.

"Are you sure the confrère spoke after Mr Marmalade was dead?"

"The what?"

"His confrère, Señor Rodrigo."

"You mean his dummy?"

"We never use that word, it's insulting. Are you sure he carried on speaking?"

"No, I'm not sure, I'm just saying that's how it seemed. It was probably the wind."

"How could it be the wind, the wind doesn't speak Spanish!"

"No I know, but it's like —"

The old man stamped his foot in a strangely uncalled-for state of agitation. "But that's a stupid thing to say, the wind goes: Wooooooooaaahhhooooo . . ."

"Or: Phweeeeeeeeeeee!" added Ben.

"Not like Spanish at all," said Bill.

"OK, you win." I raised my hands. "It couldn't have been the wind."

The two old-timers looked at each other with an air of intense earnest. Bill hissed the words, "It's the Quietus! The Quietus!"

Ben punched his fist feebly into his palm. "It's . . . it's not possible, no it cannot be —"

"And yet it must . . . this man has seen it . . . with his own eyes!"

"Are we to believe a . . . a . . . an outsider . . . one who has no love for the Art?"

"Must we reject him because of his obscurity?"

"But if . . . if . . . no it cannot be. Not to such a lowly one as . . . as . . . a private detective, who ever heard of such a thing?"

"And yet did not the Good Lord reveal himself to a mere shepherd?"

"If it is true we must put a call through to St Petersburg."

"But we have to be sure, we have to be certain."

They stopped their conference and turned to me. "It is the Quietus."

"I don't know what that is."

"No, you wouldn't. If you did you wouldn't be here, you would be on the train to St Petersburg."

"If I promise not to go to St Petersburg, will you tell me what it is?"

"The Dying Swan Quietus. It's a legend . . . no! It's much more than that . . . it's the elephants' graveyard of ventriloquism . . . no! It's much more than that, more than that, it's . . ."

His brother interjected. "You know the trick they always do at kids' parties where the vent makes his confrère speak while he drinks a glass of milk?"

I nodded, "I've seen it a couple of times."

"It's like that, only you do it when you die. Like a dying swan. It's . . . it's very sacred to us."

"You get a prize if you report one."

"But there's only ever been one. Enoch Ishmael in 1785. There was a plaque to him on the harbour wall for many years."

"But the druids melted it down to spite us."

"One day we are going to have a day-care centre and it will be called the Enoch Ishmael Day-Care Centre."

The double-handed conversation had started to resemble a vaudeville act. I raised my hand. "Whoa! Enough about the Quietus. I want to know about this man who shared the room with the monk, Dean Morgan."

They stopped speaking and fidgeted. "We . . . we . . . don't know about him."

"Please, it's very important that I find him."

"No, we don't know him. We've never heard of him." Their faces became disfigured with disgust. "He's not our friend, we hated him. Tell us about the Quietus . . ."

I stood up, walked to the door and said, "What Quietus? I didn't see any Quietus."

Gretel turned up in the office later that afternoon, wearing a fawn Spanish inquisitor's cowl over her Mother Hubbard. Her face shone with the mild intoxication that comes from a day-trip to Gomorrah. She sat in the client's chair and spun round like a child before steadying herself by grabbing the edge of the desk. "I can't stay long I've got a haunting tutorial at six."

"Sure."

"And I've got three pairs of pants on so don't even think of trying to take advantage of me."

"And I bet they're really big pants, aren't they?"

She nodded. "They were my gran's."

"Ah well, just my luck. I'll have to ask you about Dean Morgan instead."

"Have you found him yet?" she asked breezily, as if we were talking about a lost hamster.

"Funnily enough, no, I've been a bit slow this week. But I've found out a few things. It seems he only spent a couple of days at the Excelsior before checking out. According to the hotel detective he checked out in disguise."

"What do you mean?"

"A new identity. He checked in as a professor and left as a ventriloquist."

I said the word slowly and scrutinised Gretel's expression for any sort of reaction. Clients invariably know a lot more than they tell you.

"How strange. Are you sure it was him?"

I shook my head. "No but I think the detective was telling the truth and he wouldn't have been mistaken, I doubt the Dean was very accomplished at the cloak-and-dagger stuff."

"He must be in trouble, then."

"It's a possibility. But not the only one. It's always possible he just wanted to let his hair down."

"But he hasn't got any — well hardly any."

"You know what I mean. Make whoopy."

"Don't be daft!"

"People do it, you know, even in Lampeter. It's a quite popular pastime, drinking and carousing and . . . and . . . well, you know."

She flushed, from anger or embarrassment. "Yes I think I do. You're suggesting his disappearance might have something to do with a woman, aren't you!"

"It happens."

"Not to Professor Morgan it doesn't! He's a respectable man."

She was looking agitated. I made a submissive gesture with my hands. "Try not to get upset and at least consider it. You get some starchy old fossil spending years in some creaky old college . . ."

She shot up from her chair. "That's it, I'm leaving!"

"What's wrong?"

Tears of indignation were watering her eyes. "How dare you call Professor Morgan a fossil!"

I jumped round to the other side of the desk and grabbed her arm. She let herself be guided gently back to the seat. She said, "Dean Morgan isn't the sort of person to do something like that."

"People like the Dean are exactly the sort of people who do things like that."

"Whose side are you on?"

I sighed. "If you hire me I'm on your side. But only so long as you are hiring me to find out the truth and not to ignore evidence that might damage someone's reputation. You have to understand where I stand. This is a dangerous town and if you send me out there to do your business you owe it to me to tell me everything you know. I'll do my best for you, I'll even put myself in danger if I think the case merits it, but all the same you have to do your best by me: That's fair, isn't it?" It was an old, old spiel and I'd used it a thousand times before. Sometimes it worked and sometimes it didn't, but I don't think I'd had a client yet who told me everything she knew and the bits they forgot to mention were always the ones that caused all the trouble.

"Do you really think he's gone off with a woman?"

"I don't think anything at the moment. Tell me about the Bad Girl."

80

Gretel flinched. "H . . . h . . . how did you know about her?"

"You mentioned her, remember?"

"Oh."

"Yes. Oh."

"She was bad!"

"Yes, I know, and you are good and so was the Dean."

Gretel leaned forward across the desk as if there might be someone listening behind the door. "We hated her really and none of us would speak to her. She was an orphan, you see, they found her on the church steps — no really! They really did! We couldn't stop laughing when we heard, we thought it only happened in nineteenth-century novels. And there she was on a Sunday-school scholarship! But that's ridiculous, isn't it, because they are only supposed to be for holy people but who knows where she came from? For all we knew her father could have been a dirty old donkey-man like yours!" She stopped and leaned back. "But we don't talk about her."

"Yeah I can see how hard it is for you."

"And she had no sense of humour, either! After we laughed at her she wouldn't talk to us. I mean, just imagine it! Putting on airs like that and thinking you're a somebody when you don't even have a mum or dad! So then Clarissa — that's me and Morgana's friend — called her a chimney sweep and, dear Lord! Do you know what she did? She punched Clarissa in the mouth. Unbelievable! So of course we had to report her. It was for her own good, wasn't it? That's when she made the allegations."

"What allegations?"

"Well . . . you know!"

"About the Dean?"

"She was a lying bitch."

"What did he do? Make a pass at her?"

"Not only him, quite a few of them. Men! I don't know. See a girl in a short skirt and they can't control themselves, worse than goats, aren't they? But it wasn't true of course."

"Oh of course."

"No really!"

"How do you know?"

She rolled her eyes as if the answer was obvious. "Oh come on, Dean Morgan wasn't like that!"

"So you keep saying. What did this girl look like?"

"Oh I don't know. Tall I suppose, with long blonde hair, and . . . and . . ."

"Was she pretty?"

She sniffed. "She might have been, I suppose, in a cheap, slatternly sort of way —"

"Very pretty? Sexy even?"

"Some people said so but I could never see it myself."

"But she wore a short skirt?"

"How do I know what she wore! I can't remember."

"You just told me she did."

"No I didn't."

"OK, forget it, what was her figure like?"

She flushed. "Oh please!"

"Come on, you're a grown-up, aren't you? Tell me what she was like!"

"But . . . but I don't . . . how am I supposed . . ."

"She had a figure like an hour-glass, didn't she?"

"See, you're just like all the rest, typical!"

"All the rest of what?"

"Men."

"Which men? The ones at the college?"

She didn't answer.

"Look you might as well tell me, I'll find out anyway. She was blonde and cute and had curves in all the right places, yes? And she was a bit wild and all those dusty pieces of human parchment at Lampeter in their silly black hats drooled like dogs at a butcher's window whenever she appeared, isn't that right?"

Gretel banged her fist on the desk. "No it wasn't like that! It wasn't, it wasn't!"

"And all the rest of you girls were jealous and so you ganged up on her —"

"No! We didn't! She was a horrid, low-class orphan and she had to leave and we all said good riddance!" And with that, Gretel stormed out.

About half an hour after Gretel left for her haunting tutorial the Philanthropist's butler turned up. I was sitting staring at the ceiling doing a rough piece of mental arithmetic — it's an exercise I frequently do with my clients and involves guessing certain building dimensions then working out the approximate size of the client's belfry and then computing the amount of bats in it. Then I put clients in order of bat population. Gretel had just gone straight into the charts at number one.

The butler wore an old-fashioned coat, a bit like the ones worn by the Beefeaters in the Tower of London but black in colour as opposed to red. He also wore a stubby top-hat like a sawn-off stovepipe. He had mutton-chop whiskers, reading specs perpetually in his hands, a face that managed to be intelligent, obsequious and calculating all at the same time, and he spoke with an artificial plum in his mouth in a language that was vaguely reminiscent of Jeeves and yet which couldn't quite disguise, for all the exaggerated English country manor of it, his Welsh origins. If I'd ordered a Welsh butler straight from a catalogue he would have been it.

We shook hands and he told me he represented the Philanthropist who had recently purchased the old sanatorium and he had come on an errand on his behalf. I offered him some run and he accepted and I duly filled up two glasses.

"The Philanthropist is a great collector of various things — ornaments, antiques, knick-knacks and memorabilia . . ."
    "How charming."
    "Indeed. In particular he is an avid collector of all sorts of memorabilia concerning a certain nightclub singer, one known to you, I'm sure. Myfanwy Montez."

84

I managed to keep almost all trace of a reaction at bay but there was the slight narrowing of the eyelids and the tightening of my grip upon the rum tumbler. I don't know which one he noticed. It hardly mattered.

His voice had a wheedling, insinuating tone that I took exception to. "Yes I see the name is not without an effect on you."

"What do you want?"

"My master has bought up a lot of the usual stuff on the market. Signed record covers, posters, programmes, evening gowns, etcetera. But he finds his hunger undiminished. He is looking for something more intimate and personal, evidence of the private Myfanwy rather than the public persona. It is known that you had an affair with her . . ."

I stood up and walked around the desk and took hold of his glass and pulled it out of his hand.

"Don't get me wrong, Mister Knight —"

"I'm getting you wrong so loud it's making my ears hurt."

"The Philanthropist would pay handsomely. Perhaps an item of clothing left behind such as a T-shirt or a sock . . . or even something more evocative . . . shall we say, moist and intensely fragrant —"

I grabbed his coat collar and dragged him upwards from his chair offering him the choice of leaving under his own steam or under mine. He chose his own, but I gave him some help from my foot anyway.

Ten minutes later Bill and Ben turned up. It was a busy afternoon. All I needed now was a client and I'd have full house. They'd brought me a Quietus witness form to sign.

"OK," I said, "you know what the deal is. Tell me about the Dean."

The two old men swapped glances and then Bill spoke, "If we tell you, you sign the form, right?"

"If I like what you tell me."

They looked confused. "But you saw it, you saw the Quietus!"

"Some days I think I saw it, some days I think it was just the wind whistling, *amigo*. Which day it is today is up to you, but get on with it, I'm bored of talking to you." They both drew themselves up and said defiantly, "He went to join the Johnnys."

"He did what?"

"He went to be a Johnny — a Clown's Johnny," explained Ben.

"He wanted to join the circus, you see."

"Just like them all. They all want to do that. We see them, don't we?"

Bill nodded. "All the time. Everyone wants to be a lion tamer."

"Or walk a tightrope."

"Or eat fire."

"Or even just balance balls on the sea-lion's nose."

"But all they get to do is be the lousy Johnny."

"But of course, what they don't realise is, there's only one way into the circus . . ."

"Oh yeah, and what's that?"

They hesitated. Some strange force was holding them back.

86

"Go on! What is it?"

"We can't say."

"You want the prize for reporting the Quietus, don't you?"

"Of course we do, but we can't say, it's rude!"

"OK, suit yourselves. I've got three other ventriloquists coming round later on. I'll sign their Quietus forms instead."

Bill leaped up and shouted, "No! You big swine! We got there first!"

"So what's the only way of getting into the circus?"

"OK then, you asked for it," said Bill. "It's . . . it's . . . it's through a lady's thingummy!"

"A lady's thingummy?"

"We don't know the proper name," said Ben. "It's Latin."

I took out my pen and signed the form.

CHAPTER
SEVEN

Meici Moondust laughed. "Basically," he said, "the only route into the circus is through the birth canal. You have to be born into it, you see, born to a family of maniacs. A family so fucked-up they have you on the tightrope as soon as you can crawl. People who buy you sequins for your birthday and a safety net for Christmas." He lifted the cornet above his head and adroitly licked the globules of melted vanilla as they ran down before they reached his knuckles. "If you can't do the act, whatever it is, absolutely perfectly by the time you are four you'll never be good enough for the circus. But you'll always be good enough to be Mr Johnny. He's the stooge, you see. All he does is have pies put in his face or ladders swung round at him, or he gets slapsticked on his arse all season. The only reason the job even exists is because after years of taking it themselves the clowns decided they'd had enough and created the post of Mr Johnny. And people queue up for it." Meici Moondust turned aside and spat. "When I was a compère out at the Kamp I saw five or six get off the train from Shrewsbury every month. Accountants and clerks and insurance salesmen . . . you name it."

He spat again. "Clown's Johnny. If you see one look the other way."

Calamity and I stepped over the remains of the demolished wall and on to the field of cleared debris that had once been Woolie's. A thriving market had grown up in the rubble.

"I just can't believe it's gone," said a confused old lady.

"Neither can any of us," said the woman from the Saint John's Ambulance Brigade.

"It's been a terrible blow for everyone."

"We used to come to Woolie's every year. Used to drive all the way from Walsall."

"A lot of people did."

"They said I was daft because I work in Woolie's in Walsall. But it's nice to have a change, isn't it? And now it's been washed away."

"Drink your Bovril love, drink your Bovril — you'll be all right."

We ordered some tea from a stall and Calamity took out her list. "Bucket, spade, mess-tin . . ."

"We need a mess-tin?"

"That's what it says in the brochure."

"This is scarier than I thought." As a sleuth in Aberystwyth I generally went undercover a lot less than people imagined. And when I did it was usually to dress as someone come to read the meter or something. Not as a means to go and stay at Kousin Kevin's Krazy Komedy Kamp in Borth. The brochure was specific on this point: Children and pets welcome. No private investigators.

"Why can't we just go and talk to the Johnnys down at the pub in the village?" asked Calamity glumly, even though she knew the answer.

"They don't allow them out. You know that."

The first spots of rain fell from the dim, grey sky.

She tutted with resignation. "I suppose we'd better learn our catchphrases then. The first one's '*Bore da! How's your pa!*'"

I winced. Calamity dug me in the ribs. "Go on, say it."

"OK, then, here goes," I said as if about to swallow medicine. "*Bore da!* How's your pa!"

"Yeah not bad," said Calamity, "but try and sound more as if you mean it."

The windscreen wipers made a gloomy whine and our spirits sank lower and lower as Aberystwyth receded in the rear-view mirror. We drove over Penglais Hill and down through Bow Street, turning left at the garage for Borth. Calamity skimmed through the brochure.

"Do you believe the stories about this place?"

"Which ones?"

"The one about the zoo?"

"I've heard a few about the zoo."

"They say an animal charity donated some toys and the monkeys gave them to the holidaymakers out of pity."

"I heard last winter all the animals got eaten."

"What about the one about the birds not singing?"

Before I could answer we rounded the bend and saw the outline of the Kamp up ahead. Suddenly, unaccountably, we stopped talking, as if we had just walked into the room in a haunted house where once, long ago, someone had been walled up alive.

"Gulp!" said Calamity.

A guard checked our reservation at the first checkpoint and then raised the red-and-white painted bar and waved us on. A quarter of a mile further on we were at the main Kamp perimeter. We parked and, as thousands of holidaymakers before us must have done, looked up at the grim wrought-iron gates and above them, written in the same black iron, the words, "Welcome to Kevin's".

After we'd checked in and spread the straw out in our room we went for a walk round. The place was quiet, maybe because it was low season or because most of the inmates were off on a work party. The enamel hot dog sign squeaking in the wind, the doors banging and the newspapers gusting across the cheap concrete crazy paving lent a strange unsettling air to the place. Like a ghost town, or . . . or . . . Calamity put her finger on it: "Everyone's been abducted aboard a UFO." We walked into a store selling milk and newspapers to ask directions. It was open but empty, no customers and no one behind the counter. We moved across to the amusement arcade. It seemed even emptier, the bingo section shrouded in a gloom that suggested it had been many years since the lights flashed and a river of prizes fell into the excited laps of chip-guzzling families from the Midlands.

In the centre of the Kamp we found a darkened entertainment complex. Rows of seats set in clusters round tables in arrangements intended to disguise the fact that the seats had been bought wholesale from a cinema. There was also a stage with the curtain down. Finally in an adjoining saloon we found some human beings. A clown sat hunched over the bar guzzling glasses of vodka. The barman in a tatty magenta blazer filled it up each time without asking. We sat at the bar, a couple of stools down. They both looked at us with a glare of hostility before returning to their drinks.

"Can I get you men a drink?" I asked cheerily.

The clown halted his glass midway to his mouth and looked inquiringly at the barman. The barman gave a tiny almost imperceptible shrug. The clown slowly turned to me. He wore a filthy lime-green jacket with orange patches crudely stitched on. Underneath there was no shirt, just a grubby vest, with food stains on it. His face had a U-bend of a laughing mouth painted on in bright red, but his real mouth was set in a bitter sneer that went in the opposite direction, as if one of the mouths was a reflection in water of the other.

I gestured to the barman to give the clown a drink. "And one for yourself — that's if you drink while you're on duty."

Wordlessly the barman poured the clown a drink, then himself one, knocked it back and washed the glass.

Finally the clown spoke. "Just because I take your drink doesn't make you my friend."

I shrugged.

"It doesn't mean I like you."

"Of course! it means you like to drink."

"Exactly. If I said no, I would be cutting off my nose to spite my face. You wouldn't want me to do that, would you?"

"You never know, it might be an improvement."

Calamity nudged me and pointed at a woman passing the window. She walked, almost marched, with military stiffness and wore a Prussian-blue tunic and matching skirt set off by a well-polished Sam Browne belt. The left sleeve of her tunic swung emptily. I said to the barman, "Isn't that Mrs Bligh-Jones from the Meals on Wheels?"

He pretended to glance over his shoulder and without even looking said, "No that's Mrs Parker from Mansfield."

I screwed up my eyes. "No I'm sure it's Mrs Bligh-Jones. You can tell because she's only got one arm."

"No you're wrong, mate."

"But you didn't look."

"Yes I did."

She walked up to a chalet and the door opened. A man stood in the doorway in a dressing-gown. It was Jubal.

"Doesn't half look like Mrs Bligh-Jones to me; and that's Jubal isn't it?"

The barman leaned across and grabbed my chin in the vice of his index finger and thumb, jerked my face towards his and said in a cold, bitter voice, "Are you calling me a liar?"

I snatched my face free and signalled with my eyes to Calamity that it was time to try somewhere else. We walked out and carried on walking into the centre of the dreary Kamp.

We passed a small collection of fairground rides, the horses and miniature spaceships covered with dusty tarpaulins. There was a flash of movement from behind the centre of the carousel. It was a little girl, grubby and bedraggled, her hair long and wild and matted; she must have been one of the feral children said to live on the fringes of the Kamp. On seeing us she darted behind one of the cars. We stopped and I crouched down and called to her. Slowly she moved forward and peered at us from behind a prancing pony.

"Are your mummy and daddy around?" I asked.

She shook her head.

"Are you on your own?"

She nodded.

"We're looking for the clown's Johnny. Do you know what that is?"

She nodded.

"Will you take us to him?"

She considered.

"I'll give you some money to buy a hot dog."

She nodded and scampered off, assuming without even bothering to check that we would follow. We did.

The colony of Johnnys was located towards the back of the Kamp, in the cages that had formerly housed the animals. There were four of them, sitting idly about on upturned boxes and staring boredly into space. None of them wanted to talk to us, but eventually a man who said I could call him Bert came to the bars. I showed him the picture of the Dean and he confirmed that he had been a Johnny for a while.

"But he had no interest in learning the art," said Bert morosely. "He was just a dilettante. Kept going on about the fact that he was a professor and deserved better. I mean, big deal! I used to be an actuary but I don't ram it down your throat —" The man stopped suddenly, his attention distracted. I heard the sound of feet scraping deliberately on the pavement behind me and the miasma of cheap aftershave enveloped me. I turned and found myself face to face with a thin bony man in a black tie and dinner jacket. Next to him stood two Kamp security guards twirling their nightsticks. One of them went up to the bars and ran the truncheon along like a child rattling a stick along some railings. Bert leaped back and joined his friends.

The man in the dinner jacket spoke. "I'm awfully sorry to interrupt your fun, sir, but it appears your holiday has come to an abrupt end."

"Really? It's a bit sudden isn't it?"

"That's often the way of it on holiday; it seems like you've only just arrived and already it's time to go home."

"We *have* only just arrived."

"As I say it can often seem like that. It's a trick the mind plays."

"And we were having such a nice time. I can't believe it's over."

"You're not the first, sir, to remark on the fleeting nature of human happiness. If I may be permitted the observation."

I looked at Calamity and she responded by dramatically stretching her eyebrows and chin in opposite directions. I turned back to the manager. "Nice aftershave."

"Thank you, sir, I mix it myself. Nothing fancy, just a few things I find in the garden."

"Next time go easy on the slugs."

He winced slightly. "Most comedic, sir. Now if you would care to make your way to the carpark."

"Couldn't we just extend our stay by half a day?"

He shook his head in bogus melancholy. "Sadly not, we're fully booked. No room for any more guests and alas, although you would be highly suitable for the role, we are already supplied with a clown."

"And if he goes sick you could always recite your aftershave recipe, couldn't you?"

He winced again.

"I want to see the manager."

The security guard answered. "You're looking at him, pal, this is Kousin Kevin, he owns the Kamp."

"Don't sound so impressed, he can't even spell!"

Kousin Kevin took hold of my cuff. "If you wouldn't mind, sir."

"What if I do?"

The security guard waved his nightstick. "Actually, bigmouth, we'd prefer it if you did. We don't like snoopers in our camp."

We filed our way back in the direction of the car, guards on either side marching in step. No one spoke and the silence was lightened only by the soft strains of a dance tune from the swing era drifting over the eaves. As we cleared the last of the chalets we stopped involuntarily and stared before the guards urged us on. In the auditorium — deserted only a few minutes before — the ellipse of a single spotlight could now be seen bobbing across the darkened dance-floor like a drunken moon. And stepping jauntily through it, as if their shoes were glued to the light, were Jubal and Mrs Bligh-Jones, dancing to the "Chattanooga Choo-Choo".

On the drive back to town I pondered the significance of what I had just seen. Mrs Bligh-Jones was the Commander-in-Chief of the Meals on Wheels, which made her a pretty powerful person in town. But it hadn't always been so. Two years ago she was just another bit player ladling anaemic gravy over sprouts that had been boiled to death.

Her rise to prominence neatly illustrated one of the many ironies of the flood: so often the chief casualty had not been bricks and mortar, but things more intangible, like reputation. In this case the credibility of the druids. For as long as anyone could remember, they had been the town's official gangsters: running the girls, the gambling, the protection, and sending so many of their enemies to "sleep with the fishes" it made the sea snore. But it all came to an end with Lovespoon's vainglorious Exodus aboard his ark. They lost a lot of good men on that boat and the ones left behind, their credibility shot, were never quite able to compete. This was when the carpetbagger gangsters moved in and no one had a bigger carpet-bag than Bligh-Jones. She alone had been the one to recognise the simple truth: in the moonscape of rubble and potato soup kitchens that followed the receding waters there was a new weapon abroad. Hunger. And the casually issued threat of a withheld bowl of gruel could be far more effective than any blow from a druid's blackjack.

We might never have heard of her, either, if it wasn't for the tragedy on Pumlumon mountain. A story that has since become one of the defining legends of the rubble years. It started out as just a routine sweep in the Meals on Wheels van, the sort they often made into the foothills, looking for wayfarers to succour. But then a storm blew up and they received a mayday from high up on the mountain. Common sense told them to turn back, but they pressed on and before long they had passed the Bickerstaff line, that imaginary line that demarcates the point beyond which a safe return is no longer possible. Morale soon snapped in the sub-zero temperatures and the leader, Mrs Cefnmabws, lost her grip completely and ran off ranting into the storm. Then as the women argued in the fierce blizzard with icicles hanging off their eyebrow ridges it was the ruthless will of Mrs Bligh-Jones that forced them on, forced their rebelling sinews and surrendering flesh to scorn the pain. They were stranded for three months on that cruel mountain. Two of them died from pneumonia and Mrs Cefnmabws turned up the following spring preserved in a block of ice like a mammoth. The only ones to make it down were Mrs Tolpuddle, who refused to talk about it; and Bligh-Jones, who lost an arm to frostbite. It didn't hold her back, though. She returned to town a heroine and promptly began carving it up into mini-fiefdoms for her lieutenants.

The only things she didn't contest were the girls and the drinking-clubs. Either out of an inherent puritanical streak or maybe out of a respect for tradition: because everyone knew that getting drunk was essentially a pagan activity and thus the birthright of the druids. And, no matter what else had changed, Bacchus was still the most popular god in town.

We drove slowly up towards Waunfawr in a slow file of traffic stuck behind a caravan. The windscreen wipers droned hypnotically, the rain sluiced down, and the sky above Aberystwyth turned the colour of bluebottles. Perfect weather for a day at Kousin Kevin's. I thought again of what I had seen. Jubal, the man with a finger in all the pies in town, dancing with the woman who baked them.

CHAPTER
EIGHT

I walked down the dimly lit, green-tiled corridor in a pair of paper socks given me at the door and a one-piece paper suit that rustled softly as I went. I had no keys and no watch and no coins and nothing made of metal nor any material that could be filed to an edge or moulded into something that could be used to bludgeon with. If the guards could have taken my fillings they would have done. I was thirty feet beneath ground level, under the castle, in a suite of rooms designed by Owain Glyndwr for people he didn't like. I was on my way to see Dai the Custard Pie.

It felt more like a hospital than a prison, the faint smell of disinfectant and a distant generator hum emphasising the otherwise total silence. Only the elaborate electronic locking of the huge steel doors made it clear that it was a prison. But perhaps at this end of the spectrum of penal incarceration there was no real difference. The psychologists might spend their lives trying to disentangle the Gordian knot of hate, insanity, malice, neurosis, psychosis, intent and irresistibility, genes and environment that made up the peculiar evil of men like Custard Pie, but whatever their conclusions you still needed a strong door on the room.

Thirty feet beneath the town; a tomb of steel and concrete that was fitted out like an ICBM silo and manned by guards who underwent the same psychological testing to get the job. Going to see a man whom I was responsible for putting here and who I knew would never talk to me. But all the same, for the sake of the Dean — way out of his depth in the maelstrom of Aberystwyth and maybe already dead — I had to ask.

The Dean, like thousands of misguided fools before him, had dreamed of becoming a clown and then leaped into the abyss in an act that suggested that he already was one. And there was no one in all of Wales who knew more about the psychopathology of the clown's mind than Custard Pie.

I don't know what I expected, but I was shocked when I saw him. He stood just a couple of feet away from me, a wall of bars from floor to ceiling separating us. He stared with eyes glittering crazily above the leather muzzle they had forced him to wear. He wore a bright orange prison-issue boiler suit and underneath it a knitted tank-top over a paisley pattern shirt. He smelled sour and unwashed; his fingernails were a couple of inches long and had started to turn yellow and curl. Most upsetting of all, the floor of his cell was littered with excrement. I turned in disgust to one of the guards who sat a few feet away playing Solitaire.

"It's OK, mate," the guard said. "They're not real. They're fake ones, like in a joke shop."

"You allow people to give him things like this?"

"He makes them himself."

"But the regulations?"

"Regulations against most things but there's not one against making fake poo." He returned his attention to the cards and I looked at Custard Pie. The last time we had met we had been dropping through the incandescent white clouds, flying in low towards the lake of Nant-y-moch.

"I know why you're here," he said in cold monotone devoid of any inflection or feeling. "You're looking for the Dean."

"You're well-informed."

"There's nothing that happens in this town I don't know about. The only thing I don't know, in fact, is why you think I will help you."

"He may have gone to join the clowns."

"Of course he's gone to join the clowns. But why should I help you? The man who took away my liberty?"

I looked at him and considered. "He threw away forty years of scholarship to go and get his arse slapsticked all day in front of a jeering crowd. Most people wouldn't understand what drives a man to do something like that. I certainly wouldn't. But you would."

"So?"

"So you could probably find him. You could predict his next move better than anyone else in the whole world. It would be a feat of such audacious brilliance that I thought an egotist like you wouldn't be able to resist."

A contemplative look appeared in his eyes. "As a project it would not be without interest. I might even enjoy it, but what of it? I have passed the stage of doing things for the sake of enjoyment."

"With your genius for understanding the comic mind —"

"Or even the deranged comic mind —"

"If you say so."

"Tell me, Louie, do you think I am mad?"

I hesitated.

"Or are you smart enough to see the sadness where others see madness or badness?"

"All I see are good guys and crooks. I don't need it any more complicated than that."

"Oh but you do, Louie. You do." His voice took on an insinuating quality that suggested that he had thoroughly examined my psyche and found it wanting. "You do. That's your curse. I know you, Louie. I know that sometimes you lie awake at night and try to fight off this monstrous thought that just won't be driven away. How can we really be held responsible for our actions? Whether it is nature or nurture that fashions us it makes little difference, does it not? Give me the child for seven years and I will give you the man. Can I be blamed for becoming what I became? For what I had no power to avoid becoming? And if not, how can you justify punishing me?"

I smiled. "Maybe. And maybe not. But if you helped save the Dean no one could argue about the rightness of that."

"Are you really such a fool that you think he can be saved? Yes, I can find him and send him back to his college to spend another twenty years marking essays, but do you really call that saving? Some people might call it the opposite. They might say only now is he truly saved."

"Except that his new world won't make him happy. It may even kill him."

"You're right. There is no happiness for him now. He has entered the world of the clown and discovered to his dismay that, laugh as he might, there is nothing funny about it. Nothing at all. We huddle round the camp fire and laugh merely to drown out the howl that comes in the night. Save the Dean? Louie, I can't even save myself."

I waved to the guard; the interview was over and had accomplished about as much as I imagined. As I walked away the prisoner hissed a word. I stopped and he hissed it again. Three words, or four. I turned and he said, "The girl! Suffer the girl to come to me!"

My brow furrowed. "Which girl?"

And then he flung himself at the bars like a furious caged beast and rattled and kicked them and screamed, "Calamity! Calamity! Calamity!"

★   ★   ★

104

As I climbed the steps up to the street level I could hear far off from the depths of the dungeon the sound of a wolf howling.

There was a message waiting for me when I got back, from Llunos asking me to go down and bail Calamity. I groaned. This was the third time in six weeks, and I knew I'd just about run out of favours. It had taken me ages to explain to his satisfaction how I came to be in that cupboard at the Rock Wholesaler's.

A little hole had appeared in the threadbare woollen jersey of cloud, and a disc of light bathed the length of the Prom from the castle to the harbour. The railings and chrome bumpers of the cars sparkled. Eeyore was leaning against the kiosk, reading to Sospan from a book. He closed it when I arrived and greeted me.

"He's been telling me about Sitting Bull," said Sospan. "Very interesting man. What'll you have?"

"What's good this week?"

Eeyore held up his ice.

"Flavour of the month," said Sospan.

"Looks like chocolate."

"But it sure doesn't taste like it. It's Xocolatl. The original Aztec recipe. That flavour dispensed elsewhere on the Prom under the name of chocolate is but a vulgar abasement."

"What's in it?"

"Cocoa, pepper, chillies, vanilla, honey and dried flowers. They used to drink it out of a golden beaker that was used once and then thrown in the lake."

"Are you going to introduce that system?"

"I've no objection so long as you bring your own cup."

I ordered and when it arrived Eeyore and I chinked cornets like they were mugs of beer.

"So what's with the book, Pop?"

Eeyore placed his hand on it and said, "Medicine Line."

"Oh yeah, what's that?"

"It's a concept from the Old West, you see. From the old days when there weren't any frontiers and things. Apparently they had this team of men who crossed the continent surveying the boundary between America and Canada and marking it with little cairns of stones. When the Red Indians asked them what they were doing they said they were making medicine for Queen Victoria, the Great Mother across the Ocean. That's what I was reading about."

"So what's so interesting about it?"

"Well, the funny thing was, them Indians weren't all that impressed at the time — little piles of stones . . . it didn't seem like powerful medicine at all. But when they went horse-stealing south of the border the following spring, they made an amazing discovery. They found that when the sheriff and his men chased them the posse stopped up short at the piles of stone and couldn't pass. It was as if there was a glass wall there or something. For the life of them, those Indians couldn't see what was stopping the lawmen, but they had to admit the Great Mother across the Water had heap big powerful medicine. They called it the Medicine Line.

That's where Sitting Bull took them after the Battle of the Little Bighorn. Up beyond the Medicine Line to Canada where they'd be safe."

"That's a nice story, Dad."

"I was just saying to Sospan, I reckon a lot of people in this town have medicine lines inside their heads."

"I don't get you."

"You know, they live their lives penned in by fear — never get to know more than a tiny part of who they are . . . never realise the things that distinguish a man in this life lie wrapped in danger and wonder in the continent beyond the line."

"I've never really thought about it like that," I said. And added, "But I wish someone would put a medicine line round Calamity!" I put some money down, gave Eeyore's shoulder a squeeze, and walked off in the direction of the town lock-up.

It was still only late afternoon but the cell was full with the usual smattering of drunks, handbag thieves, black marketeers and an old lady who looked out of place. Calamity sat at a small table playing cards with a stoker. He was sitting in a singlet, anchors tattooed on each bicep, and, neatly folded on Calamity's side of the table, was his shirt. Calamity dealt with a stern businesslike mien and he stared at the cards, mesmerised like a child being shown a conjuring trick. It was five-card Ludo which meant he would soon be losing his ship as well, because although he was cheating there was no way on earth he could cheat better than Calamity. No one could.

★　★　★

The warder jangled the keys and let her out.

"Thanks for bailing me! Where did you get the money?"

"Out of your salary for next month."

"Hmm. Maybe it's better if I stay inside."

"Do that and you don't get a salary at all. And give the man his shirt back."

"But I won it fair and square! By the rules."

"You don't even know what the rules are! What do you want with a dirty old sailor's shirt anyway?"

"Merchandise, Louie. For every object there's a buyer, it's just a case of bringing them together."

I smiled and said, "Go home and arrange a deal between your head and the pillow. We've got an early start tomorrow."

CHAPTER
NINE

The train rolled gently to a halt at Borth station. The platform was empty except for a lone figure standing in the dawn mist. The figure of a man with a suitcase, a man who had once been a clown's Johnny. Calamity, eyes bleary with sleep, yawned like a small hippo.

The man walked down the platform and climbed aboard, the clunk of the door the only sound disturbing the early morning stillness. The guard shouted and the diesel grunted and strained and slowly pulled us out of Borth towards the bright sky in the east.

Bert spotted us and sat down in the seat in front. "This isn't what we agreed on the phone," he said over his shoulder. "I thought I said come alone."

"Calamity's my partner."

He turned to look, his face creased with suspicion. "It'll cost extra, another person and all that."

"No it won't," I snapped. "Just stop moaning."

He made a half-hearted attempt to rise and leave but it convinced no one. "I don't have to do this, you know."

"Who does? Just get on with it."

The train picked up speed and glided soundlessly through the wide watery silence. Condensation dripped in icy streams down the inside of the window and, outside, the world seemed to be taking a lie-in. The sun glimmered through the lemon mist above the estuary like a nightwatchman's lantern. Patches of water in the peat glistened and looked as if they had been cut out of the sodden turf with a giant pastry cutter. To the west beyond the dunes the sea was silent. At times like this the sight of the estuary in all its beauty made the heart gasp and long to turn back, a last final coquettish trick from that old whore Aberystwyth. Like a lover who catches you with a packed bag, tiptoeing down the stairs before sunrise, and calls to you from the landing, looking like she used to all those years ago when you first met at the Borth Carnival dance.

The rickety, tar-stained wooden bridge appeared out of the mist. We were approaching Dovey Junction, the great fork in the road for British Rail caravans. One route led north, hugging the rocky, castle-studded coast, the other went over the mountains to Shrewsbury. Bert pressed his face against the cold glass, straining his eyes to make out features in the soft misty world. "Never thought I'd finally do it," he said. "Never, thought I'd leave like this, never in a million years . . ."

"Get used to it, pal," I said, already tired of his moping. "It's Aberystwyth not Monte Carlo."

At Dovey Junction we all stepped out on to the deserted platform and faced each other in a huddled group.

"You got the money?"

I nodded. "You got the name?"

He grimaced. "No I don't have the name. I told you. All I got is the box-top."

"That's an expensive box of chocolates. Twenty quid."

"If you didn't like the deal you shouldn't have got on the train. You want to go and find her yourself, be my guest. There are only about ten thousand girls like her."

I took out the four crumpled-up fivers and straightened them out. He pulled out a piece of cardboard from his bag. We exchanged them. The cardboard had once been the top of a fudge box. And on the front, as always, a girl at a spinning-wheel in Welsh national dress. We all looked at it.

"I don't go for that type, myself, mind. But there are plenty that do. The old professor couldn't get over her. Always staring at her and begging me to give him the box. 'Isn't she a beauty?' he would say. Soon as he left I knew where he was heading. I've seen it before."

In the distance we heard the feeble lowing of the train from Machynlleth. The clown's Johnny shuffled his bag over to the edge of the adjacent platform, ready to jump aboard and swing north over the bridge to a better life. He turned to face us.

"Well, so long then."

"Good luck."

One lone, broken man against the huge clear backdrop of mountains and sky.

★   ★   ★

We caught the train back to Borth and took the bus outside the station, down the arrow-straight road that bisects the golf course, towards Ynyslas. On Calamity's lap was a bag from Peacocks containing the sort of coat that used to be popular with medieval Jews and that had now come back into fashion with druid assassins. Meirion said he thought it had something to do with the military. And in West Wales there is only one military. The Welsh Foreign Legion, famous or notorious depending on the way you looked at it, for the campaign to liberate the former Welsh colony of Patagonia in 1961.

It was all more than a quarter of a century ago now, but for the army of broken ghosts that haunted the fields and lanes of West Wales the memory burned as fiercely as ever. Five minutes in a recruiting office above Boots was all it took to seal their fate — farm boys who'd never been further than Builth Wells rubbing shoulders with a rag-bag of foreign intellectuals, artists and soldiers of fortune. Five minutes to think of a *nom de guerre* that hadn't already been taken and sign your cross on the dotted line and head off to the Welsh Vietnam. Sorry there's no *képi blanc* — that famous white pillbox hat worn by the heroes of *Beau Geste* — but here's a free knapsack of woe to carry for the rest of your life.

For two miles the scene was the same, a long line of rolling dunes, unending and unchanging, fringed with tufted marram grass like a lion's mane. The eternal dunes that were really nothing of the sort. Under the coat of scrubby grass the sands were shifting and moving even as we spoke. Come back in a year and if you had a photographic memory you would be shocked at how much everything had changed. Compared to the geological slowness with which mountains altered their shape, the dunes of Ynyslas shifted at high speed: bubbling and boiling like the cloudscapes in time-lapse photography, or like the rippling sinews of a well-fed lion.

When we reached the end we got off and walked past the man in the kiosk on to the wide flat sands of the estuary. A few cars were parked here and there was an ice-cream van with no one to serve. We spotted Cadwaladr outlined against the sky like a Red Indian on the ridge of the dunes; behind him the houses of Aberdovey across the estuary glinted like milk teeth left on a blue-green pillow.

Calamity and I fetched some ice creams from the van and then walked to the top of the dune. Cadwaladr raised an arm in greeting and we sat down on the sandy top.

"You live up here all the time?" I asked.

"Until it gets too cold. Then I spend the winter being chased out of barns by angry farmers."

"Where do you sleep?" said Calamity.

"Just a bivvy bag. That's all I need."

"But where do you keep your things?"

"I haven't got any."

The ice-cream man had smothered the ices in a home-made raspberry sauce that scented the wind with a pungent tang. Cadwaladr sniffed. "There's a smell that takes me back," he said. "Wild raspberries. It's the smell of spring in Patagonia. They used to grow everywhere." His eyes misted over. "Beautiful sight. At a time like that, even when you're a skinny seventeen-year-old, you don't half wonder about the point of travelling round the world to die in such a beautiful place."

"And then you come home and there's not even a bed for you to sleep in."

"They promised us a land fit for heroes but when we got back from Patagonia the only work they'd give us was building all these horrible holiday camps and caravan parks. All we got was a land fit for Noddy. But how can a man forget what he has seen when surrounded by such tawdry things?"

He looked at me with an urgency that suggested I might have the answer.

"How can he forget? A lifetime is not enough time, but . . . but . . . a lifetime is all we are given."

Calamity slowly drew the coat out of the bag, taking care not to let the paper disturb the moment with a rustle.

"You know," said Cadwaladr, still lost in thought, "sometimes, when you stick a blade into a man, you can feel it grating on the bone like a spade hitting the pavement when you shovel snow." He clenched his fists tightly and added, "Now when I look out over this beautiful estuary in November and see snow-clouds forming over Barmouth, my heart fills with winter."

There was a pause and Calamity looked at me. I nodded and she slowly unfolded the coat on the dunes, saying, "Have you ever seen something like this before?"

Cadwaladr glanced at it and his face darkened. He made a clicking sound deep in his throat as if this coat confirmed all the bad things he had ever thought or suspected about the world. "Yes, I've seen one like it."

"We're looking for a man who is being followed by someone wearing a coat like this. We were told it's something to do with the Ysbyty Ystwyth Experiment. Do you know what that is?"

He didn't answer immediately and we waited patiently. Then he said, "I don't know too much about it." His words sighed out of him more wistfully than the sand sifting in the wind. There was always an air of soft, otherworldly melancholy about Cadwaladr but today he seemed even more remote.

"The people who know a lot can't tell you."

"Why not," I asked. "Are they scared?"

"Possibly. Terror can do that, so I've heard. But who knows? They can't speak about it. They can't speak about anything really, just like babies before they learn to say Dad."

"So what was the Ysbyty Ystwyth Experiment?"

The old soldier took out a scrap of newspaper and a polythene bag filled with salvaged cigarette ends. I wondered where he got them from — ash-trays in buses, the cinema floor . . . or maybe the maternity waiting-room where the fathers sit and wait for news.

115

"Officially it doesn't exist. And never did. Which is strange because I know some men who volunteered for it. It was some sort of military psychological experiment. In Patagonia we called that sort of thing 'Psyops'. It was based at the old sanatorium out at Ysbyty Ystwyth."

"The old sanatorium was bought by the Philanthropist," said Calamity. "He's the new owner."

"Is he anything to do with this experiment?" I asked.

"Maybe," said Cadwaladr. "Maybe not. I don't know. All I know for sure is the guys who came back were not the same as the ones who went."

"In what way?"

"They were just different. Quiet, and brooding, and when you looked into their eyes you saw a sort of emptiness — as if all the life had been sucked out of them and all that remained was a husk of a man . . . That druid chap from the clothes shop was one of them, what was his name?"

"Valentine?"

Cadwaladr nodded. "Yeah, him. They say he went cuckoo after it. And there was Waldo, of course. Poor Waldo."

For a second or two he said nothing more, staring beyond our little group to the infinite ocean.

"Who was Waldo?" asked Calamity.

Cadwaladr pressed his eyes closed with a deep weariness of the soul. "Waldo was the saddest man ever to serve in that war. His road to Calvary began on Christmas Day when we organised a game of football in no-man's-land with the enemy. Ah! What a day that was! I remember it as if it was yesterday. When the shelling stopped and the silence rang in our ears so loud it almost hurt. Meeting our enemies face to face and clasping them in the embrace of true brotherhood. The smell of sherry and cinnamon and mince pies, mingling with the wild heather, the fresh sharp tang of distant snow. The sweet strains of "*Stille Nacht*" drifting across to us . . . And then the football. What a glorious kick-about it was. Four all after ninety minutes, both sides evenly matched, you couldn't separate them. And then, alas, in injury time one of their guys dived in the box — typical South American player. The ref awarded a penalty and they scored and that was it. They'd won. We didn't say anything, of course, because it was Christmas but a lot of guys were not happy about it. And the incident became the cancer that ate away at Waldo's soul. Waldo was the goalie, you see."

Cadwaladr shuddered and violently lofted his cornet, jerking back his head like a penguin catching a fish. He crunched off the pointy base with the venom of a wolf cracking a thigh-bone with its chops, and then sucked greedily on the vanilla marrow. "One day I will tell you the rest of it," he said, the ice cream bubbling in his mouth like lava from a fissure on the ocean floor. "But not today, my heart is too full."

CHAPTER
TEN

Once upon a time you just went mad and gave everyone a good laugh. They created a special position for you — the village idiot. You didn't mind too much because you were mad and being a buffoon was probably no worse than tilling the squire's fields for a living. Later when the world got more enlightened they got rid of the job and called you a fool or an idiot or an imbecile. And it was still OK to laugh. They weren't squeamish about where they put you either, or what they called it. Asylums for criminal lunatics, asylums for incurable lunatics, hospitals for the insane, pauper asylums, workhouses for lunatics . . . If you were rich you might end up in a chancery asylum, but it was still a madhouse. Then someone had the bright idea of charging for the privilege of laughing at you. It was quite a popular pastime for a while, even more than the zoo. By the outbreak of the Great War and the new age of science they had managed to discern four grades of madness: idiots, imbeciles, feeble-minded people and moral defectives. And nowadays, of course, there are hospitals for the mentally ill, and no one is mad any more. Although when you walk down the streets of

Aberystwyth on Saturday night you could be forgiven for thinking otherwise.

After we left Cadwaladr we picked up the car and drove out to Ysbyty Ystwyth to take a look at the old sanatorium. You might have called the Georgian country house with its ivy-covered redbrick exterior handsome if you didn't know the history. But there wasn't anyone for miles around who didn't. It's a taint by association that a house can never shake off.

It hadn't always specialised in the insane. After 1918 the house was taken over by a charity set up to treat victims of shellshock. And after that, when that particular malady lost its fashionable appeal, even though the victims didn't lose their shock, it became a sanatorium treating TB patients who couldn't afford to go to Switzerland. Later still, in the fifties and sixties it reverted to treatment of the mentally ill, and especially the fashonable new cure for depression — electro-convulsive therapy. People living nearby claim the lights in their sitting-rooms used to flicker during a busy day.

The grim, forbidding prospect instantly squashed the mood in the car. It was only a building, of course, just bricks and mortar and ivy and joists of dry wood and crumbling plaster. And yet it seemed impregnated like a sponge with all the woe that had been spilled there. The windows were dark and filled with an emptiness like the eye sockets in a skull. The deserted grounds seemed still alive with broken men from the trenches being wheeled around in bath chairs by nurses in funny uniforms. Cadwaladr's especial distaste for the place was understandable: many of the soldiers from the Patagonian conflict had been brought here and left to rot. The perimeter was enclosed by a stone wall, green with ivy and lichen and topped by newly installed rolls of razor-wire. Signs were placed at evenly spaced intervals along the wall warning us of various dire things. Private. Keep Out. Guard-dog patrols. And one sign said chillingly: "Trespassers will be shot. By Order The Philanthropist".

I dropped Calamity off in town and spent the rest of the afternoon flashing the top of the fudge box round places where the girl might be recognised. There was nothing remarkable about the picture. A young girl sitting at a spinning-wheel in an old cottage. Dressed in a shawl, coarse woollen skirt and of course the stovepipe hat. The girl was pretty, they always were. Might even have been beautiful but you couldn't tell with all the make-up. For a man whose only contact with female company was theology students she might have been attractive, bewitching even.

The same pattern of polite boredom was repeated everywhere I went. One swift uninterested glance at the picture and then a shrug. Sure they'd seen girls like this before, hundreds of them, but they couldn't say if they'd seen this one. They were ten a penny. No, make that a hundred. Stick around in Aberystwyth and you'll see a busload every week. Simple unlettered farm girls from up beyond Talybont, playing the one half-decent

120

card life had dealt them — their looks. Nothing spectacular, but good enough. Girls who dreamed of making it big as a model, maybe featuring in the ads for the tourist board or on the cover of the Cliff Railway brochure, but all they ever got were the knitting patterns and the fudge boxes. But of course you can't make a living out of modelling fudge boxes no matter how frugal you are, but a pretty girl in a stovepipe hat can always make a bit extra on the side in the druid speakeasies down by the harbour.

The men from the cheese yards were bent over the counter of Sospan's even further than usual, huddling together for the collective warmth. As if the inside was a brazier and they were watchmen sick of watching. I dropped by and mentioned the Philanthropist, but even Sospan, for once, had little to say on the subject. Everyone agreed that only a foreigner would have bought the haunted house. But they couldn't agree on where he came from. Some said he was a Texan and others a Saudi prince. All agreed he had made his money in oil. Or white slave trafficking. "I heard he's got an idiot wife locked away there," said one man. "Who hasn't?" answered another, and someone else added, "He can have mine if he wants!"

I passed round the picture of the girl and again it was the same response. Why get upset about a particular one when you can get any number down at the harbour and they all look the same anyway don't they? Once they've got the hat on and the make-up and the wig.

Then someone wishing to be helpful suggested I try Spin Doctors on Chalybeate Street, and wishing to be polite I said I would. "You mind she doesn't put a spell on you!" someone shouted after me as I left.

The shop smelled of must and dry cardboard. It could have been an ironmonger's or a bike shop but the frames in the window and hanging from the ceiling had one wheel and four legs. A bell tinkled in the back as I walked in, ducking under the foliage of hanging spinning-wheels. In the centre of the shop there was a space cleared among the bric-à-brac and a wheel stood on a podium. Even knowing nothing about them I could see this one was special. The frame was a modern carbon fibre composite, fitted with a derailleur gear-change made by Shimano of Japan. There was a racing-style aluminium footgrip on the treadle, and an alloy hub on the wheel. An enamel logo on the main frame tube said "The Sleeping Beauty".

"She's a beauty that one, sir!"

I looked down and saw the old lady, no bigger than Mrs Pepperpot, four feet nothing perhaps, clad in the traditional witches' livery of black: ebony puritan shoes with shiny buckles; charcoal stockings and black skirt; blouse, bodice, shawl and fingerless mittens; obsidian beads and studs in her ears and a sable knitting needle through a bun of hair now silver but that no doubt had once been black. She stroked the Sleeping Beauty lovingly. "Handcrafted titanium distaff. None of your injection-moulded tat. Last for ever this one will."

122

"That's good, I hate it when they fall apart halfway through a spin."

"Is it for yourself, or are you looking for a gift?"

I took out the fudge-box top. "I was actually looking for a driver." I pushed the lid under her nose and she cast an eye over. Her face fell slightly.

"I'm afraid we don't sell girls. It's too much trouble feeding them up."

"Yeah I know, they leave a trail of your best bread all the way home; tell me about the wheel."

"Cheap plastic wood, probably Taiwanese. You wouldn't get very far spinning on it but then the people who take these sort of snaps don't care too much about that, do they?"

"You ever sell one like this?"

"I'm afraid we don't handle that end of the market."

"What about the girl?"

"What about her? She's no spinner, that's for sure. Her seating position's all crooked, and her hands are in the wrong place. The way she's clutching the distaff like that you'd think it was a man's 'you know what'. Still, you can hardly blame her, I suppose, it's probably what she's used to, isn't it! Treadle trollops we call them." And then added, "I've just put the cauldron on, if you'd like a cup of tea?"

"No thanks," I said turning to go. "I'm in a hurry."

"Well, would you like to sign the petition?"

"Petition for what?"

"Mrs Llantrisant. We're hoping to get her sentence reduced."

"But I'm the one who put her there."

"Oh I know, but you couldn't have known they would stick her on that cold damp island. It's giving her all sorts of problems with her joints."

"I'm sorry," I said, "I don't think I can sign it. I mean, what if she starts another flood?"

She followed me to the door and held it open. "Are you sure I can't interest you in the Sleeping Beauty? We do hire purchase."

"I'll let you know, I still need to look at a few others first."

She smiled knowingly, and shouted after me, "Good luck with your search. If you bring me a piece of the girl's hair I can probably ask the spirits for you."

If the girl was selling herself down by the harbour, the best man to ask was the one who had a professional interest in fallen women — Father Seamus. I strolled with renewed sense of purpose up Great Darkgate Street towards the ghetto in the shadow of the castle. I bumped into him coming out of one of the houses where he made pastoral visits. Like many of the houses that had managed to withstand the flood, it now had five or six families instead of two or three. He greeted me and we shook hands. The problems he had to deal with were not that different from the ones his medieval forebears had faced and had the same cause: too many families living in one room, the clothes drying on one radiator, the horrible thick unhealthy fug poisoning the air. But he soldiered on.

"Still fighting the good fight, are we, Father?" I asked cheerfully.

"Oh struggling on, struggling on," he said, the words delivered with the affected soul-weariness of the man who dons the cloak of the martyr and finds he likes the fit so much he gets a matching pair of gloves made.

"How about yourself, Louie?"

"Struggling on, struggling on."

He put a fraternal arm on my shoulder and led me down the street. "Don't give up now, we need men like you."

"Do we, Father? Do we really?"

He stopped and took a closer look at me, his finely attuned antenna warning him of an impending loss of faith. "Are you all right, Louie?"

"Of course." I showed him the photo. "I'm looking for this girl."

He took it wordlessly, peered at it and then handed it back. "Sorry, Louie. You know how it is. I've seen loads like this."

"Yeah I know how it is."

"Sorry I can't be more help. Is she in trouble?"

"I don't know. Probably. Isn't everybody?"

"That's why we need men like you, Louie. Men who scorn the comforts of the hearth and the softness of straw beneath their heads. Men who stand guard so weaker men can sleep. Men who climb the cold stone steps to the battlement and stand watch, blasted by the icy wind, their eyes unvisited by sleep and smarting in the winter frost. Silent centurions, Mr Knight, to hold out their shield. Men like you and Mr Cefnmabws at the lighthouse flashing his light to guide the ships safely home."

"Amen," I said.

We stopped at the street corner and prepared to part.

"And don't forget to include yourself in that list, Father," I added.

He smiled wanly. "I do what I can with the strength God gives me. It isn't much."

I said goodbye and walked through the churchyard behind the old college. As I walked the words of his sermon echoed in my mind. It was a pretty speech, but it didn't really ring true. Was I really a silent centurion, scorning the soft straw to climb up the icy battlement? I didn't think so. I certainly didn't feel like one. But one thing I was pretty certain of. When I showed him the picture of the girl and he said he didn't know her, he had been lying.

I reached the bit of the Prom where it bent like an elbow jutting out into the frothing water. There was a girl standing on the D-shaped buttress, staring out to sea, wearing an old fur coat from the Salvation Army shop. It was Ionawr. I touched her gently on the shoulder so as not to make her start. But she did anyway and looked round. Then she squealed and hugged me and when we broke off she still held one of my hands in hers.

"I've been looking for you everywhere," she said.

"I was out at Ynyslas."

"I've got someone who wants to meet you. Well, he doesn't really want to but I told him he had to."

"Who is it?"

"Remember after Mrs Beynon's you told me about that monk with the suitcase?"

I nodded.

"I know who it is, it's one of my regular . . . er . . . you know . . ."

"Friends?"

"Yes. He'll be in the new Moulin tonight." She jerked her head back slightly to indicate the pier behind her where the replacement for the famous old club in Patriarch Street had recently sprung up. "You don't go there much, do you?"

"Not really, too many memories, I suppose." I showed her the fudge-box top and this time I got a reaction.

"I don't know who the girl is," she said, "but I recognise the location. I've done some work there myself. It's the Heritage Folk Museum."

I went to the Cabin in Pier Street and met Calamity. Her expression told me straightaway that she had something on her mind.

"Why didn't you tell me?" she said when I sat down.

"Tell you what?"

"About Custard Pie."

I breathed in sharply.

"He asked to see me, didn't he?"

"Yes."

"So why didn't you tell me?"

"You know damn well why I didn't. Because if I had, the next minute you would be down there visiting him."

"And what's wrong with that?"

"Everything's wrong."

"That's not an answer."

"I don't want you having anything to do with him. It's too dangerous."

"I'm not a kid, you know."

"So you keep telling me. You're sixteen and three quarters. It may seem a lot to you but, believe me, it isn't."

"What happened to us being partners?"

"The first job of a partner is to take care of the other one."

"But what can he do, he's behind bars?"

"I don't know what he can do. I'm not smart enough to think of anything, but *he* is."

"Louie, you know I have to go, we're on a case."

"There's no point going anyway."

"No point?"

"Of course not. You think he's going to tell you something that will help us?"

"No point?"

"Not even a microscopic one."

"Well you're a crap detective then," she said, eyes watering with resentment and confusion.

My eyes widened in surprise. "What's that all about?"

"Well, you went to see him, didn't you? Why did you waste your time if there was no point?"

"I . . . er . . . It was only after I went that I realised that there was no point."

She blew a raspberry.

"How did you find out anyway?"

"I'm a detective."

I sighed and Calamity stood up. "I'm going."

"I forbid you!" I said as she left, knowing full well that nothing I said would make any difference. But I said it all the same. "I forbid you." It was an old trick I'd learned from King Canute.

I sat there staring at my tea for a while and then ran out and down Pier Street towards the sea. I could see Calamity just about to turn left on to the Prom, so I turned into King Street behind the old college and cut through the Crazy Golf. From there I walked across the road and turned towards the pier. A few steps and she almost bumped into me. She turned and started to walk away but I caught her arm and pulled her over to the railings. She stood there not struggling but keeping her gaze stolidly averted, finding something improbably fascinating in the side of the pier.

Neither of us spoke and finally she said, "What do you want?"

"I just want to tell you to be careful."

She turned and looked at me, her eyes wet and gleaming. "So I can go then?"

"What's the point of stopping you, you were going to go anyway, weren't you?"

"No, I wasn't. You forbade me."

I put my arm over her shoulder. "Just be careful and keep away from the bars, and whatever you do, don't believe a word he says. OK?"

She nodded.

Meirion was enjoying his usual early-evening aperitif at the Rock Café, his big belly wedged in between the immovable plastic seat and the edge of the table. Spread out before him a gazette of English and Welsh seaside towns preserved in pink sugar: Blackpool, Llandudno, Tenby, Brighton. I sat down and ordered the aniseed one with black and white stripes.

He had just finished a piece for the morning edition on the death of Mr Marmalade. It was, he said, a typical Meirion piece — hard-hitting, authoritative, tough but fair, and like all Meirion's hard-hitting, authoritative, tough and fair pieces it would never be published for fear of upsetting all the bigshots who owned the town. Still, he had to write them if he wanted to collect his salary.

He told me what he had managed to dig up on the Ysbyty Ystwyth Experiment. "I spoke to the chap who covered the story," he began. "It seems to have been some advanced neuroscientific research conducted by the military at the sanatorium. They chose that place because folk were already scared of it so they would keep away. Then something went badly wrong and the project was wound up in a hurry. It's all officially denied, of course."

"So where does this Philanthropist fit in, the one who bought the place?"

"Dr Faustus? He was in charge. No one knows much about him, he's supposed to be some sort of

130

experimental neuroscientist who had some pretty far-out theories about false memory syndrome. Apparently he was thrown out of the scientific establishment for being too crazy. After the thing was wound up the folks living out there started seeing things. Well a 'thing' actually. A monster they said, or a ghost or something, living in the woods. The most celebrated case was a family out at Pontrhydygroes who saw something while on a picnic. They were making a home-movie. Didn't notice anything at the time but when the film came back they saw something in the trees behind them, something moving. That's what they say, anyway. The whole family disappeared not long after that. Their breakfast half-eaten on the table, the tea still warm in the pot. Never seen again. No sign of the film either. A lot of people who made statements to the police were later by questioned by a strange otherworldly man, dressed in medieval dress. He sounds a bit like this chap you mentioned in the Peacocks' coat. They didn't say what he wanted but after that they all withdrew their statements."

"So there's a time-traveller walking around in the woods."

Meirion tore off a piece of bread to scrape up the last bits of rock from his plate. "That's what they say. Of course, I prefer rational explanations myself. It may be possible that the military have been experimenting with some sort of time-travel device, and now there's a sixteenth-century Jew haunting the woods of Ysbyty Ystwyth; but if you ask me, it is far more likely to be a prowler wearing one of those coats they sell in Peacocks."

The Heritage Folk Museum was housed in an old whalebone godown overlooking the harbour. In a series of rooms various scenes from seventeenth- or nineteenth-century rural life were acted out by the sort of people who couldn't hold down the type of jobs the twentieth century had to offer. Sitting at a spinning-wheel, lying on a bed pretending to die in childbirth, or with a face covered in fake smallpox weals . . . It wasn't very demanding so long as you didn't have to say anything.

In the entrance hall there was an artist in dungarees putting the finishing touches to a mural of Mrs Bligh-Jones. It was done in that heroic style you get in Warsaw Pact town halls, where the worker holds aloft a hammer and leads forward the proletariat to a Socialist promised land. The artist had chosen to depict the moment just after the fateful decision to abandon the van: Mrs Bligh-Jones, Mrs Gorseinon, Mrs Tolpuddle and Mrs Montgomery strung out against the backdrop of the mountain; roped together at the waist, and wearing bowling shoes instead of crampons. I smiled politely at the artist but, to be honest, it was pretty crap.

Someone touched my arm lightly and I looked round. It was Marty's mum.

"Hello, Louie. How are you? Haven't seen you for so long."

"I know, I've been meaning to visit, but . . ."

She squeezed my arm. "It's OK. I understand how busy you must be."

We stood side by side and looked at the picture and when the artist went out for a cigarette. Marty's mum glared at her. "I would never say anything but, if you ask me, it's wrong. It didn't ought to be allowed."

"What didn't?"

"What they've done to Mrs Cefnmabws! She's not there."

She nodded indignantly at the mural. She was right, there should have been five figures in the landscape, not four.

"I know she lost her bottle," Marty's mum continued, "and ran off raving into the blizzard, but that didn't happen until later, did it? When they left the van she was still in charge. Mrs Bligh-Jones should be at the back, not the front."

"Maybe it's something to do with perspective or something."

"Perspective my foot! They've airbrushed her out of history, that's what they've done. That Mrs Bligh-Jones is such a busybody!"

I took her for a cup of tea and in the café she told me what brought her to the museum.

"There's been some fresh evidence about Marty."

I turned and looked more closely at her. "Fresh in what way?"

"They've released some of the official papers from the inquiry. The statute of limitations is up, isn't it? I finally found out the answer to a mystery that has haunted me ever since that morning he left for school and never came back." She leaned closer and lowered her voice. "That night before the cross-country run, he was out in the frosty woods collecting kindling for his granny. Away for hours he was. When he got back home he was half-starved with cold and his new coat was torn in half. I wasn't half angry with him, the perisher, but he wouldn't say how he did it. But now I know, don't I?"

"So what was it?"

"Apparently there was this piece of evidence at the inquiry that they didn't release for fear of embarrassing the Church. It was the testimony of a friar — one of them mendicant ones — and he had been lost in the woods that same night. Blue with cold he was, because he didn't have a proper coat. Well, they're not supposed to, are they? It's all part of the mortification. It seems when Marty saw him he tore his own coat in two and gave half to the friar."

I patted her hand. "He was a fine boy."

"They kept quiet about it so as not to upset the poor chap. He was embarrassed, you see, because he thought all the other mendicants would laugh at him for taking charity from a little schoolboy."

"I expect he would have been mortified."

Marty's mum nodded without understanding and then carried on excitedly, "Anyway, I've just been speaking to the people who run this place and they're thinking of making a tableau of it — to illustrate the theme of suffering and charity through the ages. I've just been giving them some of his old clothes."

After Marty's mum left with my promise to visit her soon I wandered into the exhibit hall. I showed the pictures of the Dean and the girl to the doctor carrying a jar of leeches. He recognised them, and said he seemed to vaguely remember them working there for a while, drifting in and drifting out as people tended to do. Workers seldom stayed long — life there was hard and the working conditions primitive. The girl had been spinning and the man had mended coracles. The last he'd heard the Dean had got a job working as a satyr in the Beltane speakeasy.

CHAPTER
ELEVEN

As I sat in the office that evening I felt my spirits sinking with the barometer and then a phone call from Llunos sent them lower still. One of his men had pulled in some junior tough guy who had been boasting about the hit on Marmalade. He said it had been pre-planned and meant to scare him off talking to me. The kid wouldn't say who paid for it. Of course, it would be stupid to blame myself but that didn't stop me doing it. The actual cause of death might have been a weak heart, but he was an old man who would still be alive today if I hadn't gone to see him. If I wasn't to blame, who was? I put on my hat and coat and then the phone rang again. I snatched the receiver and barked into it and then listened. The line was awful: hissing and squawking faded in and out as if I was tuning a short-wave radio and a girl's faint voice said, "Louie, it's me."

"Who's me?" I said as the hairs on the back of my neck stood to attention.

"It's me, oh Louie, it's me." A voice so faint, drowning in a sea of static.

"Who?" I tried again.

"Me, Louie, it's me. Myfanwy."

"What?!" I shouted. "I can't hear you!"

"Myfanwy. Oh, Louie, help me!"

Then the line clicked dead. I sat frozen, immobile for a split second, and then jabbed my fingers uselessly on to the prongs of the telephone the way they do in the movies but that never works in real life.

Out on the Prom the breeze was moist and heavy with the tang of salt, and laced in tantalising bursts with another smell almost as primal: hot dogs. That oh so heartbreaking smell, the pure essential oil of night falling on the Prom, gathered long ago in those lost days when you were small, and on holiday with your mum and dad. Gathered in the magical falling dusk when the seagulls have gone to roost beneath the ironwork of the pier; and you all take a stroll after dinner, way past your normal bedtime, towards an amusement arcade that flashes and chimes and dings. Out at sea angry rumblings light up the clouds in distant flashes, like celestial pinball. You watch it all in awe, and little know that nothing in your life will ever be as good as this again.

The smell of onions frying . . . a scent that years later still unleashes a craving — like the snatch of an unknown melody — for a lost Eden that has no gate. That has never had a gate. Because the truth about hot dogs is this: no smell in the world promises so much and delivers so little. Even as a kid when you buy it you find it tastes of nothing at all. Absolutely nothing. The biggest zero ever. A warm, bland mush as far removed from the perfume it adds to the night air as the lotus flower from the slime that spawns it.

It's as if some master perfumer and necromancer had foreseen all the broken promises of your life to come, all the pangs of unrequited love and unreturned letters; the torment of watching a phone that never rings; the bright expectancy of fresh hope at breakfast, in ruins by sunset . . . it was as if he took all these things and blended them into a single fragrance and called it whatever the French is for Disappointment — *Désolé* or *Chagrin* or something. The smell of hot dogs on the Prom at night. The scent of pure *Chagrin*.

There was a consternation at the pier. Police "scene-of-crime" tape, a flashing blue light and Father Seamus taking charge. I worked it all out in the blink of an eye. The workmen rebuilding the pier had moved the entrance to the bingo parlour two feet to the left. A swarm of confused grannies were there now, buzzing around like bees who come home at the end of the day to find the hive has gone. The priest offering comfort. The ambulance just arriving. Down on the green slimy rocks, exactly below the point where the old entrance had been for fifty years, an old lady face-down and not moving. The sea washing over her, stained pink.

I didn't give a damn. There were a lot worse ways to go in this town. I just shrugged and walked under the arch of coloured lights, down the wooden tunnel that ran along the side of the pier, to the new Moulin at the end.

Behind in the distance I could still hear Father Seamus giving comfort, could almost hear his two fingers swishing up, down, left, right — drawing crosses in the air as cheaply as a washed-up actress gives out air-kisses. I smiled grimly to myself. I had an appointment with him tonight but he didn't know it yet. Tonight he would discover that wearing a brown dress with a rope round the belly didn't guarantee immunity in this world. He wouldn't like it, but I didn't give a damn. There were plenty of things that I didn't like too. And it wasn't because he was a liar, or had spoken earlier with such unchristian contempt over the spot where Bianca died in my arms; and it wasn't because I was heading down the corridor now to a club I had vowed never to visit. And it wasn't because somewhere out there tonight, probably smelling the same fried onions, was a man in trouble called Dean Morgan, because I didn't really give a damn about him either. Just as the lifeboatman doesn't give a damn about the stupid fool he fishes from the sea. It wasn't because of any of this, although it all helped. It was just because tonight I didn't give a damn, the way sometimes you don't. So I walked down the tunnel towards the new Moulin and squeezed my fingers into a fist in anticipation of the priest's soft pink jaw.

What makes a club? If it's the spirit of the people who gather there, then the new Moulin was very much like the old. The décor was cheaper and more makeshift than the original; and perhaps there wasn't quite the same panache about it; but it still had the most

139

important ingredients: darkness and a mix of people from every walk of Aberystwyth life, all unified by the common desire to leave their scruples at the door. And most importantly there were the Moulin Girls lolling about in their stovepipe hats and shawls and not much else. Sweet soft things who for a little money would do sweet soft things.

Just like in the old club, tough guys in penguin suits stood at the door, and once inside it was hot, crowded, loud and sweaty. Waitresses walked round with trays of food, others took drink orders or ushered you to a table. In the centre of the room there was a space cleared for dancing, and set around it were tables with flickering candles, and hanging from the ceiling were twirling disco balls. Towards the back was a stage and in front of this a private table for Jubal and his guests. I felt a rush of cool air over the top of my head and looked up to see two men in satyr trousers sitting on giant swings, arcing slowly and gracefully above the crowd. They were Bill and Ben. A cowgirl walked past lighting cigarettes with a cigarette-lighter pistol, and another girl took my hand and led me through the throng to a table. I sat down and ordered a rum as a squeal alerted me to the high jinks over at Jubal's table. Father Seamus had arrived and by way of a welcome drink was drinking Vimto out of Mrs Bligh-Jones's shoe. She was squealing at the depravity of it. Once he'd drained the shoe he leered and beat his chest like Tarzan and everybody laughed but when his gaze caught mine he lost some of his sparkle and sat down

140

uncertainly. Never was it more truly said: a man is known by the company he keeps.

My drink arrived and I looked around for Ionawr but couldn't see her; no doubt she would find me easily enough. I watched the stage where there was an unknown starlet singing. A Myfanwy wannabe without the looks or the voice. But she sang all the usual songs and the crowd were pleased. And then Mrs Bligh-Jones took the mike. She made an improbable nightclub singer. She stood rather stiffly, the spotlight glinting on her Sam Browne; her tunic sleeve flapping emptily. One of her spectacle lenses had been taped over to cure a recurrent lazy eye. She spoke into the mike like a schoolgirl addressing assembly and explained that she wished to sing a few hymns to give thanks to her Lord and Saviour for her deliverance from the blizzard on Pumlumon. A murmur of pious approval drifted round the room. During her act Ionawr turned up and led me by the hand to the back.

As we threaded our way through the throng Mrs Bligh-Jones took a bow. Applause erupted like firecrackers and was then cut instantly by the appearance of a man on the dance-floor. It was Jubal, in black tie and burgundy cummerbund. Everyone drew breath in expectation as he passed through them with slow determined steps — a comic pantomime, familiar to everyone, of the man who emerges from the swing doors of the saloon and walks down the dusty street to rescue his kidnapped bride. On the stage, half-blinded by the spotlight, Mrs Bligh-Jones sim-mered with expectation like a Saxon maid when the Vikings are banging on the door. Ionawr and I halted our progress at the edge of the room and watched. Jubal stopped at the lip of the stage, paused half a beat longer to milk the moment to the full, and then reached into the air and drew a figure of eight with his index finger. A collective sigh came from all the ladies around the floor. Jubal turned his finger into a pistol and fired an imaginary bullet at the bandleader who laughed, clutched good-humouredly at his heart, and in the same instant struck up the band. Mrs Bligh-Jones squealed and jumped down into her lover's arms with the faith of a trapeze artist and was instantly swept away in a giddy tango.

Ionawr tugged at my hand and we pushed our way through the doorway at the back and down the corridor, past the private rooms. The sound of revellers clapping in time to the Latin beat pursued us. But as we trudged deeper and deeper into the labyrinth of the pier the sound faded and gave way to the moan of the sea, a thick intoxicating boom — like blood pounding in our ears — as if the corridor was an artery leading us to a giant heart. At the very end, the entrance guarded by a curtain of clacking wooden beads, was the toffee-and-opium-apple den. We clacked our way through.

The room was filled with hot sickly-sweet smoke and in near-pitch darkness, the only light a few candles and

142

the red glow from the ends of the pipes. There was no music or any sound at all except the noise that recumbent people make when they change position or draw on a pipe; or suck a toffee apple before groaning softly.

Ionawr led me to a man somewhere in the room, I couldn't say where. He lay reclined on a mat on the floor, a tray of toffee apples before him, and next to it an opium pipe. He looked up slowly and the flickering reflections in his eyes said that he was still with us, after a fashion.

"This is the man I was telling you about," said Ionawr, although it was unclear which of us she was talking to. He reached out a feeble hand and we shook.

"You want to know about the Dean?" His voice was husky and thin but steady.

"Yes," I said.

"It was all a terrible mistake," said the monk. "A terrible, terrible mistake. If the man is dead it will be on my conscience for ever."

"Tell me what happened."

The monk took a bite from one of the toffee apples and then said dreamily, "I just drifted into it, really. For a while I was a monk down at Caldy Island, until I found out how they had lied to me. All the tales about them making Benedictine — it wasn't true. You never get near the stuff. All they sell in the gift shop is home-made mint sauce and scented soap. And the communion wine is piss . . . So I ran away and ended up in Aberystwyth at the Seaman's Mission. And before long I became a gofer for the druids, a runner I suppose you'd call it. Doing errands and things, making drops and that. That's how I got the valise. I was supposed to deliver it to a Raven. You know what that is, I suppose?"

"It's the name for a male agent who ensnares a female agent by seducing her."

"Yes, an assassination technique more properly known as a honey-trap, although it is more usual for the man to be the victim, for him to fall victim to a beautiful girl he unaccountably befriends in a bar. I was told to expect this man and to give him a valise."

"Who paid you to give him the case?"

"I've no idea. I'm just a link in a chain. I know only the link that comes after me, not the one that comes after him nor the one that preceded me. That's how it works."

"And you gave the case to the Dean by mistake?"

The man cried out in pain. "But how the hell was I supposed to know, dammit!? Look out for a dark, cruel, cold-blooded killer, they said. With a feather in his cap. And then this chap turned up and I was having a drink with him that night in the bar and I said, "What do you do for a living, then?" And he said, "My trade is death. To me it holds no sting; to me flesh is just meat and the cold impersonal cut of steel as commonplace as the pen is to the clerk." Well, what would you have done?"

"But he was an undertaker."

The monk's voice rose in anguish. "I know, I know! You think I'm not aware of that? It was just a harmless piece of shop talk to him. And the bloody feather he just found on his window-sill that morning. That's pretty, he thought, it's such a lovely day I think I'll put it in my hat. The fucking idiot!"

"And after that, the Raven turned up?"

"That's right. Wearing one of those coats they sell in Peacocks for nineteen ninety-nine. I thought it was a bit corny myself, dressing like that, but who am I to judge?"

"And what was in the valise?"

"How would I know?"

"You mean you didn't look?"

"Are you mad? It was sealed. You think I would be stupid enough to break a seal, like?"

"I would have."

"That's because you don't know these people like I do."

I stood up, dizzy and disorientated in the darkness, and made for the glimmer of light that betrayed the outline of a door. Just before I reached it a hand grabbed the edge of my trousers. I looked down and beheld a sight that has haunted me ever since. The wreck of man I had once known: Valentine. He lay there so thin and emaciated his face had become a gargoyle and on his lower arm the flesh had grown so thin you could see the candle shining through. Valentine the former style-guru of the druids, his Crimplene safari suit now filthier than the carpet in a pub toilet. His mouth pulled back in a rictus of pain like a snarling dog. I kneeled down, staring in wide-eyed horror at this shattered piece of humanity.

"Valentine, what happened out there at the sanatorium? What did you see?"

The words kindled a feeble light in the empty pits of his eyes. A tiny, quivering gleam like the stormlamp of a wanderer taking refuge from the tempest in an empty house.

"What did you see out there? What was it, this Ysbyty Ystwyth Experiment?"

The grip of his hand on my trouser-leg tightened slightly, like the claw of a wren. Then, slowly, his mouth opened and through teeth the colour of caramel he whispered, "The horror! The horror!"

Then there was strength inside him for no more. His head fell back to rest on the bench; he closed his mouth, exhausted at the effort of those six syllables. I tugged my trousers away from his childlike grip and left him staring at the ceiling with eyes bigger than saucers, waiting for release of death.

As I left the club I saw the cowgirl's holster hanging up by the door and, making sure no one saw, I slipped the toy gun into my pocket. Outside, the pavements were wet with spray from the sea. Patrons were starting to leave. I kissed Ionawr and pressed some money into her pocket and told her to go. I had things to do that night that it was better she didn't see. But no sooner had she left than I was cheated of my dark design. In a riot of drunken giggling, Mrs Bligh-Jones climbed awkwardly into the back of Jubal's car and stuck her legs through the wound-down window, wiggling them until a shoe fell off into the gutter. And Father Seamus, with whom I had an appointment tonight, got in the front and the car sped off.

The shoe lay in the gutter next to the drain, a tawdry spoor of a Cinderella with size twelve feet. I took a half-step and scooped it up on to the pavement with the toe of my foot. Then I kicked it towards the cleansing sea. It toppled through the air like a rugby ball, over the white crossbar of the railings. It did little to lift my despondency. The moment called instead for an act of penance. I walked up to the stand and ordered a hot dog. As I waited, breathing in the rich perfume containing all the disappointments of my life, I thought of Myfanwy. Who had been on the other end of the line? Was it her? Where was she calling from? South America? How could it be and yet why could it not? There was no way of knowing, and yet my heart was deeply troubled. I took the hot dog and walked off into the night and thought of Mrs Bligh-Jones, the heroine of Pumlumon. True, she might have lost an arm up on that mountain, I thought grimly, but who could deny that in return she gained a kingdom?

CHAPTER
TWELVE

It was just a comment passed in an Aberystwyth bar. After half a lifetime presiding over the mortal remains of Aberystwyth folk, he decided to go and see where the course materials came from. Just a passing comment made to a harmless stranger in the sort of bar where the strangers never are. My trade is death.

I stirred the tea in the pot and set out two cups then leaned back in my chair and let the hot fug of the paraffin heater lull me. Calamity walked in and I poured the tea as she emptied her schoolbag on to the desk: copper wire, anti-rheumatics, nylons, chocolate, fake library tickets . . . and a packet of sugar marked "Property of the Red Cross, Geneva". The last item out of the bag was a packet of bird seed. I asked her what it was for.

"Custard Pie asked me to get it." She looked at me slyly.
   "You went to see him, then?"
   "You said I could."
   "I know."

"It wasn't as bad as you think. He was quite friendly, really. The guards think he's lost it. Do-lally." She twirled an index finger next to her temple to demonstrate his mental state.

"And he asked you for bird seed?"

"There's an air vent leading up to the ground, he thinks he can tame some birds like the Birdman of Alcatraz."

"I suppose he can't eat it and fly out of there. But just be careful. Make sure you sell it dearly. Tell him to give you some information about the Dean and then when he does, say: 'You call that good information! The whole town knows that, give me something I don't know.' Or something like that, OK?"

"Right."

"And be careful, whatever you do, don't trust him."

Calamity took her tea and stood staring out of the window.

"Actually, Louie, I was thinking, seeing how dangerous this project is, I may need a heater on this one."

"Put on a jumper, like your mum keeps telling you."

"You know what I mean, stop messing around."

"What are you talking about?"

"Not that sort of heater — you know, a heater."

"A heater?"

"Protection . . . an equaliser . . ."

"A what?"

She sighed loudly. "A rod, an iron, a gat . . ."

"You mean a gun?"

"Yes."

"Sorry, kiddo, you're only licensed to carry a catapult."

"I'm serious, this is a crucial aspect of the case."

"Is that so?"

"I get the feeling it all hinges on this, we can't afford any mistakes here. I could take yours."

"I haven't got one."

"Yes you have, it's locked in the sea-chest. Mrs Llantrisant told me. The key's taped behind the picture of Noel Bartholomew."

I changed tack. "Calamity, as long as you work for me, you'll never carry a gun. I never carry one and it's probably the only reason I'm still alive."

A floorboard creaked and we both looked round. The door opened and Gretel stood framed in the doorway. "Hi! Can I come in?"

She was wearing a hessian trouser suit and a wide-brimmed hat and had painted her nails scarlet. I had an awful feeling it was an attempt at glamour. There was also something slightly stilted and unnatural in the way she walked, as if her recent exposure to the tarnished streets of Aberystwyth was causing her to affect a growing worldliness. I poured out another tea and Gretel told me the news. The Dean had telephoned her and pleaded with her to call off the sleuths.

"He was very angry with me," she said. "He said there were some very bad men looking for him who wanted him dead and having two bungling private detectives hunting him was just making it easier for them."

I nodded thoughtfully.

"He knew you'd been to the hotel and the Seaman's Mission and the Komedy Kamp at Borth. And he said Mister Marmalade was . . . was . . . what's the word?"

"Whacked," said Calamity.

"What!?"

"Whacked. He got whacked. That's what we call it in this business."

I looked at Calamity who ignored my questioning gaze.

Gretel looked puzzled. "I don't think he said that, it was something else."

"What does it matter," said Calamity. "Whacked, smacked, topped, zapped, greased, rubbed-out or bought the farm, he's dead and they did it."

"Who?"

"We don't know."

Gretel put her fist into her mouth and made a sort of weeping sound. "Do you think they'll . . . they'll . . . what was it?"

"Whack him," said Calamity helpfully. "Who knows? But don't worry, we know what we're doing."

Gretel went to the bathroom, and Calamity said simply, "What a dipstick."

"And she's paying us money, so be nice."

"She's definitely holding back on us."

"You think so?"

"You don't? All this weepy stuff for a professor? It's all fake."

"How do you know?"

"Whoever heard of someone hiring a private detective to find their teacher?"

"In the real world people do all sorts of things you wouldn't believe."

"And her body language is all wrong. The crying, that's always a tough one to fake."

"They looked like real tears to me. Or has she got an onion in her fist?"

"They're real but she's doing them in the wrong places. Textbook stuff. Crying inappropriately and not crying at the appropriate time. It's a giveaway."

"She just did that?"

The toilet flushed and we stopped and when Gretel came back it was to a silence that fooled no one, even someone as unworldly as her.

"Talking about me, are we?" She sat down. "I've been thinking, maybe we'd better call off the hunt."

Calamity went and sat down on the edge of the desk and invaded her personal space like the cops do. "Getting cold feet? Losing your bottle?"

"B . . . b . . . but what if they whack him?"

"If they really want to kill him," I said, "it's even more reason for us to find him first. Calling us off will just make their job easier."

"That's if he was telling the truth," said Calamity.

"What do you mean?" blurted Gretel. "Of course he's telling the truth. Why wouldn't he?"

Calamity put a mean face on. "How do I know? Why would anyone ever dream of telling a lie? It beats me. Right from the cradle we're taught to tell the truth, and yet there are all these people out there who don't do it. I don't get it, what about you, eh, Louie?"

I tried again to flash a warning look at her but she deliberately avoided it.

"The Dean never told a lie in his life," said Gretel.

"Yeah, but what about you?"

"What about me?"

"You haven't exactly been telling us the truth, whole and nothing but, have you?"

"W . . . w . . . what do you mean?"

I slid down in my chair, trying to get my foot towards Calamity under the table.

"This Bad Girl stuff for instance —"

"I don't talk about her —"

"That's a lie for a start — you never stop!"

I managed to get my foot across and kick Calamity. She jumped slightly and shot me a furious look. Then she eased herself down off the desk and stamped on my foot.

"I . . . you . . . how dare you?" said Gretel.

"You didn't tell us he made a pass at her one night and tore her blouse, did you?"

"He didn't . . . who says . . . how did you know?"

"It's my job to know, I'm a detective." She took out a notebook and read from it. "She was a hussy and she shouldn't have been there, huh? More interested in drinking and partying than learning about Abraham; and when it came to the Ten Commandments she only knew how to break them. And then there was the incident with the Dean; by rights he was the one who should have been thrown out on his ear but the wives of

153

all the other tutors got together and hey presto! off she goes. Not that she cared of course, it's what she wanted all along . . . am I getting warm?"

Gretel stood up angrily. "I won't stay another second to hear the Dean's good name dragged through the mud like this. Good day to you both."

After she had slammed the door I held my hand out for the notebook. Calamity snapped it shut and put it in her pocket. I stood up and took a step towards her. She moved round to the other side of the desk.

"Let me see."

"What for, don't you trust me or something?"

"There's nothing in it, is there? You made it all up."

She shrugged. "So what if I did? They're in it together, you mark my words." She walked out.

I took the cowgirl's gun out of my pocket and put it on the table. It was a real beauty. Replica cowboy Colt 45, the "Peacemaker". It had been adapted to light cigarettes with a flame that appeared where the hammer hit the pin. Everything worked as on a real one: the chamber spun, the blanks slid in and out, the trigger mechanism worked. You'd need to know a lot about guns to tell it wasn't real. I slid it into my jacket pocket and went out to make my peace with Father Seamus.

The inside of the confessional booth was warm and dark and comforting, like the inside of a womb, and almost as intimate with its air of shared secrets. I

154

leaned my head against the wooden side and said, "Father I need spiritual guidance."

"That's why I am here, my son."

"It's not easy."

"Take your time."

"I need to know whether shooting a priest is a mortal or a venial sin."

The sound of forced, uncertain chuckling came through the grille.

"I suppose it depends which priest," I added.

"Louie, that's you, isn't it? What are you doing? This is God's house."

"How come he let you in?"

"This is no place for jokes."

I stuck the gun through the grille. "Who's joking?"

"My God! Dear Louie, what on earth has got into you?"

"I could ask you the same question."

"This is about last night, at the club, isn't it?"

"How was the Vimto?"

He forced a laugh.

"Or did you turn it into wine first?"

"Louie, when the Lord calls upon you to do his work, you cannot quibble at the sort of establishment —"

"Of course not. Jesus was never too proud to enter a house of fallen women."

"That's what I tell myself."

"Yeah, I bet you do. I don't remember the bit in the Bible where he drank Vimto from their shoes, though. Must have missed that bit. Still," I said, slowly twisting the gun chamber and letting the sound of the clicks fill the booth, "you must get thirsty standing on that battlement all night. Eyes smarting in the frost. Denying the soft pleasures of Mrs Bligh-Jones's palliasse."

"Mrs Bligh-Jones is a very holy woman," he said coldly. "Now I must remind you that this is the House of God. If you've come to make a confession —"

"No," I said, pulling back the trigger. "I've come to take one."

He gasped. "What do you want!?"

"I want the answer to a question. If you choose not to answer or give me one I don't like I'm going to shoot you. If you don't believe me, I'll shoot you. That makes three ways to end up dead and one that doesn't."

"Have you gone mad?"

"Yes. I have. Now here is the question. Yesterday morning I showed you a picture of a girl. Just the sort of fallen woman you seem to specialise in. You said you'd never seen her before, but you were lying. Now you're going to tell me the truth. Who was she?"

"Would you really shoot?"

"Yes."

"But why? Over a girl?"

"I'm just an incurable romantic."

He took a breath. "If I tell you, it's imperative . . . you must promise . . . this mustn't go any further."

"Anything you say is automatically protected by the sanctity of the confessional. You should know that. Now tell me."

"That girl you showed me. It's true I had seen her before. I know her because I worked with her once."

"Where?"

"In . . . in . . . a place."

"What sort of place?"

"Oh, Louie, don't make me say. A terrible place. A wicked, wicked place where a priest has no business being."

"And where's that, apart from Mrs Bligh-Jones's bedroom?"

He paused and I could hear the sweat droplets breaking out on his forehead. "Where does someone go in this town when they've reached the bottom and have nowhere left to go?"

"There are lots of places."

"For you, yes! For you there are the bars and the girls and the toffee and the bingo and the whelks. For you there is a great choice. But for her. Ah! but for her? You cannot imagine what this girl was like. A filthy, lecherous Jezebel. A girl who oozed iniquity from her every pore. Who came out at night and ensnared the hearts of men with her malevolent scent like a carnivorous flower shining in the tropical moonlight . . . where would such a dirty bitch go?"

"I don't know but I'd like to!"

"There is only one place where she would end up. The movies."

I paused for a second. "Which ones?"

"Those filthy detestable engines of lust."

"You mean the 'What the Butler Saw' machines?"

I could sense his whole being twisting in pain. "Yes them. And not the ones from the pier. The ones in those private rooms where filth boils over like a cauldron of hot tar, where men come willingly to submit to the mortification of a bridle and other upholstery of the Devil . . ."

I started to snigger.

"Oh yes, you can laugh, you can laugh! Jeer away! But be warned, those who begin by mocking the degradation of the human spirit soon end up supping themselves from the cup of vileness!"

"That's a bit rich coming from you, isn't it!? What about supping from the shoe of vileness? Look, Father, you had a little tingle under your cassock and went to see some dirty movies. Big deal!"

The priest banged his fists against the side of the box. "Oh you fool, you unutterable, execrable mean-spirited fool!" he cried in abyssal anguish. "You loathsome dolt, you —"

"Hey, who's holding the gun here!"

He exhaled like a schoolmaster finally broken by the lifetime of ignorance from his charges.

"Louie, Louie. I didn't look at these things, you fool! I was in one of them! I was . . . was . . . the gimp! Oh my God, Louie, what have I done?"

He wailed like a lorry full of sheep when the scent of the approaching abattoir reaches them. And then he added quietly, breathless, as if his spirit was now so crushed it didn't matter what he said, "The girl is called Judy Juice."

158

I withdrew the gun and stood up, adding as I left, "Say three Hail Marys and give up the Vimto."

I spent the next three nights, red-eyed and weary, trailing the gossamer thread of rumour that fluttered behind the name Judy Juice. I knew the name, of course, but it was obvious now that the girl in the leopard-skin coat at Jubal's party had not been her. It should have been obvious then, too. How could she have been when the real Judy Juice wouldn't give him the time of day? It was just a clever trap, maybe not even all that clever — one of those gaping manholes Jubal left lying around in his conversation and which I had obligingly walked into. I had to hand it to him: he was a polished operator.

Everyone I spoke to had heard of her, but no one could say where she was at the moment. They said she was bitch, they said she was a babe, they said she was gorgeous and equally they said she was vile; but they didn't say where she lived. Some people said she was slime and others said she was smart, smarter than all the men who longed to paw her; and being a bitch was all really just an act. Some said she put herself about and others said she never went near any man except on screen. They said she was easy but from the resentful looks in their eyes you somehow doubted it. They said she'd been raped as kid and that's why she hated men and others said it wasn't true and why would she need an excuse like that anyway? Some said she was beautiful and all said she was contemptuous.

Some said she stayed in the hotels, a different room every night, depending on who was paying and the house Johns at the hotels said they'd never once seen her. Some said she lived on the council estate at Penparcau and others said she was rich and owned a house on Llanbadarn Road. One person said she lived at Borth and someone else said she had a houseboat at the harbour. Another person told me she lived out at the caravan park on the south bank of the Rheidol and the security guard there told me it was true but he hadn't seen her for weeks. In short, after three nights in which I got no sleep and even less joy, the only thing I knew about her for sure was the one fact everyone in town agreed upon. The thing between her and Jubal.

Everyone you talked to said Jubal was a bag of slime, but everyone you talked to smiled and cringed like a beaten dog whenever he appeared. Jubal the movie man with his hunchback and his pea-size head and his glasses thicker than portholes. Hi, Jubal! How's it going, Jubal? Saw the latest flick, Jubal, fantastic! You're looking great, Jubal! It might not be true to say every waitress was an out-of-work actress and every waiter had written a script, but Jubal slept with a lot of waitresses and it was difficult to see what else they found attractive in him. He wasn't scared of a challenge either. They said he'd promised to make Mrs Bligh-Jones a star, but it hadn't happened yet so maybe the job was too big even for him. Yeah, Jubal was the movie man in Aberystwyth, and so vain and girlish were the hearts of the townspeople he could have anything

160

he wanted, any woman and any thing. Except Judy Juice's heart. He tried buying it, he tried bribing, he tried threatening and cajoling. But nothing worked so she got all the parts she wanted; passed the auditions without ever having to disrobe, or even turn up. It was the only thing in Aberystwyth money or influence couldn't buy.

After three days of getting nowhere I drove east along Llanbadarn towards the mountains of Pumlumon. I pondered the case and started to wonder, as I sometimes did round about this stage, whether it was really all that it seemed to be. Maybe there was something all a bit too glib about it. Almost rehearsed, this story of a man within whose soul the repressed Bohemian dream breaks free. This plummet from the top of Mount Parnassus via the ventriloquists' ghetto and the Komedy Kamp to the swirling waters of the "What the Butler Saw" sewer. Even though I hadn't found him, it seemed a bit too easy, a bit phoney. His trail led like the footprints of a man in deep-sea diver's boots across wet concrete. And the fact that, despite all that, I still felt nowhere nearer to finding him only confirmed my suspicions. Maybe he wanted to be trailed, but wasn't ready to be found. Maybe he was playing with me; or someone else was not being straight with me.

Rain had started to spit at the windscreen as I pulled into the lay-by and looked ahead at the sanatorium. Now that I was here I suddenly saw what a forlorn task

161

it was. A twelve-foot perimeter wall, razor-wire on top, guard-dog patrols . . . I sighed and stepped out of the car. The air was cold and fresh, the ground sodden. I squelched over the turf and wandered along the wall for a while, looking for entrances. There weren't any. At one corner there was a tower and I could see a guard watching me through binoculars. It was hopeless. I doubted even Llunos could get in. I walked back to the car. I hadn't been away more than five minutes but another car had arrived in the meantime and parked behind mine. Two men had got out and were leaning against my car. One was dressed in a police constable's uniform and the other wore a shabby raincoat. It was Harri Harries.

CHAPTER
THIRTEEN

Wedrove south through Ysbyty Ystwyth, towards Pontrhydfendigaid, and then turned off on to a minor road into the hills; driving too fast for any chance of jumping from the moving car.

"Why have you picked me up?" I asked. "Or is that a stupid question?"

"It's a stupid question."

I flexed the muscles of my forearm; the cuffs, deliberately on too tight, bit into my flesh.

"This isn't the direction of the police station."

"Well done, pathfinder. This is not the direction of the police station." Harri Harries turned in the front seat of the prowl car and said to the driver, "I told you he was smart."

He squirmed awkwardly round to face me over the passenger seat. "You'll like this place better. It's remote and it's quiet. Far from the hurly-burly, and from the madding crowd. It's a place where two men can unwind and get to know each other. And, best of all, it's the sort of place where if you hurt yourself you can die safe in the knowledge that your whimpers won't disturb anybody's peace."

"And you wouldn't hold the odd whimper against a dying man."

"Every man has a right to whimper, peeper. Even you. Especially you."

A few miles down the road we pulled off and drove up a rough dirt track. The car's suspension was not good and we jumped and jerked around like drunken puppets. But the driver seemed not to care and Harri Harries sat up front with a smile on his face that didn't reach his eyes which were cold and intense.

We skidded to a stone-splattering halt outside a building that looked like an electricity substation, surrounded by a chain-wire fence, topped with barbed-wire. The twin gates were chained with thick anchor chain and a padlock the size of a sporran. A mournful electric hum filled the air. We passed through the gate and Harri Harries pointed to the sign that read: "Danger. Keep Out." "Don't say you weren't warned, shamus."

I decided I'd seen enough and as soon as they pulled me out of the car I made a run for it. But they had been expecting this . . . They were both on me within seconds, and with my hands cuffed behind me ruining my balance I was soon sprawling and eating cinders. A blackjack rained down a few times and I was groggily dragged or pushed towards the building. Crudely painted slabs of concrete cemented together to make a wall. Steel-frame window, the panes filthy and broken and replaced with cardboard. Dirty green paint that had all flaked off to reveal the desiccated wooded subframe. Signs showing stick figure people in attitudes of pain being hit with z-shaped electric rays coming down from the sky. A building whose rough brick architecture seemed to be designed solely to make lonely places in which to beat up the innocent. The deputy opened the second door and they shoved me through. The space inside was taken up with piled-up boxes and packing-cases, overflowing files and sacks of paper. There was a cleared space with a workbench and a chair that looked like it had been borrowed from a pre-war dentist's. It had leather restraining straps. There were dark stains of splattered liquid on the cement floor, stains that could have been blood, and over in the corner was a table covered in fancy-dress clothing. A wolf's outfit and a little girl's dress — a dirndl, the sort that Heidi used to wear. They pushed me into the chair and fastened the straps. The nausea of fear began to well up inside from the pit of my stomach, up and up to my throat. I swallowed hard.

"Like the chair? We got it from the sanatorium. They're not allowed to use them any more — illegal."

I was too scared to answer.

Harri dragged up a chair and sat, legs astride it, facing me from the side. I nodded towards the table in the corner. "Are we going to have a party?"

He gave a quick glance and said, "Yeah but you're not on the guest list."

He took out a pack of cigarettes, gave it a rapid shake, and grabbed a protruding cigarette between his lips. Then he lit it and spoke through clenched lips the way they do in the movies. Why didn't he just take the cigarette out for a minute if he wanted to speak? The same reason he did everything: just one long trailer for a movie I'd seen a hundred times before.

The deputy brought over a canvas bag and dumped it with a loud metal clang on the table. There were a lot of iron things inside and my heart froze. How crazy were they? I had no idea. Harri Harries was new here. Maybe they really did keep law and order like this in Llanelli. Where was the deputy from? He was dressed like a constable but I noticed now the numbers on his arm were all zeros. I'd never seen him before and something told me if I survived this night I probably wouldn't be seeing him again. Not unless Harri Harries needed to do some more special policing.

Harri put his hand inside the bag and performed the pantomime of someone doing a lucky dip. He pulled out a monkey-wrench. Lucky old me. I put a foot on the tabletop. Harri turned the wrench in his hand and then let the flat side fall on to the exposed bone of my shin. Tears of pain filled my eyes. It was just a lazy slap but the message it conveyed was clear: if this is the hors d'oeuvre, just imagine the banquet to come.

"What do you want?" I said though gritted teeth.

★   ★   ★

166

He rested his elbow on the back of the chair, rested his chin on the palm of his hand and said simply, "I want to ask you a few things about Dean Morgan. Principally, where the fuck he is." He puffed smoke gently out towards the ceiling.

"But I don't know where he is."

He made a thoughtful face. "I thought you might say that. That's why you'll notice a slight departure here from formal police-interview procedure. It's not an easy one to spot, quite subtle, but someone with your enormous experience should be able to get it. Any ideas?"

"The fancy dress?"

He glanced again at the clothing in the corner and shook his head. He pulled the pen out of his breast pocket and held it out to me. "You see? It's this. I'm not taking any notes."

Again I said nothing, just wished he'd cut the comedy.

"Now there's a good reason for that. My experience with interviewing peepers is that they generally know a good deal of information that would be useful to the police but that they are reluctant to release it, either because they are selfish or because of something that is called protecting client confidentiality. They usually lay great store by this which is an area where they differ greatly from me because I don't give a fuck about it. And that, my friend, is the reason that in contrast to established procedure I'm not taking notes. Because the first ten minutes of any interview is usually bollocks. And then after I have used some of the plumbing tools

167

in the bag here interviewees start to open up a bit. A bit like unblocking a drain."

The deputy snorted in appreciation.

"You just love to hear yourself talk, don't you?"

"Wrong, peeper. I love to make other people talk; shy retiring people like you."

"What is it you want to know?" I said.

"I want to know where the Dean is."

"I've been looking for him for two weeks. I don't know where he is. No one does."

"You see what I mean? You're just like all the rest. They start off saying they know nothing and by the end of the interview I've got an aching wrist from taking notes."

"Why are you looking for him?"

A sudden flash of anger seized him and he smacked the wrench against my shin again. "Don't you fucking start interviewing me! I'm not the one tied to a chair." He stuck his face up close to mine, so close I could feel the heat of his anger burning on his skin. "You creepy little snoopers never stop, do you? Always poking your dirty little snouts into where they don't belong, prying and snooping and spying . . . isn't that right? You'd just love to put your eye to my keyhole, wouldn't you?"

"I don't need to, Harries. I wouldn't see anything I hadn't seen a thousand times before."

"Oh is that so!"

"You're just another two-bit Sunday-school teacher that took a wrong turning, Harries; brought up in some quagmire of a valley above Ebbw Vale, in the shadow of the chapel, living in a grey house beneath a dripping

168

grey sky drinking grey spoons of gruel fed to you by your grey mam and singing grey songs of thanks every grey Sunday for the shitty grey life the good grey Lord so kindly gave you. The highlight of your week was getting beaten with a leather strap to make you good and the only girl you ever kissed went 'Baaa!' —"

The wrench smashed down again. I gagged like a sobbing child and screwed my eyes up as the tears squelched out of the corners. As I groaned he brought his face up close and hissed in a cloud of nicotine, "It may help your memory to know that the wrench is the friendliest tool in the bag. Five minutes from now and you'll be begging me to use that nice old wrench. Do you understand?"

I nodded. I was no tough guy. I was ready to tell him anything. The trouble was, I didn't know anything. A few scraps of nothing that would only serve to convince him I was holding out on him and make him madder, because I was sure now that when he got mad like he just did it wasn't an act. Make him madder and introduce me to the whole range of his DIY plumbing skills. He reached into the bag and pulled out an electric sander. The deputy's face lit up and Harri looked around for a plug. He found one on the wall behind the bench.

"Would you 'effin' believe it!" he cursed. "It's a round-pin." He held the flex of the sander and let the plug that he couldn't plug in dangle uselessly just to help me realise how close I'd come. He threw the sander back into the bag and did another lucky dip. This time he pulled out a blowtorch. His mood brightened. "That's better! Old-tech, can't go wrong." He pumped the plunger to build up the pressure and lit the gas, then adjusted it until he got a perfect spear-blade of hot blue flame. He held it next to his ear. "They say that the worst part about being burned with one of these is after it stops, when the flesh cooks itself slowly like a leg of lamb in the oven."

"Please don't do it, I'll tell you anything you want to know."

He waved the flame at my face. "OK, so where is he?"

"He's out at the Komedy Kamp. Buried under the floor of chalet 7c," I said in desperation.

A look of surprise lit up the cop's face. "You're kidding? How did he get there?"

"It's like this," I began. "This Dean acted the part of the big holy monk, you know the type — wouldn't know one end of a woman from another. Holier than thou and all that, but it's all for show. Inside he has a special hobby, something he likes to do, something that he is ashamed to even think about but he still likes to do it ..." I looked at the cop. He had put the blowtorch down and was sitting there drinking up the story. This was easier than he'd expected.

"So what was it then, peeper?"

"Stiffs."

Cop nodded, trying to look businesslike, as if this what he had suspected all along.

"Of course, he's not the only person around town who likes them a bit cold. It's quite a popular pastime in some quarters, so I'm told. But not many people are in such an excellent position to do something about it. Old men, young girls, you name it, he was into it. And that might have been an end of it. He could have carried on like that and no one would have been any the wiser. But he gets greedy. Maybe he's planning on a retirement and needs a better quality nest egg, or maybe he's just tired of scrimping and saving all his life. Either way he could do with a little extra money. Couldn't we all? He finds himself approached by a couple of guys who want in on the game. They happen to have some clients who also fancy a night of passion in the morgue and they're willing to pay. So these two new guys ask him how about it? Like to share the spoils for a bit of extra cash? And he thinks why not? As long as everyone is discreet about it no one need know and everyone is discreet of course because they are all respectable men in respectable positions. And so it goes on for a while but then the two new guys think of a new angle. A special-request service. You see someone walking around you fancy, have a word with us and we can arrange the death and a subsequent night of passion."

The cop whistled. This was worse than anything he'd yet encountered. And if he knew the first thing about the underworld he'd know it was pure invention and not very good at that. But he didn't.

"Of course this is way out of the Dean's league. Bonking a few corpses, yes, he didn't have a problem with that, and for a man like him for whom death was a way of life, it wasn't a big deal. But this was something else entirely. Murder to order? No way. The trouble

171

was, the two guys had made a mistake. They'd miscalculated and let him in on the plan; that gave them a problem. So they invite him to town to discuss the matter. And they get persuasive. Very persuasive. The Dean's no fool, he realises they are planning to silence him, silence him for good. He tries to run away and hide out in town. But what does he know about the cloak-and-dagger stuff? He's just a crusty old academic fallen in with a bad lot. It was only a matter of time before they got to him."

The cop nodded thoughtfully as he took it in. He was deeply disturbed. "So who are the two guys?"

"I don't know the names, but one of them is the garage mechanic at Kousin Kevin's Kamp, he's the muscle. The other is the security guy there. He's the brains."

The cop made a determined frown. "That little jerk — I know him!"

"Of course he'll deny it all," I said.

Harri Harries picked up the bag of tools. "We'll see about that."

It was still early evening and sleet was falling as they padlocked the gates and dropped me off at the bus stop. The sort of bus stop that looked like bus arrivals were charted with a calendar rather than a clock. I hobbled over to the red telephone box. The door squeaked like a seagull and the inside stank of urine. Llunos's voice had the tone of one who really didn't want to get up and answer the phone at 8p.m. in the evening, knowing full well it wouldn't be anything

172

good. I looked at the distant row of yellow lights from behind sitting-room curtains and I knew what he meant. But this had to be done. I told him briefly about what had happened and told him to get up from his tea, the newspaper and the TV, put on his coat and go and find the two guys from Kousin Kevin's. He didn't say no, he just sighed and said, "Why me, Louie?"

"Who else is there?" He knew that was true.

"You're asking me to arrest a couple of guys who've done nothing wrong."

"Well it wouldn't be the first time, would it?"

"This isn't funny, Louie."

"Who's laughing? Look at it this way, you'll probably be saving their lives. Or at the least preventing a serious assault taking place. Just keep them banged-up until we can sort this out. If you keep them under your nose they should be safe."

Sometime after midnight I parked outside the Moulin and walked in. It was quieter tonight than the last time, smoky and slightly sleepy, as if all the moods of all the people there had become synchronised and the flavour of the night was dreamy-mellow. I ordered a drink, listened to the singers and let my gaze wonder sleepily around the room. It came to rest on a girl dancing and my eyes stayed there for a while with my thoughts wandered elsewhere. Then slowly those thoughts returned and my attention focused on her. Suddenly I understood how a rabbit feels when it stares transfixed at the headlight of an oncoming car.

She was tall but not too tall and slim but not skinny. Her figure was voluptuous and statuesque like one of those space-travelling goddesses in newspaper strip-cartoons, the ones whose job it is to save the universe. She wore a tight bodice of soft white lace, partially unbuttoned so that the cups of her brassiere, like the hands of a malevolent dwarf, thrust her breasts forward to taunt the men who watched in awe. The waist-button of her jeans was undone and the button below that too so that the edge of her white panties flashed in the ultraviolet light. Her midriff was bare and taut, and her faded Levi's 501s had been cut off at about the level that her bicycle saddle reached when she was seventeen. A saddle that had, no doubt, been stolen long ago and was now worth ten times more than the bike.

She danced wonderfully and provocatively with a flowing Polynesian languor, her hair glistening like moonlit water. Occasionally the cascading blonde hair would swamp her soft brown shoulder and the strap of her bodice would be washed away in the flood; and when that happened, her breast remained impossibly in position, mocking and taunting, like a puppet that continues to dance after its strings have been cut. Every time I tried to look away my gaze returned of its own accord, like a compass needle pointing north.

The boy she was with was one of the camp, symbolist painters who sold their work to the tourists on the

174

Prom. He was wearing a ruffed shirt and stage make-up and no doubt had left a portfolio with the hat-check girl containing five dreary views of the bandstand with the moon hanging behind it like a rotten fruit. Scarcely eighteen or nineteen, hardly old enough to have made an enemy in this world, and yet in the Moulin tonight this boy was despised by every man there. Because we all knew from the expression on the goddess's face — the truculent, savage aristocratic disdain — that she had chosen him purely to demonstrate her contempt for the rest of us. Chosen this effete, cross-dressing, half-grown milksop to show us how she despised us for being such hopeless fools; for surrendering ourselves so abjectly at the sight of her flesh. She had chosen him not as a dance-partner, but as a scalpel with which to expose like an Aztec priest our hearts to the common view and make us see, even though we already knew, what pathetic and feeble objects they were. Our palpitating flesh as craven as that of a guard dog who allows himself to be bought off with a bone and licks the hand of the man come to kill his master. And though our humiliation was already more than complete, she intensified it further by ordering round after round of exotic drinks — flaming black sambucas and B52s — which they knocked back in one, and which she paid for from a wallet stuck in her back pocket. And after that, eyes smouldering with contempt, she pressed her chest hard against the boy's bony ribcage and slid with lugubrious, side-to-side slithers up into his undeserving, pimply face. I stopped a waitress and asked the name of this girl in the tones of a shepherd asking about that new star in the east. And she told me without even bothering to look, told me with the air of one sick of explaining the obvious to the ignorant. "It's Judy Juice, the movie star."

She left shortly after and so I paid for my drink and followed at a discreet distance. By the time I got to the street she was gone, and someone else hailed me from just outside the gateway. It was Calamity, leaning against a lamppost. I looked at my watch — it was gone one and I was about to remonstrate with her for being out so late but then I saw the stricken look in her eyes, her complexion the pallor of cigarette ash.

I opened my mouth to speak but nothing came out and she opened hers silently too. Then she collapsed into my arms with the words "Custard Pie".

"It's OK," I said. "It's OK."

Then she pulled herself away from me and looked up and told me in one long gushing stream, as if the faster she said it, the less damage it would do.

"He saw the bird seed and begged me for it and I said, 'You have to buy it, buster.' And so he said, 'If you want to find the Dean, ask for the girl called Judy Juice.' And so I sneered at him and said, 'You expect bird seed for that? I've seen fresher news written on the side of a Babylonian tomb.' And then he sort of danced a bit and said I was a cutey and said, 'All right, little girl, you want some real news? Tell that smart-arse private eye to stick this in his pipe and smoke it.' And then he got all excited and rubbed his hands together and said, 'You want to know what the Ysbyty Ystwyth

Experiment is all about? What's been going on at the sanatorium? What this "thing" is that people keep seeing? You want to know that, little girl?' And I said yes and he said, 'Give me the seed.' So I made a deal. I gave him a quarter of it and said he'd get the rest when he told me about the Ysbyty Ystwyth Experiment. And so he did." Then she stopped and said, "I think you need a drink."

"I've just had one."

"I think you need another one."

But before I could drink or she could speak there was a disturbance in the entrance to the club. Judy Juice walked out in a hurry, putting her coat on as she left. Behind her, arms outstretched in supplication, came Jubal. "But Baby!" he cried. "But Poppet!"

Judy Juice carried on walking and Jubal ran and caught her sleeve. "Munchkin!" She shrugged off his hand and swept past us without noticing. He tried to grab her sleeve again, shouting, "Look here, you bitch!" Calamity put a hand out to stop him. "Lady doesn't want to talk to you, Mac." Jubal pushed her aside and she grabbed his arm. He shoved her roughly again and she kicked him furiously in the shin. Jubal threw out a backhand slap and in the same instant, before even I had time to react, Judy Juice spun round and shoved Jubal crying, "Leave the little girl alone, you cockroach!"

Judy Juice was quite a big girl and Jubal fell back in surprise and over into some sacks of refuse left out for the bin men. Calamity made a move towards him but I held her back. He lay there dazed for a second or two as Judy Juice stepped into a taxi, and then he stumbled to his feet, ran towards the car and shouted, "But Baby I'm sorry! Please, Baby . . ." The car sped off and Jubal sank to his knees, shouting "Baby, I'm sorry, I beg you!" And then, still kneeling, he buried his face in his hands and wept.

Back at the office, once I'd convinced her I'd had enough rum, Calamity told me what Custard Pie had said. Told me the news that made my heart stop for so long that I sat there listening for the beat to start again like a hundred-metre sprinter listening for the gun.

"This 'thing' out at the sanatorium," she said. "It's Herod Jenkins, your old games teacher. He's still alive."

CHAPTER
FOURTEEN

I tossed and turned all night and cried out in that half-asleep, half-awake state in which the night terrors visit us. And maybe an hour before dawn — the darkest hour — I slipped beneath the membrane of sleep and dreamed of a day in late January many years ago when the whole school was kept in during afternoon break. An eerie hush consumes the old school building, a silence so absolute you can hear the footfall of the spiders in the cupboards where the Latin books are stored. Forbidden to move from our desks, or even look at the window, we hold our breath and strain to hear above the deafening drumbeats of our own hearts . . . and then there it is, at first so faint as to be almost imperceptible, but growing and growing, getting louder until there can be no mistake: thwump, thwump, thwump! The sound of choppers. Suddenly, in a cacophony of slamming desklids that drowns out the shouting of the teacher, we all dash to the window. Thwump, thwump, thwump! The dying sun has turned the frosty sky amber like a puma's eye; spread beneath it the iced-over games field sparkles like frozen lemonade . . . thwump, thwump, thwump! From far in the glowing west, growing all the time, getting bigger

179

and bigger, that small speck that grows and slowly resolves itself into the shape of a helicopter, flying in low over the trees. Realities merge in the way they do in dreams, so that the chopper is now silhouetted against an orange tropical sky, like the film poster to *Apocalypse Now*, advertising a film about a journey upriver in a coracle to a Cambodian temple, in search of a crazy man in a track suit called Kurtz. Thwump, thwump, thwump! "Get back to your seats this instant!" Mr Kurtz cries. We look out and gasp. Against the burning sky, almost overhead now, the chopper. And slung beneath the fuselage the bier of Marty, the one who never made it back from the cross-country run.

Llunos was hunched over a pint in the Castle pub, just inside wooden doors. He looked up, smiled, saw the expression on my face and lost the smile. "Oh," he said. "Looks like you found out. Should have known you would."

"All I want to hear from you is it's not true."

"It's true. No one in town wants more than me to say it's not. But that doesn't change a thing. It's true."

"Didn't we push him out of a plane?"

He nodded glumly. "I thought we did."

"How long have you known?"

"Six months or so. At first it was just rumours . . ."

"Why didn't you tell me?"

He took a while to speak, as if he knew the answer but had forgotten it. "What good would it have done?"

180

"How could this happen? From a plane, for fuck's sake!"

He picked up his pint and brought it to his lips and then stopped. He spoke over the top. "It's not that rare to fall out of a plane and survive. Read the *Guinness Book of Records*. And this was over a lake, and we were flying in low for a bombing run. Work it out."

"Wouldn't the concussion kill him?"

"A normal person, perhaps. But a games teacher . . . ?" He stopped and took out a card and wrote an address on the back. "Look, I can't say any more at the moment. It's better for you to hear the whole story. What you've heard so far is nothing. Meet me tomorrow at this address, at 10a.m."

He handed me the card and stood up to leave. The address was a room in the old college building. "In the meantime, keep it under your hat. We don't want to start a panic."

The old college stretched along the Prom from the pier to the putting-green. With its massive stone walls and conical turrets it looked like a Rhineland castle and had stood up well to the flood. It had originally been built as a hotel and when they found they couldn't make it pay by accommodating folk taking a two-week vacation from the real world they used it instead to house the dons who took one for a lifetime. Inside the main building bronze statues of long-dead and forgotten academics gazed down at me with looks of stern and vague disapproval. An attitude built on the failsafe premise that whatever it was I was doing or thinking they would almost certainly have disapproved of it. The floor squeaked as all floors in buildings devoted to serious study should and the walls were hung with wooden boards gilded with forgotten acts of sporting glory. All from a distant time when athletic prowess for students entailed more than a run from the pie shop to the pub.

The room looked out over the ocean through arched, leaded lights with panes of stained glass. There were seven people waiting in the room when I arrived, seated around a table on which stood a movie projector. Llunos motioned me to take a seat and introduced me to the others. There was professor of some sort from the Clarach Institute. A Tillamook Indian with a face the colour of polished rosewood and wearing a racoon-skin hat. There were also two lab technicians and some men in dark suits who looked like they came from the security services.

"The first thing you need to know about this meeting", Llunos began, "is it never took place." The people round the table nodded grimly. "We never met, we never spoke, and we're not here now." More nods. "I don't wish to make this any longer than it has to be, but not everyone is up to speed here and so I will need to fill in some of the background." He walked to the front and stood in front of a blackboard.

"At first it was just a few rumours. Some of the peasant communities in the hinterlands beyond Nant-Y-moch

182

started reporting strange sightings. A manlike creature loping through the forest, usually at dusk, a shy creature that shunned human contact and used the cover of twilight to get about. Such reports were easy enough to dismiss at first — especially by people who didn't want to look too closely. Then there were the odd footprints — big ones, and even the deep wide imprint in the mud of a waterhole of his backside." Llunos gave a signal to the lab technicians who lifted a plaster-of-Paris cast the size of a small card-table. Llunos continued. "Farmers also reported losses among their livestock, but of course such things are commonplace." He turned towards the man in the racoon-skin hat. "Laughing Bear has experience with the sasquatch of North America, popularly known as Bigfoot. Laughing Bear, I imagine the pattern I'm outlining is familiar to you?" The man nodded gravely and lines appeared in the corners of his eyes.

"As I said, it was easy enough to dismiss at first. But then this happened." He gave another hand signal and the blackout curtains were drawn. One of the technicians started up the projector and we watched a grainy, ghostly 8mm film of a family horsing around beside a lake at nightfall. They had that awkward jerky movement of people shot with old cine cameras and were laughing and playing tag and pulling faces for the camera the way all families do.

"At the time they saw nothing unusual but when the film came back from the chemist, they saw this." He pointed his stick at the tree-line behind the family antics. It was a forestry plantation with the characteristic uniform rows of conifers. Where the tree-line stopped there was a wire fence and some fire-beating equipment. And there, moving uncertainly between the trees, was a figure. If it had been any more shadowy it would have been imperceptible. If it had stood still it probably would have never been noticed. But the very act of moving detached it from the background gloom and give it substance.

"The quality's terrible, of course. But anyone can see that this is no fox, or deer, or any of the explanations people normally like to pin on things like this. We had it image-enhanced and analysed and all the usual stuff. The boffins couldn't tell us much, except to say it's definitely a biped." Llunos paused for a second and pressed his fingertips together as if the next sentence was especially difficult for him. "Gentlemen, we had reason to suspect, and we soon came to know, that this was Herod Jenkins. And that he had survived his fall from the plane." No one said anything and the film ran out, filling the silent room with the repeated clack, clack, clack of the revolving celluloid whipping the tabletop.

The man in the racoon-skin hat was invited to take the stand. I half-expected him to speak with the heap-big Hollywood accent used to accuse us of speaking with forked tongue. But he just sounded like any other well-educated Canadian.

"This is the point where I was called in," he began. "I spent some weeks in the Nant-y-moch badlands tracking the creature. I found out that although the adults were scared of him, the children knew him well. They called him Mr Dippetty-doo — a helpless happy old fool eating dirt and wearing clothes of woven twigs. In stark contrast to his former persona, about which you are all better informed than me, Dippetty-doo would happily tousle the hair of the village urchins, or pull out pennies from behind their ears . . . even the farmyard dogs would no longer bark at his passing but would scamper up and lick his hand . . . in short, gentlemen, it became clear to me that the fall from the plane had caused him to lose his memory and no trace of it remained. He was in fact harmless."

The woodsman sat down and there was a mild ripple of table-rapping in applause, although I didn't see what for.

Llunos stood up and cut the applause with his hand. "This left us with a serious problem. What guarantee was there that at some point he wouldn't recover his memory? The prospect was alarming and in order to allay our fears we contacted Doctor Pritchard who is an expert on neurophysiology at the Clarach Institute of Behavioural Neuroscience. What he told us hardly put our fears at rest. Doctor."

The man in the white lab-coat stood up and smiled thinly. "I'll try and do this in lay terms as far as I am able. No doubt you are all familiar with the TV-soap version of memory loss. The patient lies on a hospital bed and his family sit around him showing him old photos and playing the records that were once his favourites in the hope that some emotionally charged event will somehow turn the key that opens the gates of memory. It's actually not as fanciful as it seems and is a well-proven clinical technique. But have you ever wondered what would happen if the family sitting round the hospital bed were impostors? And the lost memories they patiently tried to coax back were bogus? All those old songs he never sang and the specially doctored photos showing cherished childhood moments that never took place? That in essence was what we did." There was a subdued gasp round the table at the audacity of what the doctor was telling us. He continued unabashed as if used to such a reception and perhaps slightly proud. "The project was conducted under the supervision of Doctor Faustus from the sanatorium — a very brilliant and unconventional neuroscientist who has done some pioneering work on false-memory syndrome and who kindly agreed to undertake the mapping of Herod's psyche."

One of men in dark suits asked a question. "How did you get him to the sanatorium?"

The scientist smiled in acknowledgment, pleased at being given another opportunity to show off.

"Good question! Actually, it wasn't too difficult, we used a technique suggested to us by our friend here from the Tillamook Indians. Basically the same used for trapping mink. Laughing Bear told us that during his

186

observation of Dippetty-doo he noticed his quarry was secretly engaging in an occasional lover's tryst with a local woman. We approached her and outlined to her out desire to make Herod well again and she was happy to assist us in our efforts by acting as a form of bait. I believe some of you may know this woman, Mrs Bligh-Jones from the Meals on Wheels."

This was greeted with snorts from around the table of the sort that suggested "rather you than me, mate".

There were no further questions so Doctor Pritchard carried on. "Once we had successfully installed the subject in the sanatorium we invented a new past for him and hired a group of actors to sit round his bedside from dawn till dusk pretending to be his family. They were called the Flying Laszlofis — a troupe of Magyar circus performers. Day by day they sat there drip-feeding him the sweet balm of memory of all those lost tender cherished moments — hunting the black bears of the Carpathian Hills with his grandfather, Vadas; learning to dance the polka in the rustic parlour at the age of six; his old dog Ocsi, and that first sweet kiss with the seventeen-year-old Ninácscska. It was an audacious undertaking but, amazingly, it started to produce results. Before long Herod took up the violin and soon mastered the rudiments of a number of Hungarian folk songs. He began to express pangs of homesickness for those far-off Carpathian Hills. He refused to eat the hospital food and insisted on goulash and pickled cabbage. In short, the experiment had been an astonishing success; or to put it another way, gentlemen, Herod Jenkins had gone from this world, and in his place stood Zsigácska Melles." He paused and fought down a half-smile that was twitching the edges of his mouth. "Er . . . those of you who think us scientists are a rather cold-blooded, humourless lot might be amused to learn that Melles is the Magyar term for big-chested." There was a ripple of chuckling, and he continued, "It was an epoch-making moment in the annals of neuroscience; until, that is, the morning when the nurse went to his room and found him gone." The doctor made an apologetic gesture with his hands and walked to the window and spoke to the sea and the sky: "Since then there have been rumours and the occasional reports of him standing at the edge of the woods at sunset, staring, so they say, with a strange yearning at the rugby on TV in the darkened houses . . ."

I walked with Llunos down Pier Street and accompanied him to his office. As we strolled he told me about Harri Harries. The two men from the Kamp were currently in protective custody, down at the station.

"They thought it was a trick," said Llunos. "And Harries hasn't reported to work. Don't know where he is. I've sent a fax to Cardiff about it."

"Why did they send him here in the first place?"

"It's because certain people down in Cardiff are not happy with me."

"I thought you were doing fine."

188

His step unconsciously followed time with mine. "First the flood and now Herod . . . black marks against my name . . . it all adds up."

"They surely can't blame you for . . . for all this?"

"It happened on my watch. Plus they think I've gone soft. Got old. They say I don't run a tight ship any more, all this aggro between the druids and the Meals on Wheels. They can't see, it's a different world after the flood, all the old certainties have gone . . . time was you knew who was bad and who was good, even if you could never prove it you still knew it. But now, life being such a struggle, the line is blurred. And then there's the problem of you."

"Me?"

"They see me having coffee with you and generally . . . fraternising they call it, and they say that proves it. Once upon a time I would have run you out of town every now and again just to keep you on your toes."

"It's true, you would have."

"I know. But after a while . . ." He stopped at the corner and looked at me. "I mean, what's the point?"

When we got to his office we sat in contemplative silence. "We're going to make a posse, if you're interested," said Llunos after a while. "The boffins say he'll probably make for some place sacred to him."

I tried to look hopeful. "I suppose that's something."

"Yes," said Llunos sadly. "It's something."

CHAPTER
FIFTEEN

Marty's mum's house was a two-mile walk off the main road up a country lane. There were no streetlights but the wet drizzly sky gave off a soft luminescence and provided more than enough light for eyes that had got used to the dark. Despite the cold and wet it was strangely pleasant, calm and peaceful so far away from the frenetic activity of Aberystwyth. The only sound was the occasional bark of a distant dog and even that was comforting. You could tell without seeing that these were wholesome well-fed dogs who would run up to you and nuzzle your hand, not the snarling, half-starved packs of curs that slunk through the rubble of town at night. After a while I began to make out the orange light from the house, glowing through the swaying black filigree of the trees.

The door was on a chain, Marty's mum lived alone, and peered at me from inside as a wave of hot firelit air hit me. Air filled with cinnamon and baking smells and that indefinable but not unpleasant aroma that the insides of other people's houses have. Recognition took only a fraction of a second and she let out a gasp before closing the door slightly to release the chain.

190

Once I was inside she stood facing me looking up and grasped my face in her hands. We didn't speak, she just beamed at me, her old watery eyes sparkling and then her face darkened as a thought occurred to her. "I knew you'd come when I heard."

I nodded.

"So it's true then? He's alive?"

"Yes. I came as soon as I could."

She touched my cheek. "You're a good man, Louie." Then she turned and I followed her down the corridor to the kitchen at the back.

"It's funny, I always suspected it. I had a feeling . . . they say a mother always knows. Mind you, it's always good to see you, Louie, whatever the occasion."

The kitchen was filled with warmth and I sat down at the table while Marty's mum stirred some stew on the stove. There was a rifle on the table, half-way through being cleaned. We both looked at it at the same time and then our eyes met.

"It's no good you looking at me like that."

"Bit late in the year to be hunting rabbits, isn't it?"

"Bit late in life, too, that's what you're thinking, I know."

"Or perhaps you're hunting something a bit bigger?"

"This one's no bunny rabbit, that's for sure."

I put my hand on the gleaming oily barrel. "This isn't the way."

She stopped stirring and stood motionless at the stove and then said, "He took my son, Louie. Sent him

191

off on a cross-country run in weather that even the SAS on the Brecon Beacons don't go out in."

She brought over the stew and I ate hungrily. Through the steam swirling up from the spoon I could see the smiling picture of Marty on the mantelpiece above the fire. It was a washed-out colour snap of him on a beach at some south-coast English resort, seven or eight years old.

"All the same," I said, "you should leave it to the experts. I hear there's going to be a posse."

She scoffed. "Bank tellers, postmen, ironmongers, filingclerks . . . They'll try and take him alive, the fools."

"A hunt is no place for you. It's not right."

"Right or not right, I don't care any more, Louie. I'm getting old now and I've got no one here to comfort me. I lost a good husband to the mines and a good son to the games teacher. It's time to even the score."

"You'll be wasting your time, he could be anywhere between here and Welshpool."

"It's not so difficult if you know where to look. He'll make for somewhere sacred. No different from a wounded fox. Somewhere that means something special to him, from long ago. Some place he cherishes, that he holds dear from a happy time before everything got ruined."

"Sure, I said. "But no one knows where that is."

After supper we talked until late. I told Marty's mum about what I'd seen, about the fall of Valentine, and how the Meals on Wheels had eclipsed the druids. She

192

scoffed and warned me not to pay too much attention to outward appearances. Druids or the Meals on Wheels, underneath they were all the same. Like shoots growing in different parts of a garden that come from the same tree. The one to really watch out for, she said, was Mrs Llantrisant, even though she was still in prison.

At midnight, the clock chimed and Marty's mum looked slightly startled.

"Oh my word!" she said. "Almost forgot. Come! we must be quick, he usually starts at midnight."

Ignoring the puzzled look on my face she beckoned to me to follow her. She doused all the lights in the house and switched on a torch and led me up to the attic bedroom, a small garret that looked out over the hills south of Aberystwyth. The night was dark and featureless, even the lights of the scattered cottages having been extinguished, and only the ceaseless blink of the lighthouse beyond Cwmtydu reminding us that there were other people alive tonight.

"Wait for it now," she whispered.

We stared out, holding our breath, waiting and watching for I knew not what, the lighthouse the only point of focus in the darkness. And then it happened.

"Oooh! Here we go," hissed Marty's mum.

Something happened to the light from the lighthouse. Something that I had seen only once before in my life, that I struggled to find words for, seen once many moons ago at a meeting of children whose purpose was now lost to me. A shadow temporarily obscured the light, like a cloud sliding across the face of the moon. And then it passed and was followed by another smaller shadow. And then a bigger one. Marty's mum nudged me and pointed further to the south where the object that had temporarily eclipsed the sun of the lighthouse threw a shadow, one huge and measured in miles across the face of the darkened hills and all at once I realised in astonishment what it was. It was a bunny.

"It's Mr Cefnmabws," explained Marty's mum in a hushed voice. "The lighthouse keeper. He's a dissident."

The county-sized rabbit waggled its ears across the benighted hamlets above Llanfarian, and for a moment I was transported back to my seventh birthday party where a conjuror had done a similar thing with the shadow of his hand on the kitchen wall.

"What's it all about?" I asked in disbelief, as the rabbit was joined by three others who chased it.

"It's his way of publishing the truth," she said. "About the death of Mrs Cefnmabws on Pumlumon."

A shadow-chase ensued across the hills south towards Llanrhystud.

"He had a printing-press and a radio station but they closed it down. This is his only way."

The three rabbits caught up with the first and started beating him. Then the shadows disappeared and the light returned to its usual steady blinking.

"That's your lot for tonight, he'll be on again tomorrow. Doesn't do it for long in case someone notices."

194

We stayed there staring out into the night even though Mr Cefnmabws's passion play had ended.

"What's he trying to say?"

"He wants an inquiry, doesn't he? He wants them to ask Mrs Bligh-Jones the question, the one they dare not ask."

The caravans were strung out like plastic diamonds on the cheap necklace of the River Rheidol. I sat in the car for a while, listening to the radio, and waited for her to go to whichever caravan she lived in. And then I waited some more and got out.

Dew was forming on the bonnet of the car and the town was asleep. I walked up to her trailer and a man appeared out of the shadows in a way that suggested he had been watching me.

"Do you want something, mate?"

I looked at him. He didn't look the type to be accosting strangers at this time of night. He looked about sixty, with a scared face and old, tired eyes.

"What's it to you?"

"I'm the security. You don't live here, what do you want?"

I walked up to the caravan and knocked. "Just visiting a friend."

"Miss Judy doesn't accept visitors after midnight."

"That's funny, last time I came here you said you hadn't seen her for weeks. Why don't you shove off home before you get hurt."

The man reached out to grab my coat and I shoved him back viciously. "Look, old man, whatever they're paying you, it's not worth it."

The door opened and Judy Juice stood there in a silk dressinggown.

"What's going on?"

"Someone snooping, Miss Judy."

I turned to Judy Juice. "Sorry to trouble you, miss, but I was wondering if I could talk to you about Dean Morgan —"

Her eyes flashed scorn. "Do you know what time it is?"

"Yes I'm sorry, miss, but it really is important. Someone's life could depend on it . . ."

She narrowed her eyes and considered me. "Cops?"

I shook my head, said, "Private investigator," and held out a card.

She took it and read and then looked at me again, this time with a sense of recognition. "You're the guy with the little girl."

I nodded.

"It's OK, Lester. Thanks." Then she pulled open the door and let me in.

The place had a cloying, sour smell of unwashed bedclothes and not enough air and what little air there was had been burned up by the camping-gas stove. The floor was littered with discarded clothes and so many foil take-away trays they were ankle-deep like silver ingots on the floor of a vault. On one wall was a makeshift dressing-table before a mirror with a halo of

196

light bulbs set around it. And at the far end a three-piece suite was angled into the space beneath the big window. She waded through the silver sea of ingots and sat on the sofa and poured herself a gin with a shaking hand and drunk it in one go. She didn't offer me one. I sat down opposite her.

She took a deep drag on a cigarette and screwed up her eyes with what might have been pleasure.

"Was he a friend of yours?"

"No. I've been hired to find him."

"But you said no cops, right?"

"No cops."

"I'm sick of cops. They either want to lock you up or fuck you up."

"Usually both."

"What makes you come here?"

"The Dean used to have one of your fudge-box tops — he lit a candle to it every night."

She refilled the gin glass, took a violent swig, and a drag on her cigarette. "Yeah, he was sweet like that." She took another life-saving drag. "Is he dead?"

"Not as far as I know."

"Well, there's not much I can tell you. I haven't seen him for weeks. Met him at the Heritage Museum. I was spinning and he got the part as the coracle man for a while. But he didn't stay long, they never do. He was different from the others, though. I wondered what he was doing there, and then I realised it was because of me. I meet plenty of guys like that."

"Anything going on between you two?"

She looked slightly puzzled for a second and then let out a laugh. "Me and him?! Are you nuts?! What do I want with a man?"

I waited while she refilled the gin glass and then lit another cigarette. Between puffs she asked me, "Is it true he was a professor?"

"Yes, he was."

"I'd rustle something up from the fridge for you but they took it away."

"We could go out, if you're hungry."

"I haven't got the energy to dress, but thanks anyway."

"I could get a take-away. Chinese."

She smiled. "You worked out I like Chinese food all on your own?"

"It was a hunch."

I returned to the trailer half an hour later laden with a set meal for two that was so good the girl at the take-away assured me even a real Chinese person might have eaten it. Judy Juice peeled away the lids and threw them on the floor. Then she picked up a knife with a "Come to Sunny Aberystwyth" handle and used it to scrape the rice on to some plates.

"The girl at the Chinese knows you, says you eat there every day."

"It's all I eat. You ever been there?"

"The take-away?"

"No, China."

"Do I look like I can afford to go to China?"

198

"How would I know how much it costs? Someone told me the other day, when they open this tunnel to France you'll be able to get a train all the way from Aberystwyth to Peking. Is that right?"

"As far as I know."

She nodded, somehow relieved. "One day I'll go there; get on that night train to Shrewsbury and never get off. Yes sir!" The bright look faded and she said, "You know, some other guy came asking about the Dean."

"Was he wearing a Peacocks' coat?"

"I wouldn't know where he bought it, but it was long and black and he was a bit creepy. He wasn't sweet like you so I told him to sling his hook."

"What did he want?"

"Oh, you know, asking about the Dean and when I last saw him. And then he said the Dean had taken a case that belonged to him and asked me for it. And I said why would I have it, and he said he knew the Dean had left it here. I said shows you how much you know, buster, and then he said, 'Don't give me the runaround, you tart.' So I called Lester the guard here and he threw him out. Lester looks out for me because I get quite a few cranks turning up."

"Did the Dean ever mention this case?"

She sighed at the memory. "Yeah, he mentioned it. He was always going on about 'them', how they were after him because he had something that belonged to them. He once said they would kill him if they caught him. Then one day I got tired of hearing it and I told him to prove it. So he showed me some papers.

One of them was official-looking and written in runes. I couldn't understand it, but he could. I said, so what is it? And he said it was an official druid death warrant. And I said, who's it for? And he said, if I told you that, you'd be on it too."

She reached for the gin bottle again. "To tell you the truth, it all went in one ear and out the other. He was always full of crap. They all are."

From Judy Juice's I drove down to the harbour and parked by the railings, facing out to sea. The favourite spot for people from the Midlands to eat their chips; people who drive for three hours for this view and never get out of the car to take a closer look. But tonight neither did I. It was raining again and I sat there, the wipers humming, and stared at the light on the end of the jetty, thinking about what Marty's mum had said. About the question the dissident lighthouseman dared to ask, but no one dared answer. About the suspicion that had haunted him every day since that moment when they found his wife preserved in a block of ice, frozen in time like a fly in amber, and Mr Cefnmabws peered into the sarcophagus of ice and saw that expression on her face. Was that terrible frozen snarl on her face simply the agony of her death-mask? The cruel hand of hunger and cold? Or did it hint at a different explanation for her death than the official version? Something else, something altogether darker? Was it a look of horror? The terror of someone who fled down that mountain because she saw something up there no decent person should be forced to witness?

The question that Mr Cefnmabws wanted answered was a simple one. They had survived for three months up above the snow-line, alone with the bodies of their dead comrades, stranded in a world where not even the birds could survive. So what did they eat?

CHAPTER
SIXTEEN

When I opened up shop the next morning, Llunos was standing on the doorstep. He walked straight past me and up the stairs without a word. He threw his hat on the desk and slumped into the client's chair and said, "Is the girl here?"

"Calamity? Not yet."

"What time are you expecting her?"

"Oh I don't know, some time this morning. You know Calamity."

"Yes," he said in a voice without warmth or inflexion. "I know Calamity."

His tone began to worry me. "What's up?"

He grimaced. "They've sprung Custard Pie."

I jerked back slightly as if he'd held smelling-salts out to me. "Sprung him, who has?"

He ran tired fingers through his thinning hair. "I don't know, someone, some people . . . I mean, who gives a fuck, he's out!"

"I can't believe it — a Triple-A-category prisoner in a maximum-security dungeon . . ."

His face became flushed with anger and he shouted at me in a way I hadn't seen since the old days when we were adversaries.

"Now don't you start on me," he shouted. "I'm the one who put him away, remember? How do you think I feel? I'm not the one who's been giving him bird seed."

"What are you saying?"

"I ought to have your licence for this."

"You telling me he used the bird seed to escape?"

He picked up his hat and thrashed it down on the tabletop.

"Yes I'm telling you he used the bird seed to escape. The Birdman of Aberystwyth. How stupid can you get? How on earth could you fall for a stupid trick like that?"

"So what did he do, dress up as a seagull and fly away?"

He didn't answer but gave me a cold stare.

I went and fetched some glasses from the draining-board and poured two glasses of cold water.

There was a knock on the door and Llunos shouted, "Enter." One of the guards from Custard Pie's prison came in looking pretty much as you'd expect for a man charged with the task of standing guard over a single prisoner who had now escaped. He look hesitantly from Llunos to me and back again.

"Just tell it, officer," said Llunos.

The guard fidgeted and wrung his hands. "Well it's not . . . I don't know where . . . I mean the point . . ."

"I said tell it, for Christ's sake!"

"He . . . he . . ." And then it all came out in a rush. "He kept asking us to cook his eggs extra runny, said his stomach couldn't take cooked eggs. Every day raw eggs . . . I mean, how were we supposed to know?"

Llunos gave him a scowl of thunder.

The guard hopped from foot to foot. He knew he was for the high jump for this.

"Well he was keeping them, wasn't he? You know that horrible stringy bit you get, like an umbilical cord or something, that sticks the yolk to the shell? He was saving them up. And there was the play-acting as well, so we thought he must be mad, like . . ."

"What play-acting?" asked Llunos.

"He was rehearsing for a part . . . kept learning his lines, Little Red Riding Hood or something, it was."

Llunos gave me a look of enquiry, wondering whether this meant anything to me, but it didn't.

"Maybe he was just trying to act the nutter. Go on."

"That's what we thought, but we was wrong, see. It was the birds, you see, I mean we just never noticed. Well you wouldn't, would you?"

"Officer, if you don't get to the end of this story in one minute I'm going to throttle you."

"Well, there he was like, taming these little sparrows and wrens and chaffinches and things and getting them to perch on his finger and sit on his head — it was really touching, or so we thought. Such gentle creatures, birds. But then we noticed there was something really strange about them. They found their way in all right, but they had terrible difficulty finding their way back out. It was as if they couldn't see the flue any more. And they kept flying into the wall and squawking. But now we know, don't we? All that time he was billing and cooing with them he was gouging their little eyes out and then saving them up in the jar meant for his cod liver oil capsules. Then when he had enough he used the boiled egg strings and the albumen and all the little sparrow eye jelly and made himself a set of those fake gouged eye kits you get from the joke shop. I mean, what a nutter! Anyway, next thing you know we get woken in the middle of the night by this blood-curdling screaming and there's Custard Pie standing with his eyes all bloody and streaming down his cheeks. He screams, 'I've done my eyes, I've done my eyes, get me an ambulance!' That's about it really."

"That's it!?" I shouted. "That's it!? You just thought, oh he's done his eyes. We'll call an ambulance. You didn't, like, take a look or anything?" I tried to sound harsh but there was no point. No point whatsoever.

The guard answered, "I know it sounds daft. But what would you have done at 3a.m? Maybe if you was an optician it would have been different but there was us, like, woken up in the middle of the night with this nutter screaming and his whole face gushing sparrow viscera mixed with boiled egg . . . So we rang for an ambulance. Anybody would've."

Llunos turned to me. "Five minutes after the first ambulance left, a second one turns up. Seems the first was phoney. They found it burned out in Commins Coch this morning."

I asked at the pier and down by the station where the apprentice toughs hang out. And I asked in the burger bars and cafés and amusement arcades. And I asked at the harbour and round Trefechan. But no one had seen Calamity recently. I even rang the school but they just laughed at me, they thought she had left the country. Llunos tried to reassure me, saying she would be fine. Custard Pie couldn't get far because every way out of town was being watched. The railway station, the Cliff Railway, the narrow-gauge railway, the bus station and the harbour. But we both knew Custard Pie was already gone. Probably already with Herod, wherever he was. There was no reason to suppose Calamity was with them, but all the same it didn't smell good to me and when I finally gave up wandering round town asking people if they had seen her, I went back to the office and picked up the keys to the car.

The only thing I remember about the drive to Ynyslas were the looks of horror on the people's faces as they darted out of the way in Bow Street; and then the fists raised in anger in my rear-view mirror. Ten miles and thirty junctions and not once did the accelerator leave the floor. Not once were the brakes engaged until I was driving on sand. And I don't remember the dash across the wide sands of the estuary or through the sharp marram grass. All I remember is the relief that exploded inside me when I finally saw Cadwaladr.

He sat wind-blown on the dune top, a can of Special Brew in his hand. He pondered for a while what I had told him, and then said, "Are you sure they've got her?"
   I took a deep breath and spoke in monotone as if reciting a ghoul's shopping-list. "Calamity has been visiting Custard Pie. He tricked her into helping him

escape. Now Calamity has disappeared and no one can find her. What does it look like to you?"

"It's possible they haven't got her, it could be she's on a damn fool's errand to bring Pie in herself. Maybe she blames herself for him escaping and wants to make amends."

"I'd love to believe that. But I don't."

Cadwaladr sipped the beer and considered the situation. "If Custard Pie has teamed up with Herod it will be tough to catch them," he said.

"Are they really that good?"

He didn't answer immediately, but stared out to sea, eyes watering in the breeze and focusing on infinity as his thoughts drifted back across the years.

"In Patagonia I fought alongside them for a while — in the early campaigns. I used to watch them go out on night patrol — faces all smeared up with charcoal and paint. When they came back at dawn they'd always have a prisoner with them, some poor terrified conscript, trussed up like a turkey at Christmas. We never asked who he was or where he was from; we just knew if we wanted any peace and quiet that day we'd better stay out of earshot of the interrogation block." He shook his head sadly. "I can still remember the cries coming from those cells. They say in all that time there was never a man Custard Pie couldn't break." He paused and took another sip of beer. "But if you really want to know what they were like, just look at what happened to Waldo. Remember me telling you about the goalkeeper in the Christmas Day football match?"

I nodded. "You never finished your story."

Cadwaladr took a long drink from the can, as if to impart the necessary gravitas to the story of Waldo. Then he started to speak with a slow shake of the head, as if even now he couldn't believe it.

"Waldo was an Everyman. He stood for all of us. Just a little kid thousands of miles from home in a land he'd never heard of, seeing things that were too much for his heart. They say the reason he signed up for this psychological experiment at the sanatorium was he'd heard it was something to do with memory and all his life he'd been trying to lose his — trying to banish the memory of a certain week. Just one week. It didn't seem like a lot to ask. Like a lot of guys he tried to drink it away. But no matter how much he drank, it would still be there in the morning, like his shadow.

"The incident took place right at the end of the war. A few weeks before we were shipped home. Waldo was cut off in the wilds, alone, and pinned down in a ravine by a sniper. That sniper in turn was pinned down by Waldo. It was stalemate, neither could move without getting shot by the other. This went on for a week until finally the other guy's morale collapsed and he made a break for it and Waldo shot him. The bullet got him in the stomach — the wound we all feared most — but it didn't kill him. Waldo spent the next three days listening to his cries of pain coming from behind a rock. At the end of the third day, as the man's moans were getting fainter and fainter, a dispatch rider turned up and told Waldo the armistice had been signed a week ago. Waldo was shocked. All that time they had been trying to kill each other, and yet the war was over;

they had been brothers all along. A tremendous burst of love surges through the veins of Waldo and he rushes over to the stricken man and weeps. He takes out his first-aid kit and tries to save him. 'My brother,' he cries, 'my brother! It's late in the day, but do not despair!' Waldo reckons if he can staunch the bleeding, and stabilise him, they can get him back to a hospital, and he might make it. In that instant saving this man becomes the most important undertaking in his whole life. It's as if the sun has burst through the cloud in his heart. Ever since he was a kid he has been confused about who he is and what he was put on this earth for. And now he sees with a rare clarity that for one tiny fragment of time he can perform an act that has meaning, a truly moral act — perhaps the only one he will ever perform in his life. Waldo was not a bookish type, not a thinker, but squatting down in the mud of that ravine holding a wound-compress to the bullet holes in the man's stomach he understood it in a way that was deeper than words. This pure human act of salvation that could stand as a bigger symbol: to redeem all the terrible carnage and slaughter of the past three years. Then the dispatch rider comes over and says, 'Hey, isn't that the guy who dived in the box?' And by God it was. Suddenly, the piercing sharp clarity of Waldo's vision has fled. The idea of salvation and brotherhood have vanished. Instead lying at his feet is the little jerk who fucked up the Christmas Day game.

"'You dived didn't you!' they shout at him.

" 'Save me, my brother,' he pleads. 'Save me that I might go back to my little farm in the Sierra Machynlleth.'

" 'Don't change the subject, you're the little rat that dived in the box, aren't you?'

" 'Holy Mother of God,' he cries. 'I swear on all that is holy that I didn't.'

" 'Yes you bloody well did!'

" 'No, it wasn't me. It was someone who looks like me. My cousin Gabriel — he is a bad man, always making trouble, a *bastardo*!'

" 'That's it!' they cry. 'Turn your comrade in to save your skin.'

" 'No, my friends, it is not true. Please save me. Think of my wife and daughter Carmencita who is only two and knows nothing of the villainy of this world. Must she grow up an orphan because of Gabriel's treachery?'

" 'You should have thought about that before you dived in the box!' Both are incensed now. Not only that he did the terrible deed but that he should lie about it here on his death-bed to the only men in the world with the power to save him.

"So they try to extract a confession. They write it out for him and hold it under his nose. 'Go on,' they said. 'Admit to the dive, and we'll save you.'

" 'On the bones of the saints, I swear I didn't,' he cried, his breath getting weaker and weaker, since Waldo has removed the wound-dressing now and the man's rich crimson gore is staining the bed of that ravine.

210

" 'You Latin footballers are all the same,' says Waldo. 'You're always diving! This is your last chance to absolve yourself before you go to meet your maker.'

"But he refuses. And while he slowly dies, they break open a bottle of tequila and drink to victory and then dip their arms in his blood and laugh. They laugh. Two years ago on the shores of Lake Bala, Waldo would have cried to see a bird hit by a car. And now he laughs. Who can ever fathom the mysteries of the human heart? The enemy soldier went to his grave refusing to accept that it was a dive and left behind a daughter Carmencita and a legacy of knowledge concerning the villainy of the world about which she had known nothing and now knew all.

"When word got out about this incident the men were deeply shocked. 'For God's sake, Waldo!' they said. 'It was only a game of football! What were you thinking!' You see, peace had brought a new understanding to the men — the insight that the soldier Waldo killed had truly been his brother. It was the brass hats who were the real enemy: those officers who preferred to spend three years watching us get slaughtered rather than admit they'd made a mistake. In that moment the men understood what a terrible crime Waldo had committed. Just as his attempt to save the man had served as a greater symbol of Christ's mercy so the murder acquired a terrible universal significance. And they grew afraid and shunned Waldo. It was as if in spilling his brother's blood he had become the living embodiment of Cain. As if his crime would hang around the necks of all of them like the ancient mariner's albatross. They struggled to think of a way of expiating his sin. Then someone had the idea of organising a collection for the little orphan Carmencita. It was a simple solution but instantly the fear fell away from their hearts. Though no one had much to give, they all gave gladly what they could. Except for Dai the Custard Pie and Mrs Llantrisant. They jeered at the collectors and called Waldo a hero. But Herod did not join in their derision but seemed silent and thoughtful. Later he sought the men out in the quiet of the evening and said that he had been deeply moved by the story of Carmencita and although he had nothing to give he would regard it as an honour if they would let him deliver the money. At first the men were dubious, but taking the view that the Lord rejoiceth more for one sinner who repents than nine who never strayed they accepted his offer. Two days later the owner of the cantina brought him back to the base in a wheelbarrow and left him snoring and reeking of tequila outside the gates. No one needed to ask what had happened to the money."

"None of this really helps me find Custard Pie."

"I'm telling you this because you need to understand what sort of people these are. Know your enemy, Louie, first rule of survival. Custard Pie will be with Herod, he must have a base somewhere, up in the hills. That's where they'll be."

"But how do I track down Herod?"

"Not easily, that's for sure. Normally you need bait."

"What sort of bait?"

He looked at me without expression. "You'd be good."

"Me?!"

"If it was my mission, I'd be using you."

"You think he will just come and get me?"

"You did knock him out of an aeroplane. He might have lost his memory but I bet you anything he never forgot that."

"I don't have the time to sit and hope he comes to me, don't you understand that?"

"In that case you're going to have to outfox him. The only way to do that is to speak to someone who knows him better than he knows himself."

"Oh really. Do you have any suggestions?"

"Just one, because there is only one person in Wales who knows Herod like that. His old commanding officer, the one who trained him."

"The man who trained him?"

"Taught him everything he knew."

"And who's that?"

"Mrs Llantrisant."

CHAPTER
SEVENTEEN

Would she talk to me? The obvious answer was "never in a million years". But maybe today was the million-and-first. Maybe those postcards she had been sending me, babbling on about her little garden and the potatoes and the two puffins signalled a final mellowing in the iron heart of Mrs Llantrisant. Or maybe it was just another cheap attempt to get a ticket out of jail by feigning insanity. But there was only one way to find out and I owed it to Calamity to try, no matter how remote the chances. The only problem was how to get there. Since she was a category Triple-A prisoner, the only way on or off Saint Madoc's Rock was by the police launch. It was a rule strictly enforced and anyone who broke it would risk losing his mariner's permit.

I drove down to the harbour for a scout around. Within seconds I found out just how strictly enforced the prohibition was: Ianto the boatman was sitting on an upturned lobster pot, next to a blackboard on which was scribbled in chalk: "Trips round the bay, deep-sea fishing, mackerel fishing, trips to Borth, Clarach and to see Mrs Llantrisant." As I arrived he was drawing a chalk line through the last item. There was a storm heading in, he explained, and best not to go out so far. I pushed ten pounds into his hands and urged him and he agreed so long as we didn't stay more than an hour.

As we chugged out from the harbour, past the bar and on towards a sky that looked ominously dark, Ianto explained about the approaching storm. She wasn't due for a while yet, but she would be a big one, he said. We were approaching the autumn equinox which made the tides unusually high, and the moon was almost full which made them higher still. And the equinoctial storms could be fierce, he said. Add all those together and the town would be in for a battering tonight. He stopped and pointed with his pipe towards the horizon. Saint Madoc's Rock.

It was still more than half a mile away, but we could see Mrs Llantrisant. She stood like a heron on the cliff looking out to sea. Ianto handed me his binoculars and I trained them on her for a while. She remained there buffeted by the fierce wind, unmoving like a grim statue, her face expressionless and impassive, seemingly impervious to the constant beating of the gales off the Atlantic.

Ianto said she stood there every day, from dawn till sunset. And then added, "I wouldn't like to be on that island tonight."

Ianto beached the boat on the pebbles and pointed to the path, then took out a flask of tea and his newspaper and prepared to wait. He had no interest in seeing the island. To an old seadog like him, a featureless rock outcrop meant nothing, and to him Mrs Llantrisant was nothing too, just some sad, mad old woman who had somehow managed to start a flood three years ago that washed away his garden shed.

At the top of the cliff I walked towards Mrs Llantrisant. She took no notice of me, even though it was clear she could see me. It was typical of her, by which I meant not the shrivelled old gossip who swabbed my step for all those years but the other one, the secret one who lived inside her and used her charming stupidity as a perfect piece of camouflage. Lieutenant Llantrisant, or Gwenno Guevara as she once was in her freedom-fighting days. She would easily have found the discipline to stand still as stone on a mountain-top if it suited her purpose; would just as easily have had the mental discipline to force her features to betray no surprise at my sudden arrival, to force herself even to pretend I was not there. I shook my head in reluctant admiration and as I did a man appeared at the top of the path, wearing rouge and dressed in a ruffed shirt. He walked up behind Mrs Llantrisant and put his arms round her waist. Then he hoisted her into the air, put her under one arm, and started walking down the path. Still she remained ramrod straight — as stiff and erect as a toy soldier — but as she became outlined against the bright grey of the sky, I could see that instead of feet she had a metal stand like the base of a tailor's dummy. The man who picked her up whistled cheerfully and then stopped about two yards in front of

216

me. His eyes shot open but, to his credit, surprised as he was, he didn't drop Mrs Llantrisant.

"Do you need a hand with that?" I asked cheerily.

"W . . . who are you? What are you doing here? This is private property. What do you want?"

I eyed him coldly and said, "Two men meet for the first time on a cliff-top. One of them is carrying a straw effigy of Mrs Llantrisant. We are in uncharted waters here. All the same, I can't help thinking it's not you who gets to ask the questions." I smiled and he considered my point. Then having considered it he threw Mrs Llantrisant aside and started running.

I chased him up the path to the top of the island and the disused crofter's cottage that had been Mrs Llantrisant's home. Inside I found him frantically searching round for a weapon but he didn't have one and even if he had he didn't look like he had the guts to use it. It wasn't the same boy I had seen dancing with Judy Juice, but he was from the same mould, hired for the job, no doubt, from the back seat of a blacked-out car somewhere along the south bank of the Rheidol. I made a rush for him and he tried to dart to one side and I caught him. He was a skinny, effete, effeminate youth who looked like he should have been twirling his hanky as an extra in a Shakespeare love comedy. He bit my hand like a girl and I grabbed his hair, pulled his face back and smashed it into the desk-top. Then I let him go and he crawled over into a corner and cowered. I looked at him and he looked at me.

"What do you want?"

I took a step towards him. "Remember what I said about who asks the questions?"

"I don't know nothing."

"No of course you don't, you just rented the cottage for two weeks by the sea."

The desk was covered in scraps of writing and half-finished postcards. I picked up one of the scraps. It was a piece of floral, limping verse. "This yours?"

He looked at me through eyes bright with suspicion and then said, "What if it is, there's no law against it."

"You write it yourself?"

He nodded sullenly.

"It's good."

"You think so?"

"Yeah, I love it."

"It's not my best. But it's in the genre. That's how I got this job, you see. I used to be a greeting-card writer."

"I've seen some of your work before."

"Yeah, where?"

"In a fucking Christmas cracker." I took another step and he cringed backwards against the wall.

"Who gave you the job?"

"I don't know his name. He said all I had to do was sit here writing sentimental postcards filled with melancholy and plangent regret."

"Plus taking Mrs Llantrisant in and out of the rain."

He shrugged.

"And of course you haven't a clue where Mrs Llantrisant is, have you? In fact, you're going to insist on that until I get the electric bar-fire from the boat, plug it into the generator and tape it to your face. And even then you'll swear you don't know where she is. But then when I switch the fire on, well, I reckon you'll last about four seconds before you remember. What do you think?"

"Honestly, mister, I swear I don't know where she is. Do you think they'd be stupid enough to tell me?"

I started walking to the door. "No I don't. And anything you told me with or without an electric fire strapped to your face wouldn't be worth birdshit. Which means it's your lucky day. *Adiós*."

As I returned to the boat I stopped for a second by the straw effigy of Mrs Llantrisant. There really was no point questioning the boy. He was just a piece of cheap druid cannon fodder. Whoever arranged all this would have told him nothing or a pack of nonsense designed to send me the wrong way. And to beat him simply for the pleasure of it would just have wasted time. Time I should be spending hunting for my partner, Calamity. I looked down at Mrs Llantrisant, lying like a toppled statue in the thorny grass, her face a blank of straw, a nose sketched in with marker pen, and on top of that the blue translucent frames of her NHS specs. As usual I had managed to underestimate her in a spectacular fashion. But how could you avoid doing that?

I picked up the straw dummy and put it back on its perch at the cliff's edge. As we motored back to Aberystwyth, I sat in the bow and stared at her — a dark sentinel maintaining a vigil over her rock. And meanwhile, the sky behind her turned the colour of basalt and spray flew across our bows, as we butted our way home through the threatening sea.

Judy Juice was sitting in the client's chair when I got back. There was a look of horror on her face and she seemed to have aged ten years since I last saw her.

"I've seen the Dean," she said, eyes wide with fear.

I slumped down into my chair and reached for the bottle of rum. "Great," I said.

"He was in a bad way. Drunk and terrible, and out of his mind . . ."

I tried to make myself care but I couldn't. Calamity was missing and there wasn't room in my head for the stupid Dean.

"I had to come and see you, I have to tell you . . . have to tell you . . ."

I forced my concentration back to Judy Juice.

"Tell me what?"

"About the case . . . He had it with him and showed me inside. It wasn't just a death warrant, there were other things as well. There was a red hood in it, and he said the hood is worn by the sacrificial victim. And there was an almanac with the phases of the moon. And there was a movie-script. And there were detailed instructions for the Raven about how to do it — how to perform the execution. They were his orders, you see. For the Raven's eyes only." She put her hand up to her face and wiped tears away. "Oh my God."

I poured her a drink and walked round to her side of the desk and held it under her mouth. She grabbed my hands and drew up the glass and drank. Then she collapsed into me, her head resting against my stomach, and I gently held it there.

"But what does it all mean?"

"They're going to make a movie . . . for the 'What the Butler Saw' machines. You know what they call those movies where they murder someone . . . kill them for real . . . ?"

"A snuff movie?"

She nodded.

"They're going to make a snuff 'What the Butler Saw' movie?" I asked incredulously. This was altogether too bizarre.

She snivelled and nodded. "It's a remake of *Little Red Riding Hood* . . ." A series of shivers swept through her and she said, "They're waiting for the full moon, and they've got a special actor to play the wolf, and the girl who wears . . . the girl who wears the red hood . . ."

Realisation, like a horse, reared up and kicked both hooves directly into my mouth.

"Dear God!" I gasped. "Dear God! Oh my God! No!"

One of my knees buckled and I feel heavily against the desk. Judy shot up and grabbed me and hugged me, "I'm so sorry!" she cried. "I'm so sorry!"

I pulled myself up, steadied my balance, and walked across the room to the old sea-chest. My face was carved from frozen stone, my heart cold and black like a sea-creature that lives on the ocean floor where the light never penetrates.

"It's all right," I said. "Don't worry. It won't happen. No one touches Calamity. As long as there is breath in my body, no one in this town is going to harm a hair on her head. No one. Ever." I turned the key in the lock and lifted the lid. But, inside, the gun had gone. In its place a scribbled note saying, *Sorry, Louie, I need it, I won't keep it for long*.

"Fuck!" I said. "Calamity's taken the heater."

CHAPTER
EIGHTEEN

The loud sharp "crack" that rang out over the rooftops of Aberystwyth seemed louder than any electrical discharge. It was as if the sky was made of board and God had furiously stamped his foot through it. It wasn't lightning from a clear sky, it was a rifle shot. And I knew without being able to say how I knew that it was a high-powered assassin's rifle.

What happened next is seared into my memory, and like most people who were there that day I will never forget the sight until the end of my days, even though I wasn't there and never saw it. Mrs Bligh-Jones was sitting in the open-topped Meals on Wheels staff car driving down Great Darkgate Street, fiercely proud, her empty coat-arm pinned to her side and the Sam Browne shining in the shafts of sunlight that pierced the gathering stormclouds. People doing their shopping waved or shouted greetings to the heroine of Pumlumon. And then somewhere at the approach to Woolie's, from the roof of the National Westminster bank, there was that bright flash, that deafening sound, the crack that made all the war veterans dive for cover and the children burst into tears. And then Mrs

Bligh-Jones spinning like a ballerina, the grimace of disbelief on her face as a wet crimson starfish spread across her chest.

It's a scene that has become a part of our shared unconscious, along with the endless speculation about the second rifleman, because we have all seen the footage so many times — that shaky home-movie, caught by a tourist, that zoomed in on her expression just as she looked up in agonised realisation to the roof of the bank, and wailed her final two syllables: "Jubal!" Mrs Bligh-Jones wailing to her demon lover. And then, seconds after, the man emerging from the door of the National Westminster bank, that man with a hump who slipped through the crowds towards the sea having first shouted the words "I saw him! It was a ventriloquist!" The mob surged up Great Darkgate Street, towards the ghetto, with fury in their hearts. While down on the Prom I ran first down Terrace Road towards the sound, until the crowds told me what had happened. All the while I had been wondering about the identity of the Raven, and now I had my answer. The Raven who like a spider devours his mate, the lover who kills his beloved. It had to be Jubal. When the penny dropped, I spun round in the street and ran the other way, down the Prom, towards the Excelsior Hotel.

He was sitting over in the bay window, the curtains closed, the room in darkness, holding his head in his hands and moaning. The thin blade of light from the gap in the curtains was filled with dancing dust like

224

the beam of a projector and pierced my vision like a sword. I walked gingerly across a sticky carpet and stood before him. Slowly he raised his head and stared at me, his eyes like dark pools in a forest, his unwashed body emitting a thick reek of aftershave and excrement that made my hand fly to my mouth. Somewhere, lost in the gloom of the room, a gramophone played a song, the squeaky, almost Oriental ting-tong sound of a Kurt Weill opera from the thirties. I listened to the high, ethereal notes, "Oh moon of Alabama, we now must say goodbye." I flung the curtains brutally back and Jubal recoiled like a vampire before the light. The room was a pigsty. A sea of overflowing cigarette butts flowed out across the tabletops, candles and three-day-old room-service food.

He was wearing a bathrobe but didn't smell like he'd been near a bath in a long time. In his hand he held a book of verse and on his wrists were bandages from which oozed a dark moist fluid the colour of cherries.

Silently he pointed to a chair and I drew it up and sat opposite him in the window.

"I knew you would come," he whispered.

Oh moon of Alabama, we now must say goodbye . . .

"What have you done to your wrists?"

He turned his palms upwards as if showing off a new set of cuff-links.

"I opened the veins about an hour ago."

We've lost our good old mama, and must have whisky, oh you know why . . .

A cold shiver slithered up through my innards. That same shiver all decent people feel when they walk down the street past a doorway where there's been a fight and they see spots of blood or even teeth. Or when you drive past an accident and catch a half-glimpse in the corner of your eye of something red that had once been a man.

"Did you change your mind?" I asked like an idiot. Did he change his mind? What a stupid thing to say.

He shook his head wearily. "No, it's an old Roman trick, described by Petronius, I think. You open the veins and then you bandage them so you die slowly and peacefully. The custom was for those for whom no hope remained to pre-empt the vengeance of the courts and choose their own time of dying. One last night, a few hours to bid adieu. To dine, to take a last skin of wine, to listen to some poetry and perhaps amuse oneself with the slave boys. Such is the custom for the last night. But alas in Aberystwyth the choice of entertainments is . . . is . . . well, you can imagine it."

"Should . . . should I call an ambulance?"

"I would be grateful if you didn't." And then with a slight twist of his head, "Would you be so kind as to fetch me a drink?"

I went over to the drinks cabinet. And as I did he recited from the book in his hand.

> "Footfalls echo in the memory
> Down the passage which we did not take
> Towards the door we never opened
> Into the rose-garden . . ."

226

Most of the bottles were empty but there was some sherry left. I poured us a couple and handed him one. He took a sip and closed the book. "You know what he said, don't you?"

"Who?"

"Petronius. 'The pleasure of the act of love is gross and brief and brings loathing after it.'"

I said, "You don't look like a Raven."

"You think they would send a disco-dancer to ensnare Mrs Bligh-Jones? She needs to be wooed like any other woman. Or flattered."

"Or offered a part in a movie."

He nodded. "Yes, that one always works well." He put the book down by his feet and picked up a discarded shoe. It was a dancing-shoe.

"But it is not the best way . . . not the best." He traced his finger along the contours of the sole and pressed his eyes tightly shut as if stabbed by a shard of memory. When he opened the lids again, they were heavy with wetness. He held the shoe out towards me. "This is the best, my friend. To dance! Ah! Yes, to dance all night until the skylight fills with the milk rose of dawn . . . if you can do it well, with *élan* and . . . *gentillesse*, ah! it is . . . is . . . voodoo itself! I learned this when I was just twenty-one, apprenticed to the Pier Ballroom to partner the rich widows who came on holiday but had no beau. A penny a dance they gave me. Such wonderful times, such deep joy . . . I cannot speak now of . . . of . . . what does the poet say? Glory of youth glowed in his soul: Where is that glory now?"

He paused and gave the shoe in his hand a wan look; then placed it down by his foot as gently as if it were a sleeping infant.

"They closed them, you know. Closed them all, those wonderful glittering ballrooms. The people had no use any more for sophistication, or elegance, or courtly manners. They wanted rock and roll, and television and bingo. I was left with nothing but my shoes. And one other thing, a thing that every man in this world craves, but very few ever truly possess: the knowledge of how to please a lady. The people who recruited me for the Ravens understood this."

"But you used it to kill Mrs Bligh-Jones."

His features hardened. "Spare me the catcalls, Mister Knight. You dishonour my death-bed."

"I'd like to know why you killed her."

"Because my orders told me to of course. Because I am a Raven, it is my job. Do you ask the postman why he bears bad news?"

"Yes but why did she have to die?"

"Why do any of us have to die? The important thing is that we all do and the various reasons are of little consequence when set against such an implacable fact."

"You killed her because of some corny piece of philosophy?"

"No I killed her, if you must know, because her methods had become unsound. Brilliant, but unsound."

"You mean Pumlumon?"

He nodded.

"So it's true then? My God. My God!"

Jubal threw the book to one side. "Personally, I do not share the general revulsion. To me what happened on Pumlumon was nothing, just a piece of routine cannibalism —"

I gasped.

"I'm at a loss to understand such fastidiousness in the face of death. In a situation such as this, a matter of survival, such things are accepted. The literature of nineteenth-century seafarers is full of references to the practice. After sodomy it was the greatest occupational hazard a cabin-boy had to fear. Seafaring folk understand these things, but the city people get jittery. It is the one crime they do not forgive. And thus she had to die; thus once she had embarked on that road, the order, the inevitable order came: Terminate Mrs Bligh-Jones's command — with extreme prejudice."

"And yet you were her lover?"

"How else does one ensnare the heart of one's victim? Oh I admit that it was not without its pleasurable side. Mrs Bligh-Jones is a fine woman. A feisty woman, with passion and scalding-hot fire in her veins. I found much to admire in her. That clean, sharp purity of vision, that exquisite mixture of beauty and cruelty and . . . and . . . and certainty. Yes that was what I most admired. A woman of action, a woman unfettered by doubt who could eat her bowling partner of twenty years because she knew there was no other way . . ."

"How can a man love a woman he knows he is going to kill?"

"Don't be such an arse! I am a Raven, it is my mission to spring the honey-trap, it would be impossible if I did not enjoy the taste of the honey, even Mrs Bligh-Jones's honey. And now it is my turn to die. I do not complain."

"But why?"

"Because my work is over."

"Who do you work for?"

He raised his head slightly and smiled a smile of pure evil. "Mrs Llantrisant, who else? You see they call me a Raven but really my true nature is different. A soldier ant would be more appropriate. I mate and die. Steadfast in the service of my queen. Her survival is all that matters. Now that I have done my task I am content to make my exit. Although sadly I will miss the final act in Mrs Llantrisant's masterful plan."

"Calamity."

"Ah yes, Calamity."

"This was Mrs Llantrisant's plan?"

"Of course, who else would have the genius to conceive of such a mission? In this respect, brilliant though I am, I am a mere puppet. My job was to eliminate Bligh-Jones, facilitate the escapes of Herod, Custard Pie and Mrs Llantrisant; and then arrange Mrs Llantrisant's *pièce de résistance*, the Little Red Riding Hood murder. Masterly. We have a special agent up from Cardiff to play the wolf. When it is finished Mrs Llantrisant will send you the tape to watch in your long lonely hours of self-hatred."

"But what has Calamity ever done to Mrs Llantrisant?"

230

"Nothing at all! Absolutely nothing. That's the beauty of it, don't you see? The pure blinding joyous beauty of it. It's not Calamity she hates, it's you, Louie, for destroying her dream and putting her away on that island. But how can she get back at you? Kill you? Pah! Too feeble! Too altogether paltry an act — a mere spoonful of liquor with which to assuage Mrs Llantrisant's ravening thirst for revenge. No matter how slowly you died it would still be too quick. Whereas the death of Calamity, an innocent who placed her trust in you — whom you love like a daughter — ah! Think of that! No matter how quickly she died, the torment would last for ever. In your own soul, Louie, your own soul! It will burn like quicklime eternally inside you and there will be nothing you can do to undo your folly or soothe the pain. And should you ever try and forget you will always have the little tape to remind you. Oh, Louie, the beauty of it! The sheer spectral beauty of her genius!"

"Except of course that none of this is going to happen. It's fantasy."

"You think so? I think it will happen tomorrow night."

"You will tell me where they are. I'll make you."

"And how will you do that? Threaten to kill me? I've beaten you to it! What possible threat could you wield with any power against a man who has taken his own life?"

I stood up and rushed to the door. "Then I'll have to save you."

The phone had been torn from its socket so I ran down four flights of stairs to the desk and called Doc Thomas. He wasn't in so I called an ambulance and as I shouted instructions into the mouthpiece, telling them we needed an urgent blood transfusion, I saw Llunos walking up the steps of the hotel towards me. Together we rushed back to the suite on the top floor, burst through the door and found the room empty. The discarded bandages were lying on top of the TV set. Llunos picked them up and touched the red stain with his fingertip, then dabbed his finger to his tongue. He looked over at me. "Damson jam."

Pointlessly we searched the apartment. There was nothing apart from the dirty plates, the sticky glasses and the discarded clothes. Behind the sofa Llunos found the lid of a box and threw it to me. It said: *The Essential Mr Kurtz. The Pro Agent's Guide to simulating moral collapse.*

"The old Mr Kurtz routine," said Llunos. "Haven't seen that one for a while."

I turned it over and read a list of contents. Digests of Kierkegaard, Nietzsche, Eliot, Sartre . . . Hamlet's soliloquy. Posters of Mao, Guevara, Papa Doc. Recordings of Kurt Weill, Stravinsky, Marlene Dietrich . . . A concordance of degenerative diseases of the Self. The *Dummies' Guide to Despair*. I threw the box at the wall.

Llunos walked into the bedroom.

"They're going to kill Calamity," I shouted after him. "Little Red Riding Hood. Tomorrow night at full moon."

I heard him rooting around in closets and drawers and I walked over to the bay window and looked out over Aberystwyth Prom. Was Proteus the name of the Greek god who came from the sea and could change his shape at will? How many incarnations were there left? Jubal Griffiths, film-maker, and Raven, and black widow spider of the ballroom, and soldier ant . . . I picked up the dancing-shoe that was lying on the floor. Inside, the words engraved in silver were still faintly discernible: *Property of the Pier Ballroom, 1947.*

"He said there's a special agent up from Cardiff to play the wolf," I shouted.

Llunos reappeared carrying a flesh-coloured, saddle-shaped piece of plastic, with straps.

"What's that about a wolf?"

"A special agent from Cardiff."

"I think I know who it is. I got a phone call first thing this morning from the Bureau. They fished some chap wearing concrete boots out of Milford Haven harbour last night. He'd been in the water for quite some time so they just got the dental records sent over for an ID."

"Is it anyone we know?"

"Yes, a man called Harri Harries."

I stared at him thoughtfully. "Any chance of a mistake?"

"Not unless he stole Harri Harries's teeth before he went for his swim."

"So who's our friend with the plumbing-tools?"

"I don't know. But something tells me I'm going to enjoy asking him. You might like to come along."

He threw me the plastic saddle. It was some sort of medical contraption, a prosthetic.

"What's this?" I asked.

"It's Jubal's hunch." And he laughed like a morgue attendant. "Keep it. Every detective needs a hunch."

CHAPTER
NINETEEN

The needle jumped a couple of times with soggy, bass thumps and then through the clicks the crackles and pops the voice of Myfanwy emerged, singing *"Ar Hyd a Nos."* "All Through the Night", a gentle stream of notes that perfectly captures the objectless longing and confusion of a night that won't end. *"Ar Hyd a Nos,"* the mid-point in her act at the old Moulin and the song that would get me through this night with help from my faithful friend, Captain Morgan.

I raised a glass to the photo of Marty and to the picture of Myfanwy on the record cover. And I thought of Calamity. I raised a glass to them all, drained it, refilled it, drained it, refilled it, toasted them all once more and drained it, and finally it, and finally felt better. I pondered whether I should go out now and get another bottle rather than wait until there was no more left and mild panic set in. My deliberations were interrupted by the sound of footsteps echoing on the wooden stairs; the door banged open and a gale blew in scattering papers around like snow in a giant paperweight. When the door closed, the paper settled to reveal Ionawr holding a brown paper bag. She was drenched and the bag was soggy.

"I baked you some rock cakes," she said holding the bag up. "Probably ruined by now. And I found this on the mat." She handed me a letter.

"Thanks," I said without enthusiasm.

She looked at me a little uncertainly. "Having a party?"

"Just a little get-together with all the people I've let down recently."

The bright spirit slowly drained from her face.

"That's why there's no one here then, isn't it?"

I made a circling gesture with the hand clutching the glass. "Oh they're all here, Myfanwy and Marty . . . sorry to say I don't have a photo of your sister."

"You didn't let her down, you helped her. She thought the world of you."

"That just makes it worse."

"You're talking crap because you're drunk."

"I'm not drunk yet."

She took the glass from my hand. "You're drunk and feeling sorry for yourself. And if Bianca's ghost was here she'd call you a twat for talking like this."

She put the glass down and I picked it up. She grabbed it again and threw it against the wall. It didn't break, just bounced and landed on the record player. The arm jerked back to the beginning and clicked to a halt.

"You never let Bianca down, it's other people who always let you down."

"Oh sure! It's sweet of you but you don't need to."

"But it's true. That girl for instance . . ."

"What girl?"

"Oh nothing."

There was something in her tone that signalled there was more than nothing.

"Go on, you might as well say it."

"Well . . . that Judy Juice, I know it's none of my business . . . but I can't help what I hear."

"And what do you hear?"

"That you and her . . . you know . . . I mean it's nothing to do with me and I don't care what you do but they say you should be very careful of her . . ."

"They, whoever they are, always say the worst things about the best people, surely you should know that."

"Yes but sometimes they're right, and —"

"If it makes you feel better there was nothing between me and Judy. But I do like her."

"Of course, all the men do, but what sort of girl would go with Jubal?"

"She hates Jubal."

"Well that just makes it worse."

"She wouldn't give him the time of day."

"She's given him a lot more than that from what I've heard."

"You must have heard wrong."

"No I didn't. She was seen with him tonight, kissing him, and cuddling, and then they went off together . . ."

I groaned. "Oh God."

"I'm sorry, I mean if you liked her and that . . ."

"It's not that, it's just I've been such a fool today. I trusted her and it sounds like she was working for Jubal all along. Telling him everything I said . . . shit. Such an idiot."

"No you're not."

"Oh believe me, I am. All it takes to make a fool of me is a jar of damson jam."

Ionawr rushed forward and grabbed my head and held it to her. "Oh come on, Louie!"

I put my arms round her waist and squeezed and then she broke away and said, "Have a rock cake." She opened her bag and took one out. "I baked them myself, just for you."

"That was nice of you."

"They're pretty crappy actually. I've never done them before."

I took a bite. "You got the rock bit right!"

She grinned.

I put the letter down on the desk and then noticed the writing on it. There was no address, just the name "Louie" in a childish scrawl. I tore it open and groaned.

Dear Louie,

I have decided to Kwit because I no your going to fire me for screwing up like a dumbkopf. I cant believe I fell for that stupid bird seed rootine. Do not worry about me. I am going to bring custard Pie in on my own. It's the only way. We probably wont meet again for a while because I'm going to leave Aberystwyth and get a job in another

detective agensy some place where they won't
know what a bungler I am.

Thanks for everything.

I love you,

Calamity Jane

I let out a long deep sigh of despair. And then staring
at Calamity's handwriting a thought struck me; a soft
tingling hunch that you sometimes get when you least
expect it. I stood up and walked over to the bureau in
the corner of the office. She had left a file of Aunt
Minnies there, gathering dust in the way that often
happens when a kid gets a passion for something and
then moves on to the next. I took it back to the desk
and started leafing through. It was the longest shot in
the world, of course, but worth trying. Maybe there was
something in them that might help, that might give me
a clue to her movements. The photos had been neatly
filed according to time of year, time of day and
geographical vicinity. Shot after shot taken around town
of people chosen only because something was
happening behind them. On the Prom, down at the
harbour, the camera obscura, outside the Cabin, and
one at the railway station. It was clear that, try as she
obviously had, the people in the background were no
more shady than Aunt Minnie in the foreground. Just
out of focus because she hadn't mastered the depth of
field. It wasn't surprising she'd given up. I was about to
do the same. And then my gaze lingered on the picture
taken in the railway station. I blinked, snatched it up
and peered at it. My heart lurched.

It was a snap of a family leaving for a walking-holiday, four of them, two adults and two kids, all wearing hiking boots with rucksacks on the dusty platform floor. And in the background there was a woman standing and looking as if she had just stepped off the train; at her feet a suitcase. Out-of-focus, indistinct, the colour washed out; but even so you could tell she was beautiful. And, more to the point, I knew who it was.

"Oh my God!" I groaned. "It's Myfanwy."

I looked at the date under the photo. It had been taken six months ago.

The gale shrieked like a ghoul, sweeping roof-tiles like leaves into the night sky. Against the base of the Prom the waves crashed and tore out blocks of stone the size of steamer trunks, spitting them on to the road. We drove along the Prom, dodging the debris, the rocks and stones, the matchwood that earlier had been a bandstand. The hotels were dolls' houses tonight, the seaside railings broken and bent like pipe cleaners. I remembered the tales from the South Seas I read as a kid, about the typhoons in which the coral islanders lashed themselves to the coconut trees to avoid being swept out to sea. The booming and pounding of the sea was relentless, as sustained and regular as the artillery barrage that preceded the assault on the Somme. And with each fresh wave, spray soared high into the sky, rising like a geyser above the rooftops and then remaining suspended at the acme, for breathless

240

seconds, like poplar trees of milk glittering in the streetlights.

Eeyore's stables were down by the harbour on the Pen Dinas side, next to the oast houses. We found him knee-deep in straw, running a gentle, calming hand along the flanks of the frightened beasts. They were fearful and restless, flinching at the sound of every crash of the wind against the door and staring with terror in their lake eyes. The girl from the Chinese was also there in wellingtons, pouring the contents of a bucket into a manger.

"What is it?" I asked.

"Chop-suey!"

"They eat that?"

"They love it, it's a treat for when they are frightened. It's mostly grass anyway, isn't it?"

We went into the kitchen and sat at the unstained oak table listening to the fury of the storm. I told Eeyore about Calamity and asked what he thought I should do and he said he didn't know.

"The note isn't necessarily bad," he said at length. "It doesn't mean they've got her."

"But she's going looking for them, it's what they want. Obviously Custard Pie set her up."

"It still doesn't mean they've got her yet. There's still time."

I could feel his eyes on me, watching me, secretly willing me to be strong.

"Anyway," he said, "wherever she is, I hope she's not out in this." He stood up and walked to the rain-blasted windows. "You could die in a storm like this. We forget how puny we are. Everything we do in life conspires to hide from us this simple truth. And because every day we escape to live another day, the world deceives us . . . makes us believe there is some force protecting us . . . that says it can't happen . . . When it does, we feel almost ashamed at the stupidity of it, embarrassed that we ever thought for a moment that we were immortal . . ."

He stopped speaking and rested his chin thoughtfully on the top of his thumb, as if there was a part missing from his story but he wasn't quite sure what it was. After a while, just as I began to think he was drifting off, he looked up and said, "Did you see that film *A Night to Remember*? About the *Titanic*?"

"Yes a couple of times, only on TV."

"It was on at the cinema about the time I joined the Force. I went to see it with your mum when we first started courting. Marvellous film." The faint trace of a smile tugged at the corners of his eyes. "Of course we were kids then in the back row so we missed a lot of it, but . . . but . . . Stormy nights always make me think of it.

"Women and children first," said the girl from the take-away. "I said you lot were sentimental. On a Chinese ship the order given would have been, Men first, children second, women last. It makes perfect economic sense."

Eeyore chuckled and then became thoughtful again. "It was just a tiny bump they said. It's always haunted me, that bit. All those people drinking and dancing and partying late into the night, their lives so glittering and full of promise. And then a strange noise, a little bump — almost perceptible — and yet the shard of ice had opened up the ship like a tin-opener."

He turned to me, and said, "I know you're scared, son, everyone gets scared. It's what comes next that matters."

"But I don't know what comes next."

"No, perhaps not yet. But you will. You just need to go beyond your medicine line."

I smiled softly. "Sitting Bull again."

"It's like I was saying, you see. Most of the time we live like the sheriff's posse, penned in by the medicine line. Never going beyond. But there are times when it disappears. Something happens and we just pass right through it like Sitting Bull and his braves. Such a moment, I believe, took place on the ice-strewn deck of the *Titanic*. In that precise instant when the men saw that they were doomed the code that bound them disappeared. For the first time in their lives, it didn't matter what they did or how they conducted themselves. It didn't make a difference any more what society thought of them. Each man stood there naked. That's when you perceive the existence of the other code. The one that lies hidden all your life like the iceberg beneath the sea. That's when you find out what you're really made of. We know that many men became little better than snarling dogs. They panicked, and screamed, and lost their wits. But not everyone did. There were men there who ..." He stopped and thought for a second, struggling to find a suitable term to sum them up, these men who had made such a lasting impression on him. "There was some retired military chap there, for example, who stood before the lifeboats and fought those wild dogs back with an iron bar." Eeyore paused and smiled in admiration, perhaps imagining himself standing there too, his iron bar gleaming palely in the Newfoundland starlight.

"It must have been an amazing scene," he continued, "but the one that has always haunted me took place elsewhere on the ship, away from the turmoil. It was about the time the water entered the engine room and hundreds of stokers were scalded to death; and the rest surged up on deck armed with shovels with which to beat their way to the lifeboats.

"At this moment, Ben Guggenheim, the millionaire, walked into the first-class lounge with his servant. They were both dressed for dinner. The room was deserted now, the floor listing crazily, and an eerie silence prevailed, perhaps the only sound the distant strains of the band on deck playing 'Autumn'. The ship's officers pleaded with them to return to the deck and to a lifeboat, because it went without saying that such important passengers would get a place in a boat. But Ben Guggenheim said no. There he stood: the whole pre-war world of luxury, privilege and impossible splendour laid out at his feet . . . the savour of life could not have been sweeter for any man alive in the world that night. And he was being offered a place in a

244

lifeboat. But Ben Guggenheim refused to go. Instead he calmly ordered a brandy and said, 'Never let it be said that a woman or child died on this ship because Ben Guggenheim was a coward.'"

Eeyore paused for a second and nodded to himself as if making sure he had got that right. "It doesn't mean anything, son, I know, it's just a story . . ." He turned and smiled at the girl from the take-away. "And if it had been a Chinese ship we probably never would have heard of him. But so often when I see you, Louie, doing what you do here in Aberystwyth, risking your life and getting knocked on the bonce once a week by some piece of dirt who's not fit to wipe your shoes . . . well I see it and you know what I think? And you'll laugh, I know, because it's daft, but I don't care. I see it and I think to myself, there goes Ben Guggenheim!

He walked over and put a tired old hand on my shoulder, a hand that had fingered the collars of multitudes of villains in its time. "I don't know what you are going to do about Calamity, son," he said. "But I know you'll think of something . . . Because my son has never let anyone down yet."

CHAPTER
TWENTY

The next morning the storm had passed, leaving the town damp and steaming and fanned by the dregs of the gale. Llunos was already waiting for me when I got back to the office. One of his men had hauled Harries in that morning, or whoever it was pretending to be him. He was waiting down at the station. I didn't bother to wash or shave, just made coffee and picked up the Colt 45. I took out the cartridges, fetched a Ziploc bag from the kitchen and gave it all to Llunos.

Harri Harries was in Llunos's office, with a policeman standing watch outside. As he opened the door, Llunos put his arm in front of me and barred my way. "I need five minutes with him alone first."

I nodded.

He went in and closed the door, saying, "Teach him to make a monkey out of me on my own patch."

There followed a couple of minutes of loud banging from the room. The sort you might get if you swung a sack of potatoes from wall to wall. Then the door opened and Llunos ushered me in, mopping a sweaty brow as he did. What little furniture there was in the room was upturned, a notice-board disarranged on the wall; a broken table lamp flashing uncertainly. Harri Harries sat in the chair, blood coming out of his nose and mouth. One eye puffed up. His shirt torn and spattered with bright red berries of blood.

"You've got him, now," said Llunos. He walked to a cupboard and took out a dusty old scuba gear bag and emptied its contents. A rusty tank, an equaliser, some lead weights, a mask . . . all smelling mildly of the ocean floor. He held the bag up.

"Do you think he'll fit in it?"

I gave it an appraising look. "Well, it's roughly maggot-shaped and about his size."

Harri Harries looked on with fear and uncertainty. Llunos took out the Ziploc bag and slid it across the desk to me. Inside was the gun.

"It's as cold as they come. No way of tracing it."

"Thanks."

"Make sure you wipe it off afterwards."

I took the cartridges out of my pocket and started wiping them methodically with a handkerchief and then setting them up like toy soldiers in a row along the desk-top.

"Look," said Harri Harries. "I know —"

"I haven't asked you anything yet," I said in a voice colder than ice. "So shut up."

When the cartridges were all free of prints I slid one into the chamber and gave it a spin. Llunos walked towards the door. "I'll be in the next room, use one of the cushions to muffle the sound."

Then he closed the door and we both looked at each other. I slowly levelled the barrel at his face and said, "Where is she?"

He took a breath and said, "You've got to believe —"

The rest of it never came. I rammed the gun forward so the end of the barrel smacked into his mouth and then, as he gasped at the pain, the barrel was in his mouth. I'd seen this done once in a movie and it seemed to work. I don't know what difference it makes really, gun in or gun out, if it fires you're not going to know much about it. But it certainly frightened me to watch it. I pulled the trigger and it clicked on an empty chamber. His whole body stiffened like a cat electrocuted in a cartoon and his face went purple.

"You were lucky." I took the gun out of his mouth, wiped the blood and spittle off on his shirt and then slid in two more cartridges. Then I pressed it against that other favourite spot, between the eyes, and spun the chamber.

"Where have they taken her?"

He spoke quickly, trying to get as much explanation in before I shot him. "She didn't turn up, I was supposed to meet her, Custard Pie arranged it, but she never came . . . please it's the truth —"

"Like fuck it is!" I pulled the trigger. It clicked and this time Harri made the sound of a scream done with the mouth closed. Then he wept. I almost felt sorry for him.

"Please, please, please . . ." he gasped. "I'm telling you the truth . . ."

248

I picked up the remaining bullets and slid them all in. There was no point spinning the chamber now but I did anyway just for effect. "Full house," I said and aimed squarely at his face.

"Now where is she?"

"I . . . please . . . please . . ."

I squeezed and the hammer pulled slowly back like a striking snake in slow motion.

His face was the colour of green milk, his eyes bulging and he said, "I don't know. You must believe me!"

"Make me believe you. Tell me something worth not shooting you for."

He pressed his eyes tightly shut and pleaded with me. "Please, I don't know any —"

I pulled the trigger all the way and as I did Llunos slipped quietly back into the room and banged the door the moment the trigger slammed home. Harri Harries screamed and jerked forwards, landing heavily on the floor.

Llunos walked over and hoisted him back into the chair. "OK, you've had your fun. As far as I can see there are only two possible reasons you haven't told us where she is: either you don't know, or you knew the gun was a replica. And I don't believe you don't know. So we're going to play a little game of mine. It's called Welsh roulette."

He took out his truncheon and put it down on the desk. "You can think of it as a variation on blackjack."

249

He walked over to a filing-cabinet, took out some keys, and opened a drawer. He brought out two things and put them down in front of Harri Harries. There was a truncheon that had been painted red. And a kid's roulette wheel.

"The rules are simple so you won't have any trouble picking them up. We spin the wheel. If the ball lands on black seven, I hit you seven times with the blackjack. If it lands on red two, I hit you two times with the redjack. The game is over when you tell us where Calamity is."

He spun the wheel and dropped the ball. Red three. Llunos turned to me. "You see! I told you he was lucky." Then he hit him three times with the red truncheon. The next one was black four. He hit him four times. He spun the wheel, dropped the ball. Red thirty-six. "Bingo!" shouted Llunos and picked up the cosh. I turned away in dread. And Harri Harries confessed.

"OK, OK, OK!" he cried. "I'll talk, I'll talk. It doesn't matter now anyway. We had a rendezvous arranged last night — Custard Pie set it up. He told the girl if she went there she would find out the identity of the Raven. But of course it was a trap for her. I got there at midnight but no one came. Neither the girl nor Jubal. I waited and waited and finally, at about three, Jubal turns up. But he's out of his mind. Raving and screaming and crying. He was all like dressed as if for a wedding or something, you know a flowery shirt and a suit and tie, and wearing a flower in his buttonhole, but he'd slashed his clothes and covered himself in ashes. And he had a suitcase with him, said he was getting out of town. And I said, why? And he said if they caught him they would kill him, and I said, who? He said, them, Custard Pie or Herod or Mrs Llantrisant. He'd betrayed them. Everything was ruined, he said. And I said, what the hell have you done? And he cried out like . . . like . . . I don't know . . . like . . . a . . . an elephant giving birth or something, and said he'd been a total idiot and fallen into his own trap. And I said, what about the girl? And he said, she won't come now, you idiot, we're ruined, it's finished, we're all dead . . . don't worry about her, save yourself." He stopped and gasped for breath, "Honest, it's the truth."

I didn't know what Ben Guggenheim would have done this morning, but one thing was clear from Eeyore's story. He knew how to keep a cool head. The very opposite of what I had done. Chasing out to Mrs Llantrisant's island and torturing Harri Harries and generally running around not thinking. And that was the whole point really. Thinking. All along I had known about the one man who knew where Herod would have his base, the man who had studied his psyche and made a map of it. Dr Faustus, whoever he was. He must know the answer. And now he was going to give it to me.

I took the Llanbadarn Road out towards the mountains of Pumlumon, along the course of the Rheidol for a

251

while. And then cut south at Ponterwyd on the A4120 towards Ysbyty Cynfyn. A sign told me I was taking the Pont Ysbyty Cynfyn over the Nant Ysbyty Cynfyn and that was reassuring to know. Before too long, if my car didn't give out, I would be heading towards Ysbyty Ystwyth. The world was full of Ysbytys today and I wondered what it meant. Not knowing the answer in Lovespoon's classes would have resulted in the board-rubber exploding next to one's ear like flak. Ysbyty Ystwyth — the map gave it a black cross for a place of worship and a black box underneath meaning one with a tower rather than spire, minaret or dome. It also had a little symbol to say there was a public telephone. Compared to Ysbyty Cynfyn, which had none of these, it was Las Vegas. But I wouldn't be able to go and ask what it all meant, Ysbyty Ystwyth would have to wait for a brighter day. At Hafod Wood I turned off.

I pulled up in the lane a quarter of a mile from the perimeter wall and put on my old mac and hat — a standard-issue sleuth traipsing across rain-spattered, mist-smothered soggy Welsh hills. Up ahead was the sanatorium, the soft mist effacing all detail like gentle amnesia. I wasn't sure how I was going to get in. In my pocket I still had the Colt 45. Maybe I would use that. Or maybe I would just go and ask for help. Giving succour to strangers is the job of a philanthropist after all. It was easy. Just go and ring the bell. Hi, I'm looking for my partner, Calamity. She's a detective although you might not think so because she's only sixteen and really should be in school. In fact you might think I'm a louse for letting her get mixed up in all this, and you're probably right. But actually I didn't want her to, but you just can't stop her. You know Calamity, or perhaps you don't. But if you could keep an eye open. We're working on a case . . . there's a gang of them — Dai the Custard Pie, Mrs Llantrisant and Herod Jenkins. I think you know Herod Jenkins? You cured him of his lost memory, but somehow a lot of people wish you hadn't. Right now they are holding out somewhere in the hills up by Nant-y-moch. They say there's a sacred place up there, something sacred to Herod. I thought you might know where they were, you being a special friend of Herod and all that. In fact, I understand you've made a map of his psyche. What does it say? "Here be dragons"?

A dog barked in the distance, and then someone shouted. "There he is!" A shot rang out and a bullet zipped through the foliage of a nearby tree. I turned round in amazement and heard someone else shout, "Quick after him!" They were about half a mile away, a group of them. It looked like a hunting-party. I started running as another shot rang out.

Downhill, over the stream and uphill, keeping south of the thin, ruler-straight line of forestry plantation trees and heading for a copse of normal trees. More shots were fired but they were too far away. I ran fast and the hunters didn't manage to gain on me. Maybe they didn't relish the prospect of tackling me close-up. I reached the trees and climbed over the wire fence and jumped and ran on. I came to a clearing, jumped a stream and landed on the other side, and as I did so two metal shark jaws clashed shut on my shin and I leaped forward as if diving off a board and hit a tree with my head. My leg was caught in a mantrap.

I lay there on a floor of moist dead autumnal leaves, the sweet, wet reek of peat filling my nostrils. I panted and twisted in pain and succeeded only in making the teeth bite deeper and the jaws ratchet tighter on my leg. The sharp metal was rusty and had cut through the cloth of my trousers and deep into the flesh. The trap was chained to a tree and was impossible to move. Or break. I started to sweat with cold panic. You could lose a leg like this. And how ridiculous would that be? What if I called out? Would they shoot me in cold blood? What did they want with me anyway? I heard the barking of dogs and suddenly I could hear them scampering through the undergrowth. The barking got closer and now I could hear the louder sound of a man running. Then I heard him cry out in triumph and start sprinting. The dog was on me, licking my face and wagging his tail in joy at the new discovery under the leaves. And then the man appeared. He was wearing a coat that looked like the ones the Beefeaters in the Tower wear, only black instead of red. I'd seen a garment like it a long time ago, a thousand years or so, in Aberystwyth when a man came to buy some Myfanwy memorabilia.

"Oh you poor dear sir," he said. "Oh you poor man! What have they done to you! I don't know how many times we've told those farmers about their traps, but they never listen." He turned and shouted something in Welsh to a man further down the slope. "We were told to keep a lookout. They say that games teacher is loose in these woods. Some of the men thought it was you. I'm afraid I'll need help to release you from this trap, sir. You might like to take a sip of this to take the edge off the pain." He produced a hip-flask and poured some Cognac into my mouth. I drank it greedily. The scalding spirit felt good. "Is that better, sir?" I nodded but strangely the action was proving more difficult than I had expected. My head had become enlarged to the size of a small moon, and moving it was an enormous task. I tried to thank him but my tongue had been replaced with an iguana who refused to budge. My eyelids also seemed to have become alarmingly heavy. I looked up at my benefactor but he was in the sky, and his voice seemed to be coming from the next valley. The scalding spirit had felt good but now I realised there was a sharp metallic edge to the taste, a chemical taste that didn't belong there. I reached out into the sky to grab my benefactor but my hand didn't move and then someone switched the lights off.

CHAPTER
TWENTY-ONE

I was in a room. I was wearing a canvas nightshirt. It had a big black number stencilled on the front. 43. My new name. A nurse was folding my trousers over a hanger. The wound on my leg had been dressed with a white bandage. Nice job. But some idiot had left a team of roadmenders with jackhammers behind in the wound. I was going to tell the nurse, but she probably knew. It must have been a road for the dynamite trucks. Something to do with the quarry they were excavating in my head. I had a smart metal belt on to go with my canvas pyjamas. It didn't have a buckle. There was a bulge at one side. It was something electrical. Better not touch. You can get hurt if you don't know what you are doing. Better go back to sleep.

The nurse appeared in my dream. I told her to go away but she didn't seem to understand. I told her to give me my trousers back. It was hard getting through to her because she was on dry land. I was swimming at the bottom of the lake. I spoke to her in a series of soft plopping bubbles but they got lost in translation. I looked around for a fish who could help. And then I realised you need an amphibian for this job. At home on land and in water. I looked for a frog. Typical, there's never one when you need one.

I decided to go to sleep again only this time a different sleep so they couldn't find me.

It worked for a while but then the nurse came along. She was bending down towards the surface of the water and holding my wrist. That was nice. Maybe she wasn't so bad after all. I tried to groan. Nothing too ambitious. They still hadn't done anything about that iguana.

The nurse looked at me and shrugged. "*Dydw I ddim yn siarad Saesneg.*"
Oh so that's the problem.
She smiled and shrugged again.
I wasn't sure if I could remember any Welsh, but the iguana did. "*Edrychwch! Dyna'r Archdderwydd!*" he said.
The nurse giggled.
Not bad, great the way he got the "*wch*" sound. Try another one, pal.
"*Rydw I eisiau stafell ddwbwl!*"
You're better than I thought. You've even got the "*ll*" sound. I could never do that. Still I suppose if you can catch flies with your tongue this should be a piece of cake. Try again. The nurse ran out and locked the door.

I lay back for a while and hoped the people would down tools in the quarry. I looked at my watch, almost noon. The lizard had gone. I waited. And after a while,

I found I could sit up. And look around. I checked the belt round my waist. It was impossible to remove and had electric solenoids welded to it. I didn't like it. An hour passed and then the door opened and the butler walked in pushing a wheelchair. "You'll probably be a bit shaky on your feet for a while, sir, so I've brought you this. The master has instructed that you are to take lunch with him. He also asked me, sir, to advise you not to make any attempts at escape until he has had a chance to demonstrate the workings of the belt."

It all seemed like a good idea. The butler chatted to me as he wheeled me down a long corridor lined with doors. "This is the old sanatorium, sir, quite a ghoulish place if you ask me. We thought it best to put you here while you recovered. I expect, though, the master will want to move you into the main house as soon as you are strong enough." We came to some double doors and the butler pushed them open with my feet and wheeled me out into hazy sunshine. We were on a lawn some way from the main house. The cold air blew the clouds out of my head.

The Philanthropist was sitting in an electric wheelchair just inside the half-open French windows observing my progress keenly. Even from fifty yards away I had no trouble in guessing who it was. There was only one person it could be. My old adversary, the locust-sized criminal genius Dai Brainbocs; or as he now preferred to call himself, Dr Faustus. When I arrived he reached out his hand to me excitedly. "I really am most thrilled to meet you again, dear Louie." He pumped my hand and I stared at him still groggy but the fog slowly clearing.

The butler wheeled me in through the doors to a wood-panelled dining-room. Brainbocs drove alongside in his electric car. Last time we met he had been able to walk; maybe this was one of those degenerative things even his fancy Florida surgeons couldn't help. We took our places at either end of the long table that was already set for lunch.

"Before we proceed," said Brainbocs, "I hope you will understand if I quash any silly ideas that you will inevitably entertain about escape. Rhodri, if you would be so good."

The butler brought from the mantelpiece another belt identical to mine and laid it down on the tabletop. Then he brought a metal dish of what looked like liver. "These belts are quite popular with some of the police forces in South America, although this isn't an original, I made it myself out of some electronic camera flashes. It works just the same, though. Do anything to upset me and it delivers an electric shock of ten thousand volts straight to the kidneys. This isn't actually kidney on the plate, it's liver, but I think you will get the idea." He picked up a remote-control device and pressed. There was a flash from the belt and a crackle and then the room filled with the acrid smell of burning meat.

"Well I think you may start serving us lunch now, Rhodri."

★ ★ ★

Brainbocs dabbed the thick starched white napkin to his mouth and threw it to the table. In his other hand he clutched a crystal goblet of dessert wine and gulped greedily from it. It was Chateau d'Y quem, the same stuff that God drinks at Christmas. He closed his eyes with delight at the exquisite nectar and then cried as if the word was even sweeter than the wine, "Love, Louie, Love. Love, love, love oh lovey love, love! That old-fashioned obsession of the poets and dreamers but so rarely the province of the white-coated research scientist."

"You've been researching love?"

"I was exploring the furthermost frontiers of the human psyche. I was going to change the world."

"By conducting research into the neurological basis of love?"

"Precisely!"

I was about to ask the obvious question "why?" But the sight of Rhodri replenishing Brainbocs's glass took me back to that day he appeared in my office asking about the memorabilia and suddenly I knew the answer.

"Myfanwy," I said.

Brainbocs grinned and then the joy slowly seeped away and became replaced by a wistfulness as he recalled the events of the past three years. "You see, it never really worked out for us in Patagonia. Myfanwy was happy enough for a while, all that singing and being a star and that, but deep down she was never really content. Deep down, I realised, as things stood she never really could be." He put down the glass as if its contents were too sweet to accompany this particular memory.

"I did everything for her, gave her whatever she desired. She was always talking about you, you see. Always going on about how she wished she had run away to Shrewsbury with you."

He paused and stared out of the window, the silence in the room broken only by the soft crackle of the fire in the grate. He said, "She really was so desperately in love with you, so girlish. She was always trying to write to you and things. Even though I arranged that her letters, which of course were never sent, were returned stamped 'Not known at this address'. When the newspaper cuttings from the *Cambrian Gazette* arrived with news of your wedding and later the tragic accident that left you cruelly brain-damaged and imprisoned in an intensive-care unit for the rest of your life, it was still to no avail. The silly girl just blamed herself for driving you away and said it served her right. It was all terribly troublesome." He stopped and looked up. "Would you like a cigar? Or a brandy?"

I shook my head. "The dessert wine is just fine. Tell me about Myfanwy."

"Of course! Of course . . ." He smiled with benign understanding, and continued: "Galling though the situation was, I realised that my predicament was far from being unique in the annals of human woe, indeed my reading taught me that it was such a common affair as to be virtually the norm. But none of the ancient texts I consulted were able to offer a remedy. And so I set about creating my own remedy. I decided to make a love potion." He pointed an admonitory finger at me. "You think the idea absurd, I know, because the words conjure up the image of some simplistic old witch's brew. But I am talking about a love potion with rock-solid scientific credentials, one drawing on the very latest neurophysiological and neuropsychological research. Could such a thing be possible? To the poets love is ineffable, but to the scientist emotions are just physical or chemical states of the brain. Could it be brought about by design?" His voice took on a distant, dreamy quality as if he were not really here but far away in his ivory tower grappling with the philosophical ramifications of his genius. "I had to be careful, of course. I was only too well aware of the danger posed by the cold and analytical nature of scientific experimentation. My wide-ranging study of the literature on this subject made it clear to me that love was by its very nature a spontaneous thing, a wild horse that would not be caged. How then to balance the demands for scientific control and spontaneity? It was like manoeuvring a tornado, taming the tidal wave. Not just difficult but possibly impossible. For it is a paradox, is it not? By harnessing the maelstrom you exert a form of control that extinguishes precisely that which makes it a maelstrom?" He looked at me and raised his hand. "I know what you're thinking, Louie. You wish no doubt to object that the propensity to fall in love is predicated on ideals of beauty which we store in our soul since childhood; images which we derive from the earliest memory of the soft, cherished face of our sweet mother. Is that not so? And since these things are set in stone at the very dawn of consciousness, how, you ask, could I alter them? How could I possibly erase what time had written in the foundations of Myfanwy's existence more than twenty-five years ago? It's a good question, Louie, and I'm glad you raised it. I think you will be impressed by my solution.

"I managed it by artificially stimulating that sensation commonly known as *déjà vu*. I created mental sensations, coated them with the texture of 'pastness' and implanted them in the psyche by suggestion. Although bear in mind this early work was done with prairie voles; it would be quite a while before I was ready to work with Herod, let alone Myfanwy."

"You used Herod for your experiments?"

"Of course! And prairie voles — charming creatures. Did you know they mate for life? Faithful until they die, never once straying. We could learn a lot from them."

"This is crazy."

Brainbocs ignored me. "I have to say the results were quite unnerving. Any policeman will tell you how unreliable our memories are. Show three people the same scene and they will remember it with wildly differing accounts. This is well-known; all the same, I was quite shocked — even frightened — by just what a cobweb our sense of identity is. Our little worlds are built on eggshell, Louie. Our deepest beliefs and convictions may be entirely false. I started to question the fundamentals of my own existence. Was my recollection of a childhood at my mother's knee in Talybont remotely trustworthy? The squeak of the spinning-wheel on long winter evenings; the faint musk-like odour of her body; the crackle in the fireplace and the tap of wind-blown twigs against the window pane like the ghost hand of a dead child pleading to be let in? Were these really my memories or had some poetic madman implanted them in me along with the ersatz conviction that they were my childhood remembrance? What if someone had done to me what I was about to do to Myfanwy? I couldn't know.

"The rest was just a bit of O level biochemistry. A cocktail of three key hormones. Serotonin, phenylethylamine and oxytocin — which is the one responsible for the bonding between a mother and her baby. With their help I was able to effect the basic re-architecturalisation of the cortical superstructure."

"So where does Herod fit into all this?"

"He was my experimental model, along with the prairie voles which are also most suitable. You see, in my research at the National Library I came into contact with some of the government scientists who were working on him trying to prevent him regaining his memory. It was just happenstance really that I was working on the neurobiological basis of love at the same time that they were dealing with the problem of Herod's lost memory. Well, you know what scientists are like, we got to talking in the canteen and, realising how this could benefit me, I offered to help. Herod was moved to the sanatorium where he stayed for many

264

weeks. He was perfect for research purposes, you see. A man who had no memory, a *tabula rasa*, so to speak. The result was a triumph in the annals of bio-engineering. I made him love. Do you understand the full implications of that? I gave him the power to love."

"And what about Mrs Bligh-Jones?"

"Oh that was simple. Mrs Bligh-Jones was well-known to have hot pants for the gentlemen, especially those of a rugby-playing persuasion. She was a useful means of control. It was their regular trysts here that kept him docile."

"You thought by teaching Herod to love you could do the same for Myfanwy? Make her love you? It's insane."

"Not only that, but I also managed to make a few design modifications, to improve on the original. As you know there are a number of things seriously wrong with love. For a start it has a built-in statute of limitations, as evinced by Herod's return to his former self. Any weeping schoolgirl will tell you true love never lasts. It's really a problem with the instability of the oxytocin molecule. But there is a more fundamental flaw, one that is central to love's very essence: fleeting, inconstant and hostage to that cruelly arbitrary quality popularly known as 'handsomeness' — mere physical appearance that serves as an indicator of our reproductive potency. Which means, basically, that chaps who look like me never get a look in." He paused and then added, "And that's where you come in."

He signalled to Rhodri to refill the wine glasses.

"You know I haven't a clue what you are talking about."

"Yes, yes, yes. I know you are impatient to rescue Calamity —"

"You know where she is?"

"Of course. And I'm going to make a deal with you and tell you. But first you have to hear me out, or you won't understand."

I looked at him in the most profound disbelief.

"When I transferred my research to Myfanwy, I encountered an unexpected obstacle — one most resistant to my attempts to overcome it. In lay terms, I found myself bumping against a brick wall . . . a psychical brick wall. It was as if I was tunnelling into her soul . . . tunnelling to the deep, dark, hidden cave where she keeps the most powerful, primal, tender feelings and I found the way blocked by some unsuspected edifice so large it scorned all my attempts to remove it or go round it."

"And what was it?"

"Her love for you."

This was when I decided I'd heard enough. I jumped out of the chair and raced across the dining-room towards him. It was obvious he had been expecting this reaction at exactly this moment. He calmly raised and pressed the remote control. I jerked backwards, reached up to the heavens with my hands, fingers curled like claws, and screamed. And then vomited. And then fell into a writhing heap on the floor.

266

Rhodri helped me back into my chair.

"That was just a weeny one, by the way, just in case you get any more silly ideas."

I sat panting, desperately gasping for air, and staring hate at Brainbocs. He calmly flicked some lint off his blazer.

"You're agitated," he said, "that is perhaps understandable."

"What do you want with me?"

"I told you, I want to make you a deal."

"A deal?"

"You will help me, and I will tell you what you most want to know in all the world. The whereabouts of Calamity."

"What do I have to do in return?"

"You will help me extinguish what remains of Myfanwy's love for you."

"You're mad."

"You say that only because you still do not believe. And of course I cannot blame you. You need to see with your own eyes. First you need a token of my earnest in this matter. First you need to meet Myfanwy."

This time I jerked backwards, but there was no electric shock, just the even more powerful stunning effect of Brainbocs's words. "You mean she's here!?"

"Where did you think she was? Timbuktu?! Now that we have had a chance to talk we will go and see her. I know she has been dying to meet you." The butler put his hands on the back of my wheelchair, and was about to push when Brainbocs raised his hand. "One moment, Rhodri." He turned to me. "Before we go on there is a question I must ask you, a very important one. And it is this. Do you love Myfanwy like most suitors purely for her physical charms or do you love her like I do for her character . . . for who and what she is?"

It was such a strange question but he looked at me with an expression that almost defied description. I remembered the time Myfanwy described the incident when Brainbocs took off his calliper and went down on one knee to propose. The look on his face that she had been unable to describe, but tonight I knew it was the same one. A look of grief and pain of such intensity it suggested nothing that had ever happened to him in his life was as important as my answer.

"You no doubt feel it is none of my business, and you are right — it isn't. All the same I need you to answer."

"You're asking me whether I love her for her body or her mind?"

"Yes I suppose, crudely put, I am."

I didn't even bother considering it. "Her mind."

"Excellent!" He signalled to the butler and we were wheeled through. The butler opened two double doors at the end of the library and pushed me towards them. Towards Myfanwy whom I hadn't seen for three years, years during which there hadn't been a single day which didn't start and end with me thinking about her. As we passed through the doors Brainbocs grabbed the sleeve of my arm, taking care to keep the remote control beyond my reach and said, "Please, prepare yourself. The past three years have been very hard for her. She is not like she used to be. Not the way you remember her."

CHAPTER
TWENTY-TWO

The adjoining room was smaller than the diningroom but had the same high ceiling with dusty cornicing. The same oak panels round the walls. There was no furniture. At one end a set of French doors opened on to a rose garden. And at the opposite end was a console of electronic instruments. There were gauges that hummed and lights that flashed different colours, and in the centre, straight out of a second-rate science-fiction movie, there was a large Perspex cylinder containing a pale amber fluid and inside that, with wires attached, a human brain. Behind it on the wall was an enlarged photo of Myfanwy. I stood before it all and gasped. A sequence of lights, which I could only suppose connoted excitement, flashed up and down rods around the photo and a thin metallic voice said, "Hello Louie!"

I spun round and jumped out of the chair but Brainbocs was expecting this. He was holding the remote control pointed at my chest like a gun and I stopped frozen in my tracks. The memory of the lightning bolt he had sent through my body last time was fresh and filled me with an animal terror that glued my limbs. I sat back in the chair.

"How you doing, Louie!" said the electronic voice.

Nausea overwhelmed me and I looked in utter disbelief at Brainbocs. "What have you done?"

He shrugged in what appeared to be embarrassment as if his wonderful new scheme had not met with the rapture he was expecting. "I would have thought that was fairly obvious."

"But you . . . you . . . I . . ." There were no words.

Brainbocs made an uncomfortable fidgeting movement and said, "I see it is useless to try and hide the fact from you, I fucked up."

"You haven't changed a bit, Louie!" warbled the robotic voice of . . . of . . . what? Myfanwy? "How do I look?"

"Answer her!" hissed Brainbocs. "She's been so looking forward to this. Don't upset her!"

"Oh . . . well . . . you know . . ." I forced my mutinying tongue to speak. "Same old Myfanwy!"

"Very good!" whispered Brainbocs.

"You little liar!" warbled Myfanwy.

"Would you like her to sing for you?

"No."

"Yes, yes, I'm sure you would. You doubt that she can, eh? I haven't given her full colour vision yet, but she can sing." He clapped his hands. "Myfanwy, sing for our guest."

"What shall I sing?"

"Anything."

There began a thin warbling rendition of "*Una Paloma Blanca*" from the speakers. It was hideous but Brainbocs didn't think so. He rested his head in the

271

crook of his thumb and index finger and half-closed his eyes dreamily while his other hand tapped the remote control in time to the music. When she got to the "I'm just a bird in the sky" bit, I could take it no longer. "Stop it! I shouted. "Stop this . . . this . . . obscenity!"

The music petered out. "Not so good, huh?" said Myfanwy. "I know I'm still a bit rusty. I need to be able to move to the beat really."

Brainbocs looked at me with eyes narrowed to slits and the water between them glittering with fury. "You shouldn't have done that, Louie. You're a rude bastard, that's what you are."

"And you're the filthiest, vilest piece of vermin —"

He pointed the remote control at me. "Go on say it, I dare you!"

I stopped. "One day I won't just tell you, I'll write it on you with your own blood."

Brainbocs was angry now. Bubbling over with hate and confusion. "Don't come the 'I'm so pure and noble' bit with me. You're just like all the rest. I knew it but she wouldn't believe me. Just like all the other lecherous old toads down at that filthy club who saw her as a piece of meat."

"You don't know what you are talking about."

"Oh yes I do! I'm not a lusting animal like you, I love Myfanwy with —"

"Love!" I shouted. "You call this love? What do you know about love?"

"Everything!" he screamed. "I've read everything there is available on the subject!"

272

I laughed bitterly. "You didn't find out the first thing, Brainbocs. Not the first thing. This proves it. A cold inhuman monster such as you doesn't have the capacity to love. You think this is Myfanwy? A brain in a chemistry set? Myfanwy is the girl running along the sand dunes at Ynyslas with the salty wind blowing in her chestnut hair, with firm young limbs of warm flesh and blood, running joyously into the sea . . ."

"Oh spare me!" shouted Brainbocs. "Spare me the pink candy hearts! You'll be telling me next love is a many-splendoured thing!"

"It is!" I cried. "It fucking well is!"

"Oh sure, the April rose that only grows . . . Grow up, Louie Knight!"

"Myfanwy isn't a brain in a petri dish, she was the taste of salt on her skin after swimming in the sea . . . the coldness of her salty wet hair and the goosebumps and laughter and . . . and . . . and . . . Jesus, even now you haven't the faintest idea what I'm talking about. Not the faintest. This isn't love what you are doing here. It's just dissection."

There was a pause. And I could see Brainbocs visibly straining to calm himself. He straightened his tie and twisted his head sharply from side to side as he did so. "This is absurd. I won't allow you to infuriate me with your cheap gumshoe antics. I know the score. Get me upset and then make an attempt to get the remote control. Well you can forget about that."

"Oh do stop fighting, you two!" warbled Myfanwy.

"You'll understand after you've had a chance to chat to Myfanwy."

"She isn't here."

"You see," he hissed, his face once more twisting with venom. "I knew it. I told her but she wouldn't have it. You don't really love her. Just before we came in I asked you whether it was her body or her brain you admired. Well I think we have our answer now, don't we?"

"Are you so blind that you cannot see the one doesn't go without the other?"

"Oh really? Says who? You may not desire her any more but I do."

"Is she happy?"

His eyes shot open. "Since when has that been a criterion? Who's happy round here, huh? Nobody as far as I can see. Happy? Happy? I've never been happy a single day in my whole fucking life. Have you?"

"Yes, I have. Almost every day."

"Well you don't look very happy today!"

"It hasn't ended yet."

"You throw happiness at me as if it was the touchstone of man's existence whereas statistically it's the very absence of it that seems to define us. Happiness? It's crap."

"You say you love her and you don't even want to make her happy?"

"I deal in facts and certainties, Louie. Not candy floss. Any rational analysis of the world makes it clear that I cannot promise her happiness. But I can make her happier. You see, despite everything, we still have each other. And now, in her modified form, at least no one will try and take her away from me."

274

"Is that so?"

"Yes, Mr Knight, it very much is so. That, if you will forgive me underlining it, is the whole point. Because I know that despite your fine words you no longer want her. While I still do."

"What makes you so sure?"

"Oh I'm sure," he said. "Very sure. In fact, that's why I brought you here. Because I knew once you saw her you would hate her."

"I don't hate her."

"Perhaps. But you do not love her."

"She's not the same girl."

"Oh you're back-pedalling now, Louie. Back-pedalling. The tragedy for you is, she *is* the same girl. You could stay here all week and chat to her and you would never be able to deny it. The only thing that is not the same is physical. The tits and the bum — or what was that bollocks again? The cold wet tongues of hair on the goosebumpy skin. That was all you desired and it's gone."

"It's not true, Brainbocs."

"Really? Tell her then. Go and tell her that you still love her."

I paused and my indecision filled him with glee.

"You see! You can't bring yourself to do it."

"Why the hell should I?"

"To save Calamity, of course."

I turned to him and stared at the smug self-assurance on his face. Again Brainbocs made efforts to calm himself, breathing deeply and counting the breaths. And then, much cooler, he said. "You may protest and throw your teddy out of the pram, even call me a load of schoolyard names, but underneath it all you're not stupid. The deal I'm offering you is one you cannot possibly refuse. Tell Myfanwy you don't love her and I will tell you where they have taken Calamity."

I rushed at him again but again I was too slow. Or Brainbocs was too quick. Another lightning fork flashed inside my ribs, picked me up and threw me to the ground with terrifying force. I convulsed and writhed on the floor, as my heart beat so powerfully I thought my chest would explode. Brainbocs looked on impassively and, once the convulsions had subsided, said, "You stupid fool." Rhodri threw a tureen of cold water into my face and I dragged myself wearily back to the chair.

Brainbocs continued, "I can assure you, Louie, you will get tired of that before I do. But enough of this. Let us seal the deal."

"What if I don't co-operate?"

"You have no choice. You would be stupid to refuse because it is in your best interests. You love Calamity like a father. You no longer love Myfanwy, despite your brave words. So to give her up will not be so very hard except for the wound it will deal to your honour. And set against the welfare of Calamity, what is that?"

Was he right? His words had twisted me so much that I hardly knew any more what to think.

"Tell me what they have done with Calamity," I eventually said.

276

Brainbocs drove his car over to a bureau and fetched a pile of papers. "I can't tell you exactly where, you have to understand. We're not in this together, if that's what you think. Mrs Llantrisant has no more love for me than she does for you. But I know how to find out."

"How would I know you are not lying?"

"You wouldn't but when I explain it to you, you will know it to be the truth. You will feel it in your water. And besides, all you have to do is tell Myfanwy you no longer love her. If I double-cross you, you simply say you didn't mean it. You can't lose."

"So where have they taken her, what does Herod hold sacred?"

He lifted the pile of papers.

"It's not, as you might first imagine, anything to do with rugby or beer, nor even as I had secretly suspected the exciting smell of adolescent boys' fear. It was something more primal than that and dated back to a time shortly after the war in Patagonia. A time when he had all the normal appetites of a healthy young man. A man who could still laugh and love, whose soul had not yet been torn apart by the memory of that terrible conflict. This man had a love affair with someone. Can you guess who?"

I narrowed my eyes and stared in disbelief and hate at the little worm.

"Go on have a go."

"Mrs Llantrisant?"

"Close. Her sister, Mrs Bligh-Jones."

I looked startled.

"Ah, you didn't know they were sisters. Oh yes. And bitter love rivals."

"But Mrs Llantrisant had Bligh-Jones assassinated."

"Hell hath no fury and all that. Yes, Herod and Mrs Bligh-Jones did what all seventeen-year-olds with the spring sap rising in their green shoots do given half a chance. The record of it is all faithfully transcribed in here." Brainbocs waved the sheaf of papers. "Detailed descriptions of Mrs Bligh-Jones groaning and convulsing on the grassy hillside and doing out of wedlock what she spent the rest of her life hurling scorn at other girls for doing. The two of them engendering a child. Yes, Mrs Bligh-Jones and Herod had a love-child. But alas only for a while. For a single day only. A frail little kitten that popped its head out, decided the world was a vale of tears, and went back to wherever it was he had come from. They called him Onan. And Mrs Bligh-Jones gave birth to him in a cow byre because Herod had abandoned her. The only question now is, which cow byre?"

"You mean that's the sacred place?"

"Yes, up on Pumlumon somewhere. You remember all that fuss about the Meals on Wheels expedition that got stuck in the snow up there? That was all Bligh-Jones's doing. She knew he was up there, driven by some terrible, deep-seated instinct to find the place where his son was buried. That's where Herod's hideout is and where, unless you get a move on, they will kill Calamity tonight at moonrise."

★   ★   ★

278

When he finished there was silence for a while. I looked towards the console and then back at Brainbocs. "I just tell her I don't love her and you tell me where the cow byre is?"

He nodded. And then Myfanwy spoke.

"It's all right, Louie, you can say it. I already know anyway. You don't love me now. You hate me. Go on say it. No don't, please don't, please don't! Oh what does it matter? I know it anyway. Why didn't you write, you pig? I hate you for that . . . oh no I don't! Forgive me . . . I know this is all my fault. You never really loved me, it was Bianca you really loved, wasn't it? Don't lie to me, I know . . . you deserve better than this anyway, it's over for us, we're finished, look at me — just an old lump of brain in a tin of chicken consommé . . . that's what it is you know, chicken soup . . . just a brain now . . . I never was very brainy, was I? My worst feature all that is left of me . . . Go on leave me, say you don't love me . . . but say you did once . . . in Ynyslas, remember? Oh, Louie, remember how we kissed that day . . . I was so happy . . . Louie, say you did once, say you did once, Louie say you did . . ."

Brainbocs picked up a walking-stick and banged the console with it. "Sometimes the speech circuits can get overloaded."

And then Myfanwy started to sing in a voice punctuated by sobs.

> Once on a high and windy hill
> In the morning mist, two lovers kissed,
> And the world stood still . . .

"It's amazing, isn't it?" said Brainbocs. "I haven't given her full stereoscopic vision but she can still cry —"

I couldn't take any more. I walked over to the console, looked at Myfanwy and then back at the evil dwarf schoolboy. He was singing, too, now. The thin, out-of-tune, reedy sound of a youth whose voice will for ever remain on the cusp of breaking; singing the descant to Myfanwy's electronic soprano.

> Then your fingers touched my silent heart
> And taught it how to sing
> Yes, true love is a many splendoured thing . . .

It was enough. Tears in my eyes, I said into the microphone, "I love you Myfanwy. I always did. You were a bitch to me sometimes, but it never mattered. I always forgave you. So I hope now you'll forgive me too —"

"No!" screamed Brainbocs as realisation dawned. "No! You bastard, no!" He rammed the throttle forward and sped his car towards me.

"Hope you'll forgive me —"

"No!" he screamed.

I turned to face Brainbocs as he raised the remote. And I smiled at him, a graveyard smile, as he pressed and I gritted my teeth. The shock shrieked through me in spears of blue and silver fire. I spun round and convulsed, but used the force, the momentum, to carry me forward to the console.

"No!" he cried and pressed the remote once more. But he said he'd made the belt from camera flashes and even I knew you had to wait a few seconds for them to charge up again. I grinned at him and reached for the console. Brainbocs jabbed with impotent fury at the remote and then hurled it aside and raced his electric buggy forward.

"No! No! No! Stop! Please!" And then with bestial ferocity Brainbocs launched himself from his chair, his tiny hands reaching out in wild despair to grab my coat. Like a maniac he fought to clamber up me, to bring his face close to mine in a lethal embrace. He was so close now I could feel his hot breath scalding my ear. I could hear his teeth millimetres away — snapping on empty air like the jaws of a terrier trying to catch a wasp — as he tried to bite through the carotid artery in my neck. "No! No! No! Stop!" he screamed.

"Forgive me, Myfanwy," I said, and then pulled the plug out from the wall-socket.

CHAPTER
TWENTY-THREE

For maybe a whole minute or so neither of us spoke. Brainbocs lay face-down on the floor at my feet, the remote control a yard away, almost within reach. I kicked it under the sideboard. The console was now in darkness; the lights dead; the electronic hum gone. And with it too whatever it was that Brainbocs said was Myfanwy. Finally he twisted his head on the floor and looked up at me. "Curious. This funny thing called love. Of all the reactions I had computed, the one thing I didn't expect was that you would kill for it."

I bent down and scooped the broken-hearted dwarf into my arms and then put him tenderly back in his wheelchair. And then the tiredness swept over me. I could have slept standing up. The lights flickered and went out. Not just in the house but down in the valley too. I slumped into a chair and held my head in my hands. All the reserves of strength seemed to have been drained from my body.

The butler walked in holding a candelabra of lighted candles. "I fear we have some problems with the electricity . . ." He stopped as he took in the scene in front of him.

"Yes," I said. "There's been a loss of power in here too."

"So I see," he said in a thoughtful voice. "So I jolly well see."

"I'll be phoning the police in a while, if you . . . er . . . if you . . ." I was almost too tired to speak.

"Time to go, eh?" he said.

"I think so."

"Would you permit me, sir, before I leave to straighten Mr Brainbocs's tie for one last time?"

I shrugged. "Be my guest."

The butler walked up to Brainbocs and punched him with pure venom full in the face. "That's better," he said, and then walked to the door.

A fat bead of blood appeared in Brainbocs's nostril and trickled down his upper lip. Tears welled up in his eyes. I walked over and held out a handkerchief to him. He misinterpreted the gesture and flinched in anticipation of another blow.

The loudspeaker crackled on the wall and a voice, the voice of a dead girl, shouted, "Go on, Louie, bash him up!"

I twisted round suddenly and the butler pointed at a set of doors to the left of the console and said, "I think someone had better go and untie Myfanwy, don't you?"

I walked across and swung the doors open and there she was. Tied to a chair, and staring at the proceedings on a TV screen with a microphone in front of her, but seemingly unharmed. Myfanwy. I attacked the cords with fevered hands and soon she was free and in my arms and squeezing me so hard I could feel my ribs crunch. "Oh, Louie!" she groaned into my chest. "Oh, Louie!" And I pressed my face against the top of her head and breathed deeply the lost incense of Myfanwy's hair. Finally she pulled back, looked up at me and said, "You switched me off, you pig!"

I called Llunos and he told me Calamity had turned up. She had walked into the police station an hour earlier and turned herself in for the Custard Pie break-out. He was going to send me a car, the fastest one he had, because she was driving everyone mad down there and they were considering arresting her for vagrancy or something, just for some peace and quiet.

We didn't wait for the police car, we borrowed Brainbocs's 1960s era Rover instead.

"Why didn't you warn me," I asked as we drove through Ponterwyd and west towards town.

"If I gave the game away he was going to kill you. He said he had a power setting on the belt that would kill you instantly; he demonstrated it by electrocuting a pig. The deal was I had to answer all your questions and convince you that you were really talking to me. Then he would make you the deal: renounce me and he would tell you how to find Calamity."

"What would have happened if I didn't renounce you? Told you I still loved you?"

"He said you would never do it, you would never let Calamity die; but if you did he would let us go. We could be together."

"Really?"

"He said if you did that, if you sacrificed an innocent child for me, he would be quite impressed and would have to admit that maybe your love was even greater than his."

I nodded. It sort of made sense.

"Do you think he really would have let us go?" asked Myfanwy.

"I'm not sure. What do you think?"

"I think he was planning to kill us all, including himself."

We drove on in silence for a while, in a dark world of old leather, polished wood and chrome bezels.

"Anyway, I told him there was no way you would be stupid enough to fall for such a dumb trick. And he said you would."

"He was right."

"No he wasn't, you outsmarted him. You thought of something he didn't expect. That was really cool. Although I'm not sure about the bit where you called me a bitch."

"And don't forget I switched you off." I squeezed her hand in the dark.

Myfanwy loosened her seat-belt and sidled across, nestling her soft head on my shoulder.

"But to tell the truth," I added, "he had me hook, line and sinker. I fell for the whole thing — especially your bit. When you started going on about Ynyslas and then broke down and wept . . . where on earth did you learn to act like that?"

"I wasn't acting."

Calamity was sitting on a chair wrapped in a blanket and arguing with an exasperated-looking policewoman.

"For the umpteenth time," she said, "I didn't get kidnapped. I used myself as bait to smoke him out . . ."

"Look, missie, I've had enough of your tales."

"And I've had enough of yours!"

"Really? And how would you like a tanned bottom?"

"And how would you like to spend the rest of your career writing speeding tickets?"

She looked up at my approach. "It's OK Louie, I've got it under control, just briefing the uniformed guys."

"She thinks she's a detective," said the policewoman.

"She is a detective," I said.

There was a loud groan. "Don't you start as well."

"Can we get to talk to someone with a bit of seniority around here, we're losing valuable time," said Calamity.

I took her by the arm and drew her to one side. She started to expostulate about the incompetence surrounding her and I made the gesture known as "shhhh!" She stopped and looked up at me, slightly sheepishly, and said, "So, are you OK?" I smiled. "Seeing you again is the best tonic in the whole world. What about you?" "Of course!" A slight tremor flashed across her face when she said that and she swallowed something. And swallowed again. "I'm fine, why not?" Her eyes glittered. "It's been a bit of a tough one

286

this, but I think I've worked out how to find the sacred . . ."

Again I motioned her to be quiet. "That's not important right now . . ."

"Of course it is, if we don't hurry . . ."

"No it's not. Right now it doesn't matter whether they escape or whatever, the most important thing is that you are all right."

"Yes, yes, I'm fine . . . I told you, didn't I? This is still a case and . . ."

"There will always be more cases and some we'll win and some we'll lose. That's the way it will always be, we'll never change it. But I'll only ever have one Calamity."

She looked into my face and blinked back tears. "Boy! I really made a dog's dinner of the Custard Pie job."

"No," I said gently. "You did fine. You found out about Herod. That was an incredible piece of detective work."

"But I helped Custard Pie escape. How stupid can you get?"

"Trust me, Calamity. I would have done exactly the same."

"Really?"

"Really. And if it's any help to you, it wasn't you who let him escape it was the idiot on watch that night who didn't check the ambulance."

Calamity considered that and her face became childishly stern. "Yeah, we'll have to throw the book at him when this is over." Another worrying thought intruded, and she peeped reluctantly at me. "I've been thinking about my letter of resignation . . ."

I tried to look unconcerned. "Oh that! You didn't think I would be fooled by that old trick, did you?"

She looked uncertain. "You weren't?"

"'Course not! I knew straightaway it was the work of an impostor."

"It was?"

"Sure! Crummiest impersonation I've ever seen. Whoever did it didn't know the first thing about you."

"Really?"

"For a start, they couldn't spell for toffee."

She looked at me and then slightly narrowed her eyes as she considered; and then she grinned and punched me. "Oh you! Does this mean you're not angry with me then?"

I ruffled her hair. "I'm not angry about the escape. But there is one thing I am very angry about. Taking the gun like that."

Her eyes flicked wide. "What gun? I didn't take your gun."

Llunos walked over clutching a Styrofoam cup, looking tired; his tie skew-whiff, shirt buttons undone over his belly. "She says she knows where to find Herod's sacred place but won't tell us because it's her collar."

"It is my collar," protested Calamity. "I have to be there."

"Talk some sense into her," said Llunos, "or I'll make her a material witness. I do that and she'll never get a job as a dick in Cardigan for as long as she lives. I don't like it but that's the rules."

"But it's my collar," said Calamity.

I crouched down and spoke to her face to face. "No one is saying it isn't, kid. But you can't come along. You have to stay here and give these people some statements and things. Boring, I know, but that's life as a real detective. But if you tell us where they are, it's your collar. Everyone knows that." I looked up at Llunos.

"'Course it's her collar," he said. "Anyone says it isn't will have to explain to me why not.

Calamity looked to Llunos and then back to me, making up her mind. "OK. Well I don't know where it is, but I do know how to find out. Just ask Smokey Jones."

"Who?" Llunos and I asked in unison.

"Smokey G. Jones — the pro Mrs Beynon champ from the sixties. She's bound to know all about Mrs Bligh-Jones getting up the duff out of wedlock . . ."

Llunos didn't stay to hear the rest, he was off across the room, barking his orders. "Put out an A P B on Mrs Smokey G. Jones. I want everything she's got on Mrs Bligh-Jones's bastard — times, dates, places. If she won't talk, slap a charge on her; if she still won't talk run her in and make her. You've got half an hour and I want her singing like a canary. Use your truncheons if you have to, and I don't care where you stick them . . ."

"If she clams up," shouted Calamity across the room, "tell her I've got that large-print edition of *Lady Chatterley* she was asking about." She turned to me and smiled. "We'll get them yet."

"We sure will. Now tell me how you escaped."

She broke my gaze and looked down. "Argh, you know," she said trying to sound casual. "Custard Pie arranged for me to rendezvous with one of his confederates, he was going to tell me who the Raven was. Like an idiot I thought I'd nail them on my own. Then when Pie escaped I was so scared at what you would say, so I sort of hung low for a while. I knew you'd be furious."

"I wasn't furious. You just made a mistake, everyone is allowed to do that."

"So I went to the rendezvous and, you know, I was too smart for them of course . . ."

"Yeah, I know."

"No way I was going to fall for a dumb trick like that."

"No way?"

"'Course not."

"OK," I said. "That's fantastic. Now tell me the truth."

She bit her lip. "Well actually, to tell the truth," she said reluctantly, "I was warned."

"Who by?"

"I don't know. I was going to the meeting-point and this old woman in a black shawl walked past me and told me it was a trap. She didn't hang around, one minute she was there, the next she was gone. Soon as she said it I realised what an idiot I was being."

Before the half-hour was up Llunos came over and told me to put on my coat. Smokey G. Jones had been happy to talk, although she made the two officers wait while she made a cup of tea. And they had to listen to the antique case-histories of four gymslip pregnancies, two extra-marital affairs and a case of incest before they got to the bit they wanted. The love-child had been born in the hut in the Pilgrim's Pass on Pumlumon. The posse would set out at dawn, but since there was still about half an hour of daylight left . . . Llunos didn't need to say any more, we both knew what we were going to do.

I turned to Calamity before I left and said, "Is that true you didn't take the gun?"

She nodded. "You told me not to, didn't you? I wouldn't have dared."

CHAPTER
TWENTY-FOUR

The pilgrim's hut was the last of the old wayfarers' stations before the pass. It used to be the main way on foot into England but once the snows set in it was often impassable. Llunos drove fast across the rolling badlands of Blaenrheidol as the first flakes of snow fluttered from the sky.

We left the car in a lay-by and followed the National Trust footpath through the valley and up the scree towards the pass. If they were keeping a watch they would see us easily, but then where would they go? In this weather the only safe route was down back into the valley. To our left the sombre waters of Nant-y-moch reservoir lapped the shore with tiny wavelets. It seemed a thousand years since we had both passed this way before; above the clouds in an aeroplane from which Herod Jenkins plunged to what we assumed was his death. We were both deeply aware of the significance of this moment, here above the lake where last time we had failed. We walked without speaking; there was nothing left to say. It was a time for deeds.

★ ★ ★

Herod was standing outside the hut, his back to us, bent over and skinning a ferret. He was dressed as a man of the woods: home-cured furs wrapping him, with the arms and shoulder bare like a circus strongman. A twig cracked beneath our feet and he spun round, a bloody skinning knife in his hand and on his face that horizontal crease that they once called a smile.

"Well bugger me!" he said. He nodded to Llunos. "Evening, Llunos, bit parky isn't it?"

"*Nos da* Mr Jenkins! Looks like we might be in for a bit of snow."

Herod spoke to me. "Still playing detectives, are we? You should get yourself a proper job."

"It is a proper job."

"Could have fooled me."

"We've come to take you in," said Llunos.

"What for?"

"What for!?" I spluttered.

"I've paid my debt to society."

"Like hell you have!"

"I fell out of a plane, didn't I? Banged my bloody head on the water, lost my memory, lived on berries . . ."

"Tell it to the judge, Herod."

He yanked at his fur vest, pulling it down to reveal a long ugly scar on his chest. "See this? I sewed it myself with a nail and some thread made from the intestines of a sheep."

"I thought needlework was for girlies."

"Give up, Herod," said Llunos simply.

"To you two? I'm bigger than both of you, what are you going to do?"

"There are more coming, you know that. Men with dogs, and guns. They'll get you. You can't go forward into the pass, you'd be crazy. The only way is back. You want to spend the rest of your life running?"

"I like running. If the little pansy here had done more of it at school instead of moaning like a girl we might have made a man of him."

"I'm not talking about running round a track. I mean running like a hunted dog all your life. Never lying down at night without worrying if that night they'll come for you. Every day a new town, a new identity, always looking over your shoulder."

"It doesn't sound any worse than rotting in jail."

"Who says you'll go to jail? What have you done? It's not a crime to lose your memory and live in the woods. We could probably work something out."

"I'm in it up to my neck. You said so yourself."

"No you're not, if you turn Mrs Llantrisant in you'll probably get a deal."

Herod spat with contempt. "Oh that's it, is it? Turn my comrade in for an easy sentence. Well you've made a mistake there if that's what you think. I'm not a coward like Louie Knight here who was always too scared to catch the ball."

"Is that the grave?" I asked pointing to an outcrop of rock above the hut, on which now stood a new cross, crudely fashioned from chopped wood.

★   ★   ★

Herod turned and peered upwards. The sky was milky grey and filled with tufts of snow falling as gently as a dandelion flower.

"I put it up there myself last week. His spirit can rest in peace now."

"We can probably arrange something with the judge, let you come here now and again," said Llunos.

Herod's voice thickened with the emotion. "It's all I ever wanted, really, was a son. To play rugby on the lawn with. It's not a lot to ask, is it?"

"Every man has that right," said Llunos.

"But he's dead now. Because of me. I kicked her out. Kicked Mrs Bligh-Jones out when she was seventeen and with child. Poor girl with nowhere to go. Abandoned. The poor little mite was born in a cow byre . . ." Tears welled up in his eyes. "My little son in a cow byre."

"Jesus didn't start out any better," said Llunos.

"Although he had a nicer dad," I added.

Herod carried on as if he hadn't heard. "All alone she was, trying to walk through the pass to Shrewsbury. No friends, no help, no one to comfort her . . . and the boy . . . my son, little Onan . . . only lived a day."

"Let us take you in, Herod," said Llunos gently. "You won't have to serve a long sentence, you'll be out in a couple of years and then you'll be able to come and live in the hut here."

Herod became thoughtful. "Up here?"

"You could probably be the hut-keeper or ranger or something. There's always a job for a strong man."

He considered and then said, "I had nothing to do with that thing with the girl, you know?"

"Calamity?"

"That was Custard Pie's idea. I didn't want to get involved. It was rude."

"We believe you, Herod. We know you wouldn't do a thing like that. The judge will believe you too. But you have to help us help you."

"Where is Custard Pie?" I asked.

"He's inside. Broke his leg in a fall. We don't think he's going to make it. Mrs Llantrisant has gone to get some Savlon."

"If you come with us, we can get help. No point letting him die up here."

The powerful spirit that animated the frame of the mighty games teacher wavered. It was a moment of decision so intense you could see it etched into the sinews of his flesh. He stood proud and erect, as if cast from iron, and then slowly the tension within lost its edge and he shrunk slightly. As if the thought of a warm hearth when compared to the uncertainty of flight into the snow-covered badlands was sapping even his considerable reserves of strength. As if he was slowly beginning to take stock of the terrible toll the daily battle to ward off the Furies that had pursued him was taking on his aging body. And who could blame him? A man who took a wrong turning at the very outset of his life's journey, at a time when he knew nothing of the world; took a wrong turning and for ever after was sworn to follow the path it led to. What if he had not rejected Mrs Bligh-Jones all those years ago? Had taken her in and she borne him a son who would have played rugby on the lawn with him? How many years of torment would have been spared to the long-suffering armies of children who passed through the battleground of his lessons?

Could I blame him? Could any of us really be blamed for becoming what we had no power to avoid becoming? Wasn't that what Custard Pie had said? But is it enough to blame the Furies? It was hard to know, but I knew what Eeyore would have said. Think along those lines and there's no point being a detective. Might as well stay in bed all day. Each man makes a decision that moulds his life. And lives with it. No one ever said it was nice. But each man has a choice. Ben Guggenheim did. I looked at Herod. In his eyes were many things, hate, pain, bewilderment, but most of all helplessness. And then something else appeared there: the ghost of a decision.

"If I come back with you," he said turning to me, "will you give me your blessing?"

For a sliver of a second I was startled. Llunos turned to look at me as if it all now rested on me.

"Will you give me your blessing?" he repeated.

I opened my mouth not knowing what I was going to say, when a voice cried out a single word that echoed round the canyon like a ricocheting bullet.

"No!"

We all turned and looked up, and standing on the outcrop of rock next to little Onan's grave, her white hair flying wildly in the wind like an avenging Norse goddess, was Mrs Llantrisant. And she was pointing a shotgun at us. We raised our hands and she climbed down the stony path to join us.

Llunos spoke first. "Better put the gun down, Mrs Llantrisant."

"You must think I'm daft."

"You are if you don't put it down. There's nowhere left for you to go."

"Better to die on your feet than live on your knees."

"I find that a bit hard to believe coming from someone who spent her life swabbing a step."

She spat. "Pah! That was my cover, you stupid fool. If I disguise myself to look like an idiot does that make me an idiot? Or does it make you one for being deceived?"

"These are lofty-sounding words, Mrs Llantrisant, but the simple truth is you are a fugitive, and you also have bad rheumatism. You need proper medical care. Your fine rhetoric won't help you wade through the snow of this mountain pass and that is all that is left open to you."

"After all I've been through you really think I care a fig for the pain in my joints? You may succeed in sweet-talking my man into acting like a cur ..." She jabbed the shotgun at Herod, who was now silently weeping. "Pull yourself together, man, or I'll take a horsewhip to you!" Herod wiped away the tears on a pelt hanging from his waist.

298

"Don't you think you're a bit old to be Bonnie and Clyde?" I asked.

"Yes," she sneered. "You can laugh at me because I'm old, but I've got more balls than you even though I'm twice your age."

"No one doubts the strength of your spirit, Mrs Llantrisant —"

"Not half you don't. You think I don't know? How you despise us old ones because we're in the way. Want to put us in a home where we never see a normal-sized teapot again? Oh I know all about what you think. You see my weak eyes and my thin grey hair stretched across my skull and you want to hide me away from sight. And what you hate most is the idea of me, an old woman, being consumed by the fire of passion. Yes I know. But I tell you I was not always like this. There was a time when my skin was not this wrinkled parchment that you see and my dugs not these dry empty bags, but bursting with milk and fire and love. And I tell you the love I bore to Herod Jenkins was as the Nile to the Rheidol compared to Mrs Bligh-Jones's, and as a hurricane to a fart compared to how Louie Knight here felt about that whore from the nightclub."

"We don't doubt it, Mrs Llantrisant, but you must be realistic. This is no weather for you to be out in the wilds living off rabbits. You need some hot *caawl* inside you."

"I didn't see much hot *caawl* on that island prison you banished me to."

"Perhaps we were too harsh. Perhaps we can arrange something more suitable for a lady in your condition."

"Don't try and fool me with your tricks. I'm no idiot. You'll lock me up and throw away the key. But I won't let you."

"Come home with us, Mrs Llantrisant."

"No! It is impossible. I won't go. I'm free and I have my man again and we'd rather die together than live apart in chains."

Just then Dai the Custard Pie crawled out of the hut, his one leg bandaged to a splint made from a tree branch. The stomach-churning reek of gangrene flashed in our nostrils.

"What's going on?" he croaked.

Mrs Llantrisant took command of the situation. "We'll leave the shotgun with you. You cover them until we have had time to get away. Then you let them take you, they'll bring you to a hospital where you can get your leg fixed."

"We're not going to leave him, are we?" asked Herod.

"We don't have any choice. The gangrene is bad and he needs to get to a hospital."

"It's only a little break," said Herod. "He just needs to put his weight on it, that's all. I've sent plenty of boys out with worse injuries than that."

"No, Herod, the world has changed. Those things are not possible any more. He'd hold us back."

"But I could carry him on my broad back."

She shook her head. "It's the only way." She handed the shotgun to Custard Pie and the two of them started climbing through the snows of the Pilgrim's Pass, stopping briefly to bid one final farewell at little Onan's grave.

CHAPTER
TWENTY-FIVE

We left custard Pie on the mountain for the medics to find, put a call through to the mountain rangers in Welshpool to look out for the fugitives, if they ever made it through the pass, and drove back to town. The snow was falling thickly and the gritting lorries were already out.

"This stuff about the cannibalism up on the mountain," said Llunos. "It was crap."

"Yeah, I've sort of worked that out. Mrs Llantrisant made it up to smear Mrs Bligh-Jones's name. She knew she'd been seeing Herod and was jealous.

Llunos nodded. "Mrs Tolpuddle broke her silence about the mission yesterday. It seems they were out on a routine sweep, and Mrs Bligh-Jones claimed she had received a distress signal. No one else did but they went and had a look. They wanted to turn back, but Bligh-Jones kept pushing them on and on; it was as if she knew what she was looking for. Then up above the snow-line they see the "Thing". Which we now know to have been Herod. Or Mr Dippetty-doo. That's when it happened."

"When what happened?"

"The thing that made Mrs Cefnmabws flee in horror. It wasn't cannibalism, it was something else. Mrs Bligh-Jones threw off her clothes and made love to Mr Dippetty-doo in the snow."

"I expect that would make me flee, too."

"I'm pleased in a way, though," said Llunos. "I've never had a lot of time for Mrs Bligh-Jones — always thought she was a bit toffee-nosed; but I could never really picture her as someone who would eat her bowling-partner."

"Don't be too sure," I teased him. "All this tells us is that she didn't; not that she wouldn't have!"

He threw me a dark, irritated glance. He was in a sombre, reflective mood and didn't welcome my joking.

"So Mrs Llantrisant thought up this thing with Calamity just to get back at you?"

"Looks that way. She obviously thought it was the best way to hurt me, and as usual she was spot on."

Llunos shook his head in wonder and disbelief.

We reached the crest of Penglais Hill and suddenly, as it always did, that familiar sight of Aberystwyth appeared in the valley below like a faithful dog, making the heart glad: skeins of smoke drifting across the slate roofs, the battered old pier and the pointy turrets of the old college, all set against the backdrop of a dove-grey sea.

"I still can't get my head round it all, you know," said Llunos. "Brainbocs coming back and all that. Making a love potion."

"I think it will probably take us all a good few years to get used to that one."

"I haven't even got my head round the last caper, yet. The flood."

"Nor me."

"Where do you want me to drop you?"

"I need to go to Trefechan." He put his foot down and drove on, past the railway station. I took out the key to my office and put it down next to the gear stick. "When you get back to the police station, give this to Myfanwy and tell her to go and wait for me at my place. Tell her I'll be about an hour, and I'll explain when I see her."

Llunos nodded. "Don't suppose there would be any point asking what's so important that you have to go to Trefechan at this time of night?"

"Nope."

"Thought not. If it was me, all I would be able to think of right now would be Myfanwy."

"It's all I've thought about all day. But I've waited three years. I can wait another hour."

We drove past the station and I cast an anxious glance over at the clock. 11.40. Still time. Just.

"And make sure someone takes Calamity home. Tell her I'll see her at the office tomorrow, business as usual . . . This will do fine."

He nodded and pulled up just before Trefechan Bridge.

I opened the door and Llunos put a gently restraining arm on my forearm. "Imagine if they did succeed in making a love potion like that," he said with a strangely troubled look. "That made you fall in love with someone you didn't like. It would be like rape,

304

really, wouldn't it?" He shook his head slowly, pondering the implications. "We'd have to make a new law against it." Then he put out his hand and we shook.

I plodded wearily over Trefechan Bridge and along the river bank to the trailer park. The storm had gone completely now and, in its wake, an air of almost supernatural calm lay on the harbour. Even the odd car sounded distant and not quite real; on the silent air the delicate scent of the sea hung faintly, softer than the memory of rose petals.

The caravan was dark and still, and gave off the same fetid reek as last time. The door was ajar and I eased it open and crept furtively in, not knowing what to expect but prepared for anything. I tried the light switch inside the door but it wouldn't work.

"The power's off." It was a girl's voice, thick with pain and urgency, coming from somewhere in the darkness. "I suppose the bitch forgot to pay the bill." My eyes gradually became accustomed to the gloom and I made out the figure of someone standing in the middle of the caravan. It was Gretel. She was wearing something that shimmered even in the dark and enveloped her from knee to shoulder. It seemed to be a dress, perhaps made of taffeta or something.

"I guess I had you fooled all along with my sackcloth and ashes stuff?" She spoke in staccato gasps as if there was a strangler's hands at her throat, or some deep, desperate pain inside her was squeezing out the last droplets of life.

"It's not hard to fool me," I said. "All you need is a jar of damson jam."

Something glinted with a blue white light down by Gretel's wrist. It was my gun, pointing at me. Gretel looked down at it and waggled it slightly.

"Soon teach her to keep her filthy paws off my man."

I nodded and said in the sort of voice you use to coax a frightened animal, "Yeah, you sure did that." I took a half-step towards her. Suddenly the words of Eeyore came back to me, about how death when it comes can often strike us as embarrassing, as stupid, even banal. How cruel, after all this time, now that Myfanwy was waiting for me back at my office, after all the myriad ways I could have died recently, for it to happen now. I put my hand out ever so gently. As if to a cat in a tree. "Come on," I said. "It's all right."

"Thanks for letting me have the gun."

"I didn't. You took it."

"How did you guess it was me?"

"It wasn't hard. That day Calamity asked for a heater, she said it was in the trunk, the key behind the picture. You were standing outside the door."

She considered for a second, and said, "I've sent you a cheque."

"For what?"

"For helping me find her. A deal's a deal.

"The agreement was to find the Dean not Judy Juice."

"I guess I should have read the small print." The voice was getting weaker and hoarser with a hint of a whine in it like a homesick dog.

"I would have got the bitch, too! But the fucking thing jammed."

She let out a tiny gasp, and swayed slightly like a felled tree about to collapse. The gun slipped out of her hand and clattered to the floor. It was then that I noticed in the corner of her mouth a thin dark trickle oozing and bubbling with her breathing. Transfixed by the sight I let my gaze drop and saw the handle of the "Come to Sunny Aberystwyth" knife, stuck to her chest, just below where the heart should be. She let out a strange squeak and slid slowly to her knees, slumped against the cooker and stayed there between the cooker and the cupboard, wedged in by her own enormous weight. The blood in the corner of her mouth stopped frothing.

I stepped forward and put my finger under her chin and closed the ugly, gaping mouth. I didn't care so much about her eyes, I couldn't really see them. I could tell now that it was a taffeta gown, and she had a set of pearls and a brooch and various other trashy gewgaws. Only the hat was missing.

There was a rasping sound from the far end of the caravan, the sound of a match on the side of a box. A light hovered pale and gold for a second and then went out, replaced by the steadier flame of a candle. So acute had my senses become now in this near-perfect darkness that I could smell the smoke of the extinguished match. I took out my handkerchief and used it to pick up the gun.

"It's all right, you won't need it," a man's voice said. I walked up to him, sitting at the far end where I had sat with Judy Juice. The candle gave off a small halo of flickering gold that occasionally touched the edge of his face. It was Lester, the security guard.

"Not much use pointing that at me," he said. "It's jammed."

"It's not jammed," I said. "She just didn't know how to shoot."

"We both know that's nonsense. But it doesn't matter. I don't intend causing any trouble. After I've smoked my cigarette I'll call the police myself, if you like."

"And tell them what?"

"That I killed that sack of shit down there in the taffeta dress."

"You did that for Judy?"

"I don't expect you to understand. You didn't know her."

"Where is she?"

"She's gone. Where you and the other men in Aberystwyth can't hurt her. Gone far from here to a place where she won't be confronted every day by the terrible reminder of her mother's cruel death."

"I thought she was an orphan."

"She was. Most of her life. But then she came to Aberystwyth and found a mother. And then saw her gunned down in the street a few months later."

I gasped in the darkness. "Mrs Bligh-Jones was Judy Juice's mother?"

"You didn't know? Why did you think she came to Aberystwyth in the first place? To live in this stinking caravan? She came to find her mother and I came because I couldn't bear to be away from her. She got me this job, you know. I'd like to think it was because she needed to have me near. But I know it was just pity. All the same, it saved my life."

"The Raven never guessed who you were?"

"I looked him in the eye and he never knew; I even threw him out on his backside."

"I thought the baby died on Pumlumon."

"That's what Bligh-Jones told Herod. But it wasn't true. No more than it was true that he was the father. It was born in the byre, but it didn't die. She put it on the church steps and it got taken to the orphanage. Judy, my beautiful little Olivia Twist."

I put the gun on the table. "You're really going to tell the police you did it?"

"Yes."

"You'd better wipe Judy's prints off the handle of the knife then."

"I already have."

I walked back up the caravan and out into the night, closing the door as I left. Behind in the darkness lay the corpse of a fat girl in taffeta, and a man calmly smoking a cigarette. A man known in Lampeter as Dean Morgan, head of the Faculty of Undertaking; the man who once boasted that his trade was death.

I was too tired to run but time was short. I managed to hail a cab on the main road and told him we had three minutes to get to the railway station. The streets were empty and we made it in two. I jumped out, thrusting too much money into his hand, and ran under the stone portal. The concourse was awash with that sharp white fluorescent light that hurts the eyes so much late at night. The lady was closing the buffet but I could see the train hadn't left. The end of the last coach was butted up against the point where the rails stopped, squeezed against the buffers. The diesel far off in the night, panting like a horse, flexing muscle, aching to leave. Along the platform the long awning stretched out into the darkness, ancient ironwork still embossed with the initials of the Great Western region. The filmy panes of glass smeared with the accumulated generations of G W R soot; and coated with that exquisite essence that condenses in the eaves of railway stations: the distilled longings and sadness of all the travellers who have parted and departed, kissed and cried and anointed the spot with their hope. Railway stations at night: as romantic as the names of far-off towns on the long-wave radio dial; magical places dislocated in time that belong to night-wanderers; pilgrims and lovers; the lonely, the hopeful and the damned.

I searched madly for a coin to put in the platform-ticket machine, and the guard, seeing my plight and the desperation on my face, smiled and opened the gate. I ran down the platform. Beyond lay the lights of the engine sheds and the signal box, the lakes of dirty oil, the maze of lines, criss-crossing and gleaming like mercury spaghetti . . . And beyond that in the mauve autumn sky, a tangled necklace of stars.

A lone old woman in a black shawl walked up the platform pulling a small suitcase behind her. I reached her as she took a step up into the final compartment. She stopped and turned, one foot still in Aberystwyth, one foot in another world. The hat and shawl did little to disguise the liquid loveliness of Judy Juice.

She smiled, the faint smile of someone who expects to be disappointed and is at least pleased to be right.

"I almost made it. One more step and I would have been there. I'm glad it's you, though, and not a real cop. You know cops . . ."

"They either lock you up or fuck you up."

"Is she dead?"

I nodded.

Judy shrugged sadly. "I suppose I should pretend to be sorry, but I'm not."

"The Dean says he did it."

"He always was a fool."

The guard walked up the platform slamming the doors, holding a flag at the ready.

I picked up the suitcase and put it inside the train.

"He must have thought you were worth it."

"I said he was a fool."

"I can understand him feeling like that."

She grinned. "You're sweet! Where were you when I was getting thrown out of college?"

"Thanks for warning Calamity."

"Did she tell you that?"

"No, she didn't know who it was."

"Forget it, it was nothing."

"It was everything."

She reached up and stroked the side of my face. "Nice kid, you take care of her."

I took the crook of her arm and helped her up and closed the door. She slid the window down and leaned out.

"You're really going to let me go? I did it, you know. I killed her."

"I know. You had to."

"Does that make a difference?"

"She took my gun, took it and wrote a note. That was no heat of the moment thing. Then she went round to your trailer with it. She would have killed you. If it hadn't jammed you would be dead."

"You're going to let the Dean take the punishment?"

"As far as I'm concerned, only three people really know what happened in that caravan, and one of them is dead. I wasn't there."

"Will they believe you?"

"No."

"You think they'll find me in Shrewsbury?"

"Probably. But why stop there? The tracks go much further than that."

"Yeah, all the way to China so I've heard."

The whistle blew and the train clunked as the engine took up the slack.

"They'll know you let me go — the people at the station have seen you."

"And a taxi driver."

"What will they do to you?"

I sighed. "They could do lots of things. If I'm lucky they will throw every book in the library at me. If that doesn't satisfy them they'll take away my licence. It won't be the first time."

"You're doing all this for me? Why?"

I grabbed her hand on the window-edge and squeezed it gently. "Let's say it's an old trick I learned from Ben Guggenheim."

She leaned forward and kissed me and said, "He sounds like a nice guy, I'll look out for him."

The train jolted once more and then pulled out, gliding slowly, and then rapidly picking up speed. I stood there on the empty platform and thought of stories from long ago: of comets appearing in the skies when strange children were born; children with tails or covered in fur. And I thought a similar celestial marvel must have been seen once above Pumlumon, when Mrs Bligh-Jones lay down in a cow byre and a girl stranger than a changeling issued from her loins. No conjuror ever pulled anything more remarkable from a hat than that. The Bad Girl who saved Calamity's life and said it was nothing. But I knew how far from being nothing it was; knew the cruel price she must have paid. Because only one person could have told her the location of the rendezvous with Calamity: a man she despised; who serenaded her mother and then slew her; and who finally must have enjoyed that night the only girl in Aberystwyth they said he could never have.

A fine mist began to form making the lamps along the track fizz like sparklers and in the distance, somewhere around Llanbadarn, the tail-lights of the train finally winked out. From the street outside came the sound of a car door slamming, followed by the staccato clatter of high heels on concrete. The urgent footfall of someone running for a train that has already gone. I turned and saw a lone girl racing towards me, like someone I once saw running across the dunes at Ynyslas. And then I caught a glimpse of the anguished look on her face and knew she had not come to catch a train but to stop one. "Oh Louie!" she gasped, throwing her arms around me. "Louie! Please don't go!" I buried my face in the tangled skeins of Myfanwy's hair and drank the scented darkness as the horn sounded from the distant hills and the night train to Shrewsbury raced eastwards, up that bright, silver ladder of hope.